THE MISER OF
CHERRY HILL

THE MISER OF CHERRY HILL

A Dr Clyde Deacon Mystery

Scott Mackay

severn House

This first world edition published 2011
in Great Britain and in the USA by
SEVERN HOUSE PUBLISHERS LTD of
9–15 High Street, Sutton, Surrey, England, SM1 1DF.

British Library Cataloguing in Publication Data

Mackay, Scott, 1957–
    The miser of Cherry Hill.
    1. Physicians – Fiction. 2. Murder – Investigation –
    Fiction. 3. United States – History – 1901–1909 – Fiction.
    4. Detective and mystery stories.
    I. Title
    813.5′4-dc22

ISBN-13: 978-0-7278-8038-3   (cased)

All Severn House titles are printed on acid-free paper.

Severn House Publishers support The Forest Stewardship Council [FSC],
the leading international forest certification organisation. All our titles that
are printed on Greenpeace-approved FSC-certified paper carry the FSC logo.

MIX
Paper from
responsible sources
FSC® C018575

Typeset by Palimpsest Book Production Ltd.,
Falkirk, Stirlingshire, Scotland.
Printed and bound in Great Britain by
MPG Books Ltd., Bodmin, Cornwall.

To Michael Hofmann and Nancy Hutton

Acknowledgements

I would like to thank my colleagues – friends – at the Southeast Toronto Family Health Team.

Fairfield, New York, 1902

PART ONE
A Flask for Bravery

ONE

I was coming back from a house call one dull November morning when, turning up the surgery drive, who should I see but Sheriff Stanley Armstrong waiting for me on his horse. He was in uniform – drab blue serge with big brass buttons and a bobby cap. His large mustache drooped, and his red face, set, looked carved from granite.

'Cecil Fray has gone and hung himself,' he said.

As the grim nature of the news took hold, I pulled my reins and brought Pythagoras to a stop. 'In the smithy?'

He nodded. 'From the rafters.'

'Is he still up there? Or did you cut him down?'

'We were waiting for you. Ray's standing guard outside. You got time to document it for the county?'

I got myself to the ground. 'Let me get my coroner's forms.'

On the way to the Fray Smithy, I glanced at my old friend. Though we were both naturally solemn about the business ahead, I couldn't help noting dark half-moons below the sheriff's eyes. 'You look tired, Stanley.'

He nodded. 'I've got two new murders, Clyde, one in Burkville and the other in West Shelby. I'm hoping to get them all squared away before Christmas so I can spend some time with my family. I been puttin' a whole heap of extra work in on them, and it's tuckered me out.'

I surveyed the sheriff with compassionate eyes. 'You let me know if you need help. You can always deputize me any time you like.'

'Much obliged, Clyde. If my case load gets any bigger, it just might come to that.'

We reached the smithy a short while later, a building of double-brick construction with a large chimney. Brown paint peeled from the masonry, and the black roof was now white with a thin layer of snow. Conveniently for Stanley, the Fray Smithy was right next door to the Sheriff's Office.

Deputy Raymond Putsey stood guard outside, a rifle against his shoulder, a stubby cigar hanging from his lips. Putsey was a young man, twenty-five, tall, strong, broad-shouldered, with blond hair underneath his black derby. As he saw us, he threw his cigar down, squared his shoulders, and struck a military pose.

'Howdy, doc,' he called.

'Morning, Ray.'

'Any sign of Billy yet?' asked Stanley.

'No, sir.'

'Any customers show up?'

'Had to turn Lyle Fitch away, was bringing his mare in to be shod.'

The sheriff motioned at the door. 'The doctor needs to take a look.'

The deputy moved out of the way, and we went inside.

We entered first the smithy office, an untidy room with a desk, a couple of chairs, and a pot-belly stove that radiated scant heat. Disorganized papers covered the desk. On top of these was an empty whisky bottle toppled on its side, and a picture of Billy, Cecil Fray's grown-up son, in a frame, also toppled.

A door led from the office into the smithy proper. We went through this door and found the blacksmith hanging from his neck by the central rafter. A length of white sailor's rope had been used. He wore denim overalls, a pair of unlaced work boots, and a red thermal undershirt, all covered with grime and dirt. A wooden chair had been kicked out from under him.

I had a good look at his face. He was cyanosed, his complexion a bruise-tinted shade of blue. His tongue hung out, reminding me of the pig tongues Earl Hadley sold at his butcher's shop on Tonawanda Road. Though the blacksmith's eyelids drooped, his eyes bulged. He smelled of whisky. Around his neck, below the noose, I saw rope burns and a few small scrapes that looked like red exclamation points. His jaw had been broken by his abruptly interrupted fall.

I turned to Stanley. 'Did you know him much?' I motioned out the window at the Sheriff's Office. 'You're right next door.'

Stanley shrugged. 'I used to talk to him. We were downright friendly at one time. But when his wife died, he started keeping to himself. Took to the bottle.' Stanley looked around the smithy. 'And business ain't been that grand lately. Been too drunk to manage, I suppose.'

We lapsed into silence.

At last, I said, 'Let's cut him down. I see a ladder over there.'

Stanley got the ladder. I summoned Deputy Putsey to help.

We soon had the blacksmith on the ground and covered in a blue horse blanket, one with a big glue stain on it.

'No point in the two of you staying,' I told the sheriff and the deputy. 'I know you've both got things to do.'

The sheriff and the deputy thanked me and left me to my coroner's work.

I searched for a suicide note. I checked the papers on Fray's desk. I investigated the two bedrooms and parlor upstairs. I spent about a half hour looking around for a note, but there was no goodbye letter to be found. I finally ended my search, went over to the Sheriff's Office because there wasn't a phone in the smithy, called Edmund Wilson, the undertaker, went back to the smithy, and was there when the undertaker arrived a short while later.

'Any idea of the arrangements, doc?' asked Wilson.

I shook my head. 'We're still looking for his son.' I motioned to Fray. 'Did you know the man at all? I'm trying to figure out why he hanged himself. He didn't leave a note.'

Wilson, a short sallow man, slight and birdlike, maybe ten years older than me, gazed at the blanket-covered body. 'I know he was awful shook up when we buried Hazel a few years back.'

I thought of my own poor departed Emily. 'It can be hard on a man when he loses his wife.'

'After she died he took to the bottle.'

'So the sheriff told me. A man has to seek solace any way he can at such times.'

'Only problem is, he kept seeking solace, drinking and drinking. And so the business started going downhill. The sheriff tell you that?'

'He mentioned it.'

'Money became a problem.'

I looked around the forge. 'Not exactly a model of enterprise, is it?'

'No. Fact is, he was drinking himself into a hole, doctor. People would come to get their horses shod and he'd be passed out drunk at his desk, with Billy nowhere around. I came here to get my own horses shod once and found Cecil in that condition. Had to take them to old man MacFadyen on Riverside Drive. Now I go there regular. Lot of people do likewise. Don't see how Cecil managed to keep afloat, carrying on the way he did. You can't make money like that.'

'So money became a worry for him?'

'A big one, from what I understand. Wilfred Hurren says so, at least.'

'The assistant manager at the Exchange Bank?'

Wilson nodded. 'He's a friend of mine. We do a lot of fishing together on Silver Lake.'

'And he told you things were bad for Fray.'

He nodded again. 'According to Wilfred, Cecil had to take several loans just to keep going.'

I jotted this in my notebook, then asked, 'Any idea where the son might be?'

'Billy?'

'Yes.'

'Probably out getting drunk somewhere. He's a lot like his pa that way.'

I thought about this. 'I guess I'm going to have to put the word out, then. If you see Billy, tell him to get his britches over to the surgery as soon as he can.'

TWO

I was turning the lights off in the surgery that night when out the front window I heard a wagon come up my drive.

My man, Munroe, twenty, tall, skinny, and red-haired, appeared at the parlor door. 'A late call, doc?'

I parted the sheers. For a moment I thought it might be Billy Fray, at last shown up. But it wasn't. The wagon, drawn by two horses, appeared out of the gloom. I perceived Mr Ephraim Purcell, one of the town's richest businessmen, sitting on the right, and his butler, Leach, handling the reins on the left. A woman knelt over a prostrate patient in the back.

'It would appear so, George. Prepare the examining room.'

Munroe hurried to the rear of the surgery to get things ready.

I left the house by the side door and descended the steps to the drive. The air had a nip to it, and I could see my breath in the faint moonlight. Leach slowed the wagon to a stop beside me.

'Evening, gentlemen,' I said.

'Evening, doctor,' said Purcell. 'Sorry to trouble you this late, but my stepdaughter's got herself real sick. I don't know what it is, but she has me worried. Seems like women's troubles to me, but I'm not a doctor. She's losing blood, and I would have to reckon it's a lot more than she usually does when the month comes round. She's pale. She's fainted three times since we got her in the wagon. And she's not making any sense when she talks.'

I walked to the back of the wagon to make my initial assessment. The woman kneeling over the patient turned out to be Miss Flora Winters, the patient's maid, a young woman in a servant's uniform and cloak, a shawl over her head to protect it from the damp.

'Evening, Miss Winters.'

'Evening, doctor.'

Mr Purcell got down from the box and came to the other side to have his own look. Miss Winters moved out of the way so we could both have a better view.

Marigold Reynolds, Purcell's stepdaughter, lay wrapped in blankets. She was a woman of twenty, had curly amber hair, green eyes, and freckles. I reached over the side and felt her forehead. I was relieved. She was afebrile. Any infectious process was not an immediate concern. But she did appear ill. And weak.

She looked at me, but didn't seem to recognize me. 'It hurts.'

Munroe came to the door. 'Doc, the examining room is ready.'

'Good, George. Please bring the stretcher.' I turned to Purcell. 'Any idea when it started?'

'I've been asking her,' said Purcell, 'but she's all confused.' He pleaded quietly. 'You got to save her, doc. Her poor dead mother would never forgive me if you didn't.'

'I'll do my best, Mr Purcell. You can make yourself comfortable in my waiting room.'

Munroe and I soon had Marigold inside on the examining room table. Purcell, Leach, and Miss Winters settled themselves in the waiting room.

The patient was now shivering. In the glow of my recently installed electrical lights, I saw that she was indeed extremely pale. She looked at me a second time.

At first, she seemed insensible. But then she recognized me. 'Dr Deacon?'

'Yes, child. What happened?'

She stared at me, then looked away. 'I just want to die. Please, let me die.'

From the troubled expression on her face, I understood the nature of her malady was more than just physical.

I peeled away the blankets and saw that the front of her white muslin nightdress was soaked through with blood. From the look of all this, I formed a fairly quick idea of what was going on. 'Are you with child, Marigold? Or were you?'

Her eyes widened. 'I hate him. He's the bane of my existence.'

'It's extremely important you tell me what you know of your condition, dear. If you're pregnant – or if you *were* pregnant – you have to tell me.'

She surveyed me for a few seconds, then turned away, her eyes filling with tears. 'What does it matter? I'm a slave, that's all I know.'

As she remained singularly unhelpful, I proceeded to perform my examination without any useful medical history.

I lifted my surgical scissors from the tray and snipped her night-dress from hem to collar. Blood smeared her thighs. A clumsy bandage of bleached burlap had been applied to the source of her malady. I peeled it away and got a strong whiff of wood alcohol. Looking more closely, I saw a fragment of willow bark. I sighed at this clue. I then took a speculum and did an internal exam.

I grew gravely concerned about the extent of the internal damage, and also with the possibility of sepsis. I saw several small lacerations, and more fragments of willow bark. Overall, the injuries, various and many, had the telltale signs of an Oneida practitioner trying to dispense with the products of conception. Especially the willow bark, as it was well known to many Oneida practitioners that willow bark had strong analgesic properties.

I went to the drawer, got a clean sheet, and spread it over my patient. I then placed a few more coals on the fire to keep her warm.

Having now finished with my initial exam, I felt I would do better with an assistant, and so immediately thought of the local midwife, Olive Wade.

I went into the waiting area, where Mr Purcell was sitting with the maid, Flora Winters. Leach had apparently gone to see to the horses. The businessman stared at me with solicitous eyes while Miss Winters gave me a timid glance.

Purcell said, 'Well, doc? Is there anything you can do for her?' With a bluntness bordering on callous, he asked, 'Or is she going to die?'

'I don't think she's going to die, Mr Purcell. But I must send for Olive Wade to help me.'

He nodded. 'Do whatever you must, doc. Money's no object.'

I went to the corridor where I found Munroe standing by. 'George, saddle Archimedes and fetch Miss Wade. I'm going to need her help.'

'Yes, doctor.'

I returned to the waiting room.

Hoping for more medical details, I summoned Mr Purcell into my office.

I sat behind my desk while he took the chair in front. His considerable bulk occupied the entire chair, arm to arm. He now had a cigar wedged in the corner of his thin lips and he puffed with worried preoccupation.

I probed. 'Can you tell me exactly how you discovered your stepdaughter in this condition, Mr Purcell?'

He took his cigar from his mouth and, keeping it wedged between his fingers, cupped his hand over his eagle-head cane. 'I was called from my fire by Flora. I went upstairs and found my stepdaughter ill. I saw a lot of blood and understood that we must bring her to the doctor. So I had Leach arrange for the wagon.'

'And there were no visitors to the house tonight?'

He seemed confused by my suggestion. 'It's a dreary November night, doctor, hardly clement weather for visiting.'

'My initial examination would seem to indicate she's the victim of an unprofessionally terminated pregnancy. I want to verify that before I treat her.' More sternly, I repeated, 'Were there any visitors to the house tonight?'

His lips tightened. He leaned forward and gazed at me with all the unpleasantness of an artillery piece. 'Now see here, doc. She might be a high-strung girl, but she's not a stupid one. There were no visitors.' With mounting displeasure, he said, 'There were no procedures performed, no amateurs hired for the sake of discretion, and no pregnancies terminated. She would never stain the Purcell name that way.'

I wasn't satisfied with this. 'Might I remind you, sir, that her last name happens to be Reynolds, not Purcell.'

*   *   *

Olive Wade arrived a short while later. As a wealthy heiress, she did
not have to work, but did so as a midwife and occasional nurse
from time to time out of a sense of civic duty and compassion. She
was a creature of ethereal loveliness. Every time I saw her, my heart
contracted with passionate arrhythmia.

Her blonde hair was tied in a bun and her blue eyes were wide
with concern as she entered my surgery. She offered me her hand
and I, Tennessee gentleman that I was, raised it to my lips and
kissed it.

'I'm relieved you've come,' I said.

'Where's our patient?'

'In the exam room.'

Munroe took her coat and we went inside.

Miss Wade approached Marigold and took her hand. 'Have no
fear, my dear. Dr Deacon will have you well and on your feet in
no time.'

'You know each other?' I asked.

Miss Wade nodded. 'I teach Marigold piano from time to
time.'

Miss Reynolds gazed at the midwife as if she were an angel
descended from on high. 'Miss Wade, I'm so glad you're here.'

'There, there, dear. When I heard it was you, I came
immediately.'

We got the patient draped and prepped in the usual fashion, then
anesthetized the theatre of activity with eucaine. Olive operated the
speculum, allowing me the access I needed. I thoroughly scraped
the remaining products of conception from the patient's uterus with
a curette, then applied copious amounts of tincture of iodine. Once
this was done, I packed and dressed the various willow-inflicted
wounds to my satisfaction, and let Olive finish with some external
dressing while I wrote my note.

For all my thoroughness, time, and care, I was still worried. And
when a doctor was worried, the final stop in his treatment algorithm
was the hospital. I finished my note with admission orders to Sisters
of Charity in Buffalo. Once I was done, I went out and told Mr
Purcell my plan.

'You must take her to Sisters of Charity by the night train.'

This distressed him considerably. 'But the night train doesn't pull
in till just after two in the morning. And I have an important meeting
with some business associates from New York at eight.

'You'll have to change those arrangements, sir. The situation is grave. She's lost a good deal of blood. She needs expert medical attention in a hospital setting.'

Mr Purcell turned to Miss Winters. 'Flora, girl, you're going to have to manage this yourself, all right? I can't put this meeting off. I've got a hundred thousand dollars riding on it. Leach will give you money. Get her on the night train to Buffalo, and then take her to the hospital. Is that clear, young miss?'

Miss Winters gave Mr Purcell a timorous nod. 'Yes, sir.'

Later, after they had gone, I asked Miss Wade, 'Do you have any notion if Miss Winters is up to the task of getting our patient to Buffalo?'

The midwife nodded. 'She's a most capable servant, Clyde.' Miss Wade's eyes narrowed. 'You really think Marigold was with child? And that an Oneida practitioner might have terminated her pregnancy?'

I tapped my fingers against my desk a few times as I considered the case. 'I'm sure of it. Has she ever mentioned a beau in her life? During her piano lessons?'

Olive looked out the window at the November mist. 'Marigold mentions a great many things, Clyde. She's entirely capable of carrying on a conversation all by herself.'

'And does she talk of boys?'

'Oh, yes. Prattles on about them ceaselessly. Which ones she likes, who's the richest, the strongest, the smartest, the most handsome.' Miss Wade's pretty blonde brow furrowed. 'But now that you mention it, there is one boy in particular she mentions often. I've seen him waiting by the fence during music lessons.'

'Who?'

Outside, I heard snow falling against the window.

'Billy Fray.' She shook her head sadly. 'I was so sorry to hear of his father's passing.'

I was surprised by the coincidence. Billy Fray, still not found, was now linked to two tragic events in one day, the death of his father, and the death of Marigold's unborn baby. 'Would you think the child was his?'

'Assuming there was a child?'

'Yes.'

'I wouldn't know. Certainly Marigold never told me about it.'

A short while later, I had Munroe bring Miss Wade's trap around.

The two of us stood at the door waiting. Olive came up to me and put her arms around me. I put my own around her.

'Did you get your invitation to Dr Thorensen's Christmas party yet?' she asked.

'I did.' Then I chided her. 'Do you know if Everett Howse is coming?'

She gave me a playful pat on the chest. 'Clyde, there was never anything serious between us.'

'Except a rather unfortunate summer romance.'

'I believe Everett will be spending Christmas in New York.'

'Ah. You see? The humble country doctor triumphs.'

She grinned. 'You haven't triumphed yet.' She kissed me on the cheek. 'But you're getting there.' Munroe drove up in her trap and we disengaged. 'You're getting there just fine.'

THREE

Mr Wilfred Hurren, the assistant manager of the Exchange Bank, was a slight man in a grey three-piece suit. He had a showy watch chain, and, incongruously, a black eye-patch. He greeted me cordially, and when he learned I was on official county business, ushered me into his private office with an air of importance he was careful to display to all the other bank employees.

Once seated, I explained to him that I was investigating Cecil Fray's suicide, and that both the sheriff and the undertaker had indicated money troubles. I proffered paperwork. 'This document from the county courthouse allows me access to his financial records. As Mr Fray did his banking here, I thought you might be kind enough to shed some light on the matter.'

Hurren took the document and glanced it over. 'Of course, doctor.' He put the paperwork down and looked at me with his one good eye. 'Glad to be of help. And Edmund and the sheriff are right. I'm afraid Mr Fray was under considerable financial strain. He was coming every month for a loan. I did what I could for him. But in my last meeting with him I told him the bank couldn't continue to extend him credit, and that he had best start making good on the loans we had already made. As well, Mr Purcell had been raising his rent every three months for the last year.'

'Ephraim Purcell owns that building?' I considered this an interesting coincidence as well, the Frays and the Purcells, tied together in yet another unexpected way.

Mr Hurren nodded. 'He bought it a year ago. He wants to tear it down and put up a warehouse. It's in a prime location, right across from the railway station, so putting up a warehouse there makes a lot of sense.'

I thought this through. 'If you don't mind me saying, it sounds like a pressure tactic.'

'A pressure tactic? In what way?'

'Raise the rent to get Mr Fray to move out so Mr Purcell can tear it down.'

'It's not a tactic, Dr Deacon. It's a sound business plan.'

'To force a man out of his home? He and his son live in the rooms above.'

Mr Hurren frowned. 'I'm aware of that. But Mr Purcell has every right to raise the rent on that building. When he bought the place, it was far below average for that stretch of North Railway Street and he was just bringing it in line. He gave Mr Fray plenty of warning that he was going to raise it, and was kind enough to phase in the increases quarterly.' Mr Hurren shook his head. 'I was constantly advising Mr Fray to find a cheaper building because it was perfectly apparent to me that he couldn't afford the increases, but he didn't want to leave, and kept believing that the money would turn up somewhere.' Hurren shrugged. 'And so he dug himself a rather large hole, not seeming to understand that money has to be made, and that it doesn't just turn up.'

Ephraim Purcell's primary Fairfield business, the New York Hard Goods and Clothing Emporium, was just down the street from the Exchange Bank. As it was close by, I thought I might glean further information about Mr Fray's financial disarray from his landlord, and so stopped by to say hello to Marigold's stepfather.

I made my way to the back of the emporium past bins, displays, and shelves of various merchandise. I paused at the hat display. Seventy-five percent off. Every week it was the same thing. A hat sale, and only a hat sale, as if Purcell had a tick about hats. They were good hats, too. I fingered the rim of the nearest derby. He couldn't be making money. Why was it always hats? I shook my head. We all had our eccentricities.

I continued on until I came to his office at the back. I knocked, and Mr Purcell, dressed in his usual three-piece business suit, a scowl etched across his face, looked up at me from his desk through the open doorway as if I were a great imposition upon his busy day.

'Doctor. Good afternoon.' His greeting was about as friendly as a drawn pistol.

'Good afternoon, Mr Purcell. Do you mind if I have a word with you?'

His scowl deepened. 'I have a very few minutes. I'm scheduled to meet with Mayor Vanduzen at two o'clock about some zoning issues.' He made an assumption. 'You've had word from Sisters of Charity about my stepdaughter?'

'No. I'm here on business of a different nature.' I glanced into the store, taking careful survey of the curious shopgirls who had drifted to the rear of the emporium, ostensibly to dust the ceramic-ware but really to eavesdrop, then turned back to him. 'Perhaps I could come in?'

He looked at me with some interest now. He lifted his chin, took a deep breath, and acquiesced with a wave of his palm. 'Very well. Come in. I hope your business won't take longer than five minutes.'

I went inside and took the seat in front of his desk.

I was surprised by how old and well-used the furniture in his office was. For a man of Mr Purcell's wealth, I would have expected more luxury. All the pieces, except one, dated from the 1870s, and looked as if they had been repaired and reupholstered many times. The only new piece – and this surprised me even more – was a parlor organ of thoroughly seasoned oak, profusely carved and ornamented with the latest and most popular design.

He caught me looking. 'I see you admiring my instrument, Dr Deacon.'

'Indeed, Mr Purcell. Do you play?'

He nodded. 'Music was my first passion. That organ is the best money can buy. I had it shipped all the way from England. It's my one indulgence.' His tone grew a little more expansive. 'After the toil of the day is done, I sit and play for the girls while they do their final clean-up.' He raised his brow. 'I understand you're a violinist.'

I deferred with modesty. 'I'm a rather imperfect fiddler.'

He nodded thoughtfully. 'Perhaps we'll take a few hours together one day, then?'

'Perhaps we might.'

'Your business, doctor?'

I gave it an appropriately solemn pause.

'I'm sure you've heard of Cecil Fray's demise?'

His brow rose and he nodded solemnly. 'I sometimes envy Edmund Wilson his choice of occupation. There is never any lack of custom.'

'You own the building where Mr Fray had his smithy?'

'I do. In fact, it's the reason I'm meeting the mayor. I want to have the property re-zoned for warehouse use.'

'I understand Mr Fray couldn't afford the rent.'

Purcell sat back. 'Mr Fray couldn't afford a great many things, doctor.'

'So sad. It was his home. It appears you were forcing him out.'

The drawn pistol came back. 'If you're suggesting he took his life because his landlord was trying to make a decent return on his investment the way the rest of the landlords along that stretch of North Railway do, I resent it. I gave Mr Fray plenty of warning that I was going to raise the rent once I took deed of the building, and that I would do it gradually so he could make adjustments. It's not my fault he didn't go looking for another building. One must take care of one's business, Dr Deacon. I take care of mine constantly, and I can't be held accountable if Mr Fray didn't take care of his.'

FOUR

Thinking it had been unfair to impose upon Olive Wade to be my nurse – it hadn't been the first time – I placed an employment advertisement in the *Fairfield Newspacket* later that afternoon. I bought space for the same ad in the Buffalo, Rochester, and Syracuse newspapers, and in this way hoped to cover all of Western New York.

A few days later I had three applicants sitting in my waiting room. I interviewed all three, and found all three wanting.

Then a fourth came along. She was a lot more promising.

Her name was Henrietta Gregsby. In her letter of application she
indicated she was twenty-three, and hailed from Sodus Point, New
York, a beach and spa community a few miles west of Rochester
on the south shore of Lake Ontario. She had an open, pretty face,
brown eyes, and a white smile. She spoke pleasantly about herself.

'I was trained in Philadelphia. When I first graduated, I worked
with a private practitioner, Dr Emmett Cousins, in my hometown
of Sodus Point. Unfortunately, after six months, Dr Cousins suffered
a stroke.'

'How terrible.'

She nodded. 'It was.'

'Naturally you couldn't continue at his practice.'

'No. And as Sodus Point is a small community, I had to seek
employment elsewhere. I found it at Rochester City Hospital. I've
been employed there for the last year, primarily in the birthing
center, and so have wide obstetrical experience. Nothing gives me
greater joy than bringing a new life into the world, doctor.'

I warmed to the young woman. 'That's certainly an asset in my
practice, Miss Gregsby. I deliver a lot of babies. But I'm worried.'

Her lovely brow rose. 'I quite understand if you find my qualifi-
cations insufficient. I realize I'm still in my first years as a nurse
and have much to learn.'

'It's not that, Miss Gregsby. I just wonder why you left Rochester
City Hospital in the first place. It's a renowned hospital, one
presenting a great many opportunities to an ambitious young woman
like yourself.'

She looked away. For several seconds she seemed sunk in dark
remembrance. She then shook herself out of it.

'Something sad happened to me there, Dr Deacon, that's all. I
can assure you, it had nothing to do with my professional life. I
suffered a loss. A dear friend of mine died. In such a case, a change
of scene is sometimes advised. I availed myself of your advertisement and took the train to Fairfield. I'm pleased to say I'm charmed
by your town.'

I restricted the rest of the interview to professional concerns, and
was relieved to see Miss Gregsby understood the duties and privileges of a private-practice nurse well. She even had knowledge of
many of the most recent medical advances, including antiseptics,
X-rays, and germ theory.

Over and above that – and my ardour for Olive Wade

notwithstanding – I was drawn to the young woman. Despite the sad events of her recent past, she seemed a cheerful creature, and one who would be a conscientious addition in the day-to-day running of my surgery. And if she reminded me of my poor dead Emily, so young, so innocent, I suppressed those feelings under my professional exterior and remained Dr Deacon, a town physician who was in desperate need of a nurse.

As we concluded, I told her I would take the lunch hour to think about it.

'Take longer, if you wish, doctor. I'll be staying at the Grand Hotel. My train doesn't leave until tomorrow morning.'

After she was gone, I put my DOCTOR-IS-OUT sign in the window and crossed the Culver Street footbridge over the canal to Court Street, hoping to find Stanley in the Sheriff's Office.

On my way, I felt unsettled, even noting an increase in my heart rate. No doubt about it, Miss Gregsby was reminding me of Emily. I thought of Miss Gregsby's smooth cheek and how it was much like Emily's. Her hair had the same chestnut tones that Emily's had had. Even her eyes were big and almond-shaped like Emily's.

I found Stanley in the Sheriff's Office labouring on paperwork.

'I'm about to hire a new nurse,' I announced, 'and I want to get your thoughts on the subject.'

I told him about Henrietta Gregsby. As I waxed movingly about her dark eyes and hair, and how she made such a graceful figure in her shirtwaist, puff sleeves, and trimmed hat, Stanley put his pen down, leaned back in his chair, and locked his hands behind his head.

'I do believe you like the young lady, Clyde.'

'Only in a professional sense.'

'And all this time I thought you had a decided fondness for Miss Wade.'

'My fondness for Miss Wade is still a decided one.'

'And that Miss Wade had a fondness for you.'

'I believe she does.'

He unlocked his hands, leaned forward, and put them on the desk. 'So instead of asking me what I think of Henrietta Gregsby, maybe you should ask Miss Wade what she thinks of her. At one time, I believe you planned on asking Miss Wade to be your nurse.'

I shifted in my chair. 'What prevented me was her summer vacation with Everett Howse. Her time away with the young assemblyman left me confounded.'

'And not just as your nurse, but also as your intended.'

'Yes, that's true, too.'

'And while I can see that you're dang near ready to ask Miss Gregsby to be your nurse, I can't understand why you haven't asked Miss Wade to be your wife yet. What's taking you so long?'

I looked out the window, shifting in my chair yet again. On Court Street, I saw a wagon going slowly by, a boy sitting on its open tailgate dragging a stick. I wondered how we had so suddenly found ourselves on the prickly subject of me dragging my matrimonial heels with Miss Wade.

'I suppose the whole town is wondering why I haven't asked Miss Wade to marry me yet.'

'Maybe not the whole town. But I'm sure Miss Wade is.'

I shrugged. 'Like I say, it was Miss Wade's summer away. It shook me up.'

'Clyde, I thought we went through that. The assemblyman's pa was in my office the middle of September. The way he tells it, there wasn't anything serious between Miss Wade and Mr Howse.'

'Maybe not. But then there's this fellow from Boston.'

Stanley paused. 'What fellow?' I could see the fellow from Boston was news to him and I realized I should have been more discreet with Olive's private life. But the fellow from Boston had been in the back of my mind ever since I'd heard about him.

'When she came here to bury her Aunt Tabitha, she stayed in Fairfield because of this married man she knew back in Boston. It was a bad business. She couldn't go back.'

Stanley paused and lifted his chin. He tapped his desk a few times, and said, 'Best not to question a woman's history too closely, Clyde. Not if you plan to marry her.' He pointed his finger at me. 'And if you hire this young nurse, I'd be careful. I can tell you see something in her. And I can tell it has nothing to do with your professional sense.'

I thought of Olive Wade on the way home. I stopped in the middle of the footbridge over the canal and stared down at the water. Two blocks away to my left, a barge steamed by on the Tonawanda River carrying a load of coal upstream to West Shelby. I knew that if I was going to marry anyone, it would indeed be Miss Wade. So why should I be careful about hiring Miss Gregsby? Miss Gregsby had an impressive résumé. She was personable. And I knew she was the kind of woman – and nurse – who wouldn't shirk her duties, no matter how arduous or taxing they became. Where and when I would ask Miss Wade to marry me was a separate issue entirely. The point was, I needed help in the surgery, and Miss Gregsby, despite her big brown eyes, was my best candidate.

Accordingly, when I returned to the surgery, I drafted an offer of employment, and walked to the Grand Hotel to deliver it to the front desk in person.

As I turned the corner from Culver Street on to Tonawanda Road, I saw two carpenters tacking a tarpaulin to the front of Flannigan's Stationery Shop, the façade having been torn away preparatory to the construction of a new one. The two scrambled over scaffolding to get the job done, as it looked like it was going to snow any minute, and they wanted to protect the interior. One of them backed up on the scaffolding and knocked a bucket of tacks to the ground. I hurried over and helped put some of the tacks back in the bucket.

'Much obliged, Dr Deacon,' the tall one called. He jumped down and started helping me. I left off and let him do the job himself.

Although I didn't know their names, being still relatively new to Fairfield – they momentarily introduced themselves as Ernest and Oliver Fitzhenry, carpentry of all kinds, lowest price guaranteed – they certainly seemed to know mine.

'Carry on, gentlemen.'

I continued along Tonawanda.

I was just nearing the alleyway between the Grand Hotel and the Corn Mercantile Building when I felt a painful poke in my toe. I stopped, lifted my shoe, and saw that I had stepped on one of their tacks. I couldn't help seeing it as a sign – and also as a warning – not to lose my head over Miss Gregsby, no matter how much she reminded me of Emily. I took the tack out of my shoe after some struggle, and put it in the pocket of my clay worsted overcoat so no one else would step on it, or otherwise misplace their heads when encountering pretty young women who looked like dead wives and had sad stories to tell. I resolved then and there that before the old year was out, I would ask Miss Wade to marry me, and end my widower days once and for all. That way I wouldn't have to worry about Miss Gregsby.

Also, there was no point in keeping Stanley in suspense.

*   *   *

Billy Fray finally made an appearance at the surgery the next day. He was an exceedingly tall man, with muscles like a gorilla, his shoulders broad and rippling from lifting a hammer all his life. His eyes were puffy, and he looked as if he had been grieving for his father vigorously. He was in workman's pants, unlaced boots, a thick wool coat, and a cap that had a tear at the front. He smelled of whisky and tobacco.

'Is there anything you or the sheriff can do, doc?' he asked. He pulled out a piece of paper, which, upon closer inspection, turned out to be an eviction notice from the law office of Mr Ambrose Johnstone. 'Not only did he make my pa kill himself, but now he's kicking me out of my own home. I got nowhere to go.' Billy proffered the document toward me. 'Signed by Mr Purcell himself, and notarized by that crooked lawyer of his, Ambrose Johnstone.' Tears came to the big man's eyes. 'I lived there my whole life.' His voice grew ragged. 'So did my pa. So did my grandpa. Mr Purcell can't do this to me. He's made my life miserable. And he made my pa's life miserable. I seen my pa go downhill day after day, and now he's done gone and hung himself, all because of Mr Purcell.' For several seconds he couldn't go on. When he did, it was not with grief but with a great burst of anger. 'It's all Mr Purcell's fault! And sumpin's got to be done, I tell you!' In the back of my mind, I couldn't help thinking of Marigold Reynolds, Mr Purcell's stepdaughter, and how she was apparently in love with this sad brute in front of me; enough so that she was willing to have his child out of wedlock. 'It ain't fair what he done to us! I got no family, I'm out on the street, and don't have no way of making a living, all because of that old miser. And he's got to be made to pay!'

FIVE

That night, as I was in bed reading a letter from my son, Jeremiah, who would be coming home for Christmas from school in Boston in a few weeks, I heard a gunshot break the stillness out my window.

I sat up. I listened, my heart pounding. There came a second shot. Or was it the echo of the first one coming from across the river? I listened for a third shot, but everything grew silent.

Stanley was in West Shelby for the evening working on one of the two murder cases he was trying to solve before Christmas, and I had been deputized to look after the town in his absence. We had once been sheriffs together in Cross Plains, Texas, and so the choice was natural. Discharge of a firearm within town limits was against the law. As much as I wanted to stay in bed and read my son's letter, I knew I had to go investigate.

I got dressed, went downstairs, put on my boots, my overcoat, and my brown derby, then lifted my deputy's badge – a five-point brass star with the words FAIRFIELD POLICE engraved in the metal – and pinned it to my breast.

I was about to leave the surgery when, deciding that caution might be in order, I went to my study, opened my firearms cabinet, and chose my Colt Army Frontier revolver, a weapon with a seven-and-a-half-inch barrel, one that had stood me in good stead when I had been a lawman with Stanley in Texas eighteen years ago.

As I rounded the corner from Culver Street onto Tonawanda Road, and climbed south up the hill past Flannigan's Stationery Shop (tarp still up, not all the tacks collected from the road yet), I saw a small crowd in front of the Grand Hotel. Moving closer, I discerned within this thicket a man of considerable girth lying on the ground. A young woman knelt over him, pressing his chest with both hands up and down in a rhythmical manner. A few seconds later I saw blood on the paving stones, and realized I had a shooting.

I broke into a run and reached the crowd quickly. 'Stand back, please. Sheriff Armstrong has deputized me. Stand back!'

The crowd, all men, drinkers from the tavern in the Grand Hotel, or farmers from the Saturday-evening auction at the Corn Mercantile Building next door, shifted out of the way and revealed to me my victim – none other than Ephraim Purcell.

On her knees before him doing what she could to save him was my freshly hired nurse, Henrietta Gregsby.

She turned to me, blood on her hands, and some on her face. She was wearing only her muslin nightshirt and a purple overcoat, no shoes, hat, or scarf. She looked at my badge.

She then met my gaze and, in a shaky voice, said, 'I'm sorry, doctor, but the patient seems to have expired.'

I rushed forward, knelt next to her, and placed my fingers on the man's carotid artery. Miss Gregsby had indeed made a correct diagnosis – Mr Purcell was indisputably dead.

The murmuring in the crowd dwindled away to nothing. I glanced at Miss Gregsby. She was staring down at the dead man. Her lips were pursed and her blood-besmirched face had settled into a perplexed frown, as if she couldn't understand why she hadn't been able to save him. She remained professionally calm.

She turned to me. 'You're wearing a badge, doctor?' She looked at my revolver. 'And carrying a gun?'

I quickly explained my dual role in Fairfield. 'Genesee County is currently under-policed. And so when the sheriff bites off more than he can chew, I step in and help him.'

One of the onlookers offered further information about me. 'And he also used to be President McKinley's personal doctor as well.'

Her eyes narrowed further. 'Oh. So you're *that* Dr Deacon.'

I saw that she was now shivering. 'My dear, you're cold.'

She lifted her hands and gazed at all the blood. 'I do so hate to lose a patient. I take it as a personal defeat.'

I glanced at Purcell. 'Miss Gregsby, he was shot through the chest. There was little you could do to save him.'

I placed my hand on her elbow and gently coaxed her to her feet. I took off my coat, put it around her shoulders, then pulled out my handkerchief and wiped the blood from her face. She gave me a quavering smile of gratitude. Here it was again, murder, come to visit me. I remembered the president's assassination. I remembered how I had tried to save him. And how I had failed. I glanced down at the brass star on my breast. Yes, here it was again. The gears meshed. The engine turned. I pulled back. I looked at the dead man.

'Did you see anything?' I asked her. The words were out of my mouth even before I understood that I had properly formulated them.

Her eyes narrowed as she put events together in her mind. 'I was in my bed reading.' She twisted around and pointed. 'Up there, on the fourth floor. That corner room. I heard the shots, and came to my window. I saw the victim on the ground crawling toward the hat shop. I'm sorry, I don't know his name.'

'Ephraim Purcell. He's an important businessman in Fairfield.'

'He was struggling.'

'So he was still alive when you saw him out the window?'

'Yes.'

'Dragging himself toward the hat shop?'

'Yes.'

Here was some potentially useful information. I looked across the street at Jensen's Hat Shop.

I then made a general survey of the street.

Next to the hat shop was Wiley's Drugstore. Both were three-story buildings with ground-floor shops and apartments above. Yes, the hunt was on, the murder of the president goading me forward, transforming me, now not a doctor but a lawman, and one who was always seeking redemption for the way he hadn't been able to save the twenty-fifth president of the United States. South on the street, the hill rose on my left to the New York Hard Goods and Clothing Emporium, Mr Purcell's establishment, and on my right to the Exchange Bank. I then swung around and gazed first at the Grand Hotel, then at the Corn Mercantile Building next to it, and at last at the alley running between the two. How had it all come about? Why was Ephraim Purcell lying dead here in the street? Certainly Billy Fray's outburst of earlier in the day came to mind. And certainly that alley was a well-hidden vantage point from which any shooter, including Billy, might fire.

Now fully in lawman mode, I made a general announcement to the onlookers. 'I want anybody who saw anything to gather on the hotel steps. The rest of you, go home. There might be evidence around here, and I don't want it trampled.'

I was disappointed when only one farmer remained behind and the rest went on their way.

Before I started with the farmer, I had a few more questions for Miss Gregsby.

'So Mr Purcell was dragging himself away from the back alley?'

'Yes.'

'And when you heard the shot, did it sound as if it came from the back alley, or from somewhere else?'

She corrected me. 'Shots.'

I paused. 'Yes, shots. From where I was, I thought the second shot might have been an echo.'

'No. There were definitely two shots, one right after the other.'

Here was more potentially useful information. 'It's an extremely important distinction, Miss Gregsby, because if the shooter reloaded, he might have ejected the first cartridge, and finding it would be my first step in identifying the murder weapon.'

'I heard two shots, doctor. Whether they came from the back alley or not, I can't say.'

'And were you the first one on the scene?'

'No. There were a few others about when I got here. Mostly men from the tavern.'

'Very good, Miss Gregsby. You may return to your room. I'll see you in the morning. Please be at the surgery by eight.'

'Of course, doctor.' She got up and retreated into the hotel.

I now went over to the farmer, inclining my head toward him. He was a tall, grim-looking man, one I hadn't met before. 'Good evening, sir. I'm Dr Deacon.'

'I know who you are, doc.' His voice was low, like the E-string of a double bass, and I saw at a glance that he was a no-nonsense and humourless man.

'And you are?'

'Albert Swinford. Own a hunnert and fifty acres out by Reese's Corners.'

'And you think you saw something, Mr Swinford?'

'*Heard* something, doc. Heard exactly where that shot came from.' He motioned around the area. 'People was saying it came from here, it came from there. But I was a scout in Cuba in the war against Spain. I know a thing or two about pinpointing enemy position.'

Having fought in the Spanish–American War myself, I was willing to grant this man some credibility. 'And did you hear one shot or two?'

'There was only one shot, doc. That other so-called shot? That was just an echo from across the river. Take it from someone who's heard a lot of gunfire.'

'And where did the shot come from?'

He pointed to the alley. 'Right down there by those garbage cans. No doubt about it.'

'And where were you?'

'Inside the Corn Mercantile. Sittin' up by that second-story window. My son and I were bidding on hogs.'

'Did you look out the window?'

'No way I could. There's an eighteen-foot drop behind the bleachers. But I'm not wrong about the shot.'

I stared at the window for several seconds, then turned back to Mr Swinford. 'I fought in Cuba with the president's Rough Riders.'

'I think I heard that.' He gave me a lacklustre salute.

I returned the salute. 'Might as well go over and have a look, then,' I said.

We both went over.

We weren't halfway when Mr Swinford stopped abruptly, and in a hard and unfriendly voice said, 'You going to need me for anything else, doc? I should be hitching up and riding home. It's getting late.'

I turned to him. He was frowning, as if this was all a big bother to him.

'You have nothing else to add?'

'No, sir. I heard the shot from the back alley. That's about all I can tell you.'

I stared at him some more, and now I detected an unexpected nervousness. 'I can't hold you, Mr Swinford. If you have to go, you have to go.'

'Reese's Corners is a fair piece. This morning's snow might have melted here in town, but the Wiccopee Road is fairly bad.'

'You've been most helpful.'

Mr Swinford nodded and moved off.

I proceeded into the alley.

I wasn't hoping for much. Through experience, I knew a lot of criminal investigation was an uphill battle. But there on the ground beside the nearest trash bin was not an ejected cartridge, such as I had originally anticipated, but an unfired round. I lifted the bullet, turned it over, and saw an 'H' stamped on its brass bottom. My brow rose. Having made a study of a wide variety of firearms, I knew the round was from a Henry rifle, a much-coveted Civil War era weapon.

My eyes narrowed as I realized I had made my first step forward in the case. A Henry. Not the rarest rifle on the rack, but certainly less common than a Winchester.

As such, I hoped it might eventually narrow my field of suspects.

SIX

Once I had pocketed the bullet and had finished with a further rummage around the alley, I returned to the street and searched Mr Purcell's body.

I discovered on his person a thirty-two-caliber Smith and Wesson hammerless revolver with a three-inch barrel. I checked the chamber and discovered that the weapon was fully loaded and that there was no evidence of a recent discharge – the murder had happened so fast and unexpectedly the poor man hadn't had a chance to defend himself.

I checked to see if the bullet had gone straight through. It hadn't. There was no exit wound.

I then went through Purcell's other pockets and found a pocket-book, a gold watch with emerald inlay, loose change, business cards, cigars, and matches. As everything still seemed to be here, I concluded that he hadn't been robbed, which meant I had to consider another motive.

I again couldn't help thinking how Billy Fray had come to the surgery earlier that afternoon to tell me Purcell had to be made to pay. I could hear his words echoing in my head. 'I got no family, I'm out on the street, and don't have no way of making a living, all because of that old miser.'

I sent a boy from the hotel to fetch Deputy Raymond Putsey – he lived on the edge of town and probably hadn't heard the shots. I sent another boy to get Deputy Ernie Mulroy, who was on duty manning the Sheriff's Office telephone tonight.

When the junior deputies arrived, I had Mulroy go get Edmund Wilson, the undertaker, over on Talbot Lane. Putsey and I then gave the alley another going over, looking for tracks. The mud in the alley was like slop, with all the snow melted from earlier in the day, and finding a proper trail, or evidence of an escape, proved impossible.

A short while later, Mr Wilson and his assistant, Lloyd Pearson, preceded by Deputy Mulroy, appeared with a team of two pulling a large market wagon. They came to a stop in front of Jensen's Hat Shop. Edmund Wilson, who I had already seen that week in regard to the Fray suicide, got down off the wagon, and came toward me. Pearson stayed with the wagon.

As Mr Wilson approached, he said, 'We do meet in the oddest places, don't we, doctor?' He motioned at the hat shop. 'We left the wagon over there in case you weren't finished with the scene yet.'

'Most thoughtful of you, Wilson. I believe nothing else useful will be obtained.'

I had my junior deputies start knocking on doors. Putsey began first by speaking to Mrs Jensen in the hat shop. Mulroy spoke to Cora Wiley in the drugstore. Both ladies shook their heads and I could see that they didn't have much information for us. The deputies then fanned out both north and south along Tonawanda and left me to deal with the undertaker by myself.

'You may attend to the body, Mr Wilson.'

The undertaker turned and raised his arm. 'Lloyd, bring the wagon around.'

Mr Pearson shook the reins and the horses started toward our victim.

The undertaker squatted by the body.

After inspecting Purcell for a few seconds, he said, 'Went through the chest, did it?'

I nodded. 'But there's no exit wound. The bullet's still in there. Do you think you and Mr Pearson are up to the task of recovering it for me? I'll need it for my investigation.'

He nodded. 'If we have any difficulty, we'll send for you.' He looked at Purcell. 'Poor Ephraim. I never thought I'd see the day. Fairfield won't be the same without him.'

'You knew him?'

'Oh, yes. We're both members of the Welland Street Club, and we fraternized often. I just hope he's left his business concerns in competent hands. He was a great economic force in town. A lot of people will be nervous about that, wondering if they're going to keep their jobs and so forth.'

By this time, Pearson had moved the wagon next to the body.

Mr Wilson pulled out a cloth sack with a draw-string. 'I'd like to remove Mr Purcell's personal effects and valuables first, if you don't mind, doctor. I know he has some gold and silver pieces he carries, and I'd hate to be accused of not itemizing them correctly when the family comes to collect them.'

'A wise precaution, Mr Wilson.'

Mr Wilson went through the victim's pockets, writing down in pencil on a claim-slip each item he removed: a gold card case with calling cards; a gold pen and pencil case; the gold pocket-watch with emeralds; a cedar-lined cigar case big enough for five cigars; spectacles; a mother-of-pearl medicine box containing numerous pills and tablets; a miniature portrait of his dead wife, Francine Reynolds.

Then Mr Wilson checked the pockets of his topcoat.

As the undertaker went through one pocket after another, a puzzled line came to his brow.

He then felt through the man's coat more assiduously.

'Mr Wilson?' I said.

'Strange.'

'Is something wrong?'

The undertaker frowned. 'It's just that Ephraim always travels with his whisky flask. He's never without it. It's an extremely special item to him, made of sterling silver, engraved, an article he won in a bet a number of years ago. Every time I run into him on the street, or in the club, he draws me aside, pulls it out, and says, "A flask for bravery, Mr Wilson?" and we take a nip.' Wilson shook his head. 'He carries it wherever he goes. But now it's not here.'

'Are you sure he carries it with him always?'

'Yes, always.' He looked up at me and cocked a brow. 'Perhaps he's been robbed?'

Billy Fray's outburst notwithstanding, I now considered this a second motive. But I was a little puzzled. 'You have a cloth sack of other valuable items.'

'Yes.'

'It's odd.'

'Extremely.'

'Why take just the whisky flask? Why not everything else as well? Can you more accurately describe the flask, Mr Wilson?'

The undertaker searched his memory. 'I've never inspected it closely, Dr Deacon. I was always making sure the coast was clear, so to speak. A man in my profession doesn't like to be caught taking a nip in public. So I can only describe it in rough strokes. Like I say, I know it was sterling silver, and that there was some engraving on it.'

'And he always had it with him?'

The undertaker nodded solemnly. 'It was an incontrovertible law of the universe that he never ventured from Cherry Hill without it, doctor. He used to say to me, "I always carry my flask, Wilson. Some men may pray. But why do I need to pray when I have my flask?"' Mr Wilson motioned at the corpse. 'I guess he should have taken up prayer.'

SEVEN

Later, when the undertaker and I had Ephraim Purcell in the mortuary, I examined the victim's wound more closely. Deputy Putsey was standing by.

The dead man, laid out on a steel embalming table, was now without his clothes. I pulled my Kodak Brownie camera out of my medical bag and took some clinical photographs of the fatal injury. The oval perforation, wiped of its excess blood, gaped above and to the left of the cardiac structures, below the scapula – a clean shot into the upper part of the lung cavity. There was no evidence of gunshot or powder burn on his skin, and taking my magnifying glass to his topcoat, I couldn't immediately detect any dark stippling there either. This eliminated the possibility of a close-range shot, and supported the existing evidence of a shot fired from the back alley.

I took pictures of both the wound and the coat.

After I was finished with the camera, I examined the rest of the body checking for signs of a struggle but saw not a scratch, contusion, or other collateral trauma.

These findings again supported a long-range shot.

I then inserted a hose with a hand pump down his airway and evacuated several hundred cubic centimetres of blood. In this way I determined that cause of death was asphyxiation on his own blood, which would account for the way he had crawled a good distance before finally succumbing.

I made notes of all this, then drew a narrow piece of bamboo from my bag. Wilson, Pearson, and Putsey looked on with interest. I lightly coated the first few inches of bamboo with hair pomade, then inserted it gently into the bullet wound, breaking past the initial coagulation so that the wound started to seep again. Careful to find the wound's slant no matter where it took me, the bamboo now stuck out of Purcell's chest at a fairly extreme angle, up past his chin and forehead. I was surprised. This left me to conclude that the bullet had perhaps not been fired from the back alley after all, such as Mr Swinford the farmer had asserted, but from an elevated position.

The discrepancy left me puzzled.

Later on, when I was finished with the undertaker, and was riding over to the Purcell residence to give the servants the news, I said to Deputy Putsey, 'It doesn't make sense, Ray. Why would Albert Swinford, a scout, mind, trained in pinpointing enemy position, schooled in gunfire, insist the shot came from the back alley when the evidence is telling me it came from either an upper window or a rooftop?'

'Maybe he got it wrong.'

I shook my head. 'I know the training these scouts get. They're never wrong about enemy position or pinpointing gunfire. Plus there was something odd about his manner. The way he was so intent. And then he got nervous. It's made me suspicious. Do you know him at all?'

Putsey shrugged. 'He and his family live in the loneliest part of Reese's Corners. The only time they come into town is for church, the Corn Mercantile, and sometimes to visit the Wileys.'

'The Wileys? From the drugstore? They're friends with them?'

'It's more just the wives, doc. Albert Swinford ain't exactly the friendly sort.'

I shook my head. 'Swinford certainly made a point of telling me the shot came from the back alley, didn't he? Why do you suppose that is, Ray, especially when it's now looking like the shot came from a roof or upper window?'

'I don't know, doc.'

'Do you know anything about bloodhounds, Ray?'

'Not much, sir.'

'I raised them in Tennessee. There's only one way to fool a bloodhound.'

'How's that, doc?'

'Cover your tracks with cayenne pepper. And I'm starting to think Albert Swinford is sprinkling cayenne pepper around.'

I let Putsey go and rode over to the Purcell mansion by myself.

By this time it was well after midnight.

The Purcell mansion, a gracious if somber residence at the top of Cherry Hill Road, was three stories tall and had three wings.

Sidney Leach, Mr Purcell's butler, answered the door.

I got straight to the point. 'I'm afraid your master's been murdered, Leach. Shot to death in front of the Grand Hotel. I'm sorry.'

The butler behaved as all must in these situations, the jolt of the news rendering him immobile for several seconds, his stare widening, comprehension slowly sinking in by degrees, understanding finally coming and made manifest by how his shoulders at last eased with shocked resignation.

'Where is he?'

'At Wilson's mortuary. Has Miss Marigold returned from Buffalo yet? It's my duty to inform next of kin.'

At first too distracted to answer, he said after a few seconds, 'No . . . no.' Now with greater agitation, he added, 'Oh, dear. This is appalling. Have you apprehended his killer?'

I shook my head. 'I'm afraid Mr Purcell's murderer is still at large. One of the first steps I must take in order to catch his killer is to determine your master's movements this evening.' I gestured toward the interior of the house. 'Do you mind if I come in? If anybody has any direct knowledge of the way Mr Purcell arranges his day, I'm sure you do.'

Still shocked, and now apparently deep in thought, it took him a few seconds to respond. 'Of course, doctor. I'm sorry. It's cold out. Come sit by the fire.'

He made way for me and I entered. We settled on the bench in the capacious front hall. The hall fire was made up, and I was thankful for its warmth. Dual staircases wound up either side, and a large chandelier hung from the ceiling. I saw a salon through French doors to the left, a ballroom to the right, and a conservatory full of plants further on. Above the hall fireplace was a full-length portrait of Francine Reynolds, Marigold's mother, Ephraim's late wife, done in Academy style, a painting showing a well-proportioned young woman in an 1880s bustle dress, with the same orange hair as Marigold.

We began by discussing Mr Purcell's routine.

Leach said, 'He's up at five every morning, has a vigorous constitutional down to the river and back, the same breakfast of porridge and orange juice day in and day out, followed by two cups of coffee, a cigar, and perusal of the *Fairfield Newspacket*. By eight o'clock he's in his downtown office at the New York Emporium. He's back here by three to work in his home office, and then after that he takes another constitutional down to the river and back. If the weather is fine, we go for a ride in the motorcar.'

'What about today in particular?'

'He spent most of it in the emporium looking after Christmas orders. Then he came back to dress for dinner. Saturday night he has dinner at the club and then walks over to the Grand Hotel to check the week's receipts.'

'He owns the hotel, too?'

'Yes, doctor.'

I made a note of this, then revealed to Leach one of the more perplexing aspects of the case. 'It appears his whisky flask was taken. The sterling silver one. Nothing else. I find it odd. Do you know anything about the flask?'

Leach shrugged. 'Only that he prized it very much. He won it in a bet six or seven years ago. I'm not exactly sure of the details.'

'Do you know what it looks like?'

'Sterling silver, with a picture of Abraham Lincoln on it.'

This detail was at least a little more useful than the vague ones Mr Wilson had given me about the flask. But it didn't narrow the field too much, as many Union Army veterans had flasks with pictures of Old Abe on them. 'And do you know if Mr Purcell has any particular enemies?'

A weary grin came to Leach's face. 'A man like Mr Purcell has many enemies, Dr Deacon. But then again, he has many friends, too.'

'Would Billy Fray be a particular enemy?'

The butler's eyes widened. 'The blacksmith's son?'

'Yes.'

Leach thought about it. 'Mr Purcell was irritated Marigold had shown an interest in the young man. That's about all I know about it.'

'Did Mr Purcell have any connection to the Swinford family of Reese's Corners?'

Leach was puzzled by the inquiry. 'The Albert Swinfords?'

'Yes.'

Leach searched his memory. 'I believe he hired Clarence Swinford, the man's son, to work at the hotel one summer. In an accounting capacity. A very bright young man. It's one of Mr Purcell's talents, spotting the bright ones. Other than that, no.'

Although this didn't seem like much, I made a note of it as well.

'Do you know anything about Mr Purcell's estate, and how he's got it arranged? I understand he employs a great many people in town. I think a reassuring statement should be made to the

Newspacket, just to allay fears Mr Purcell's demise might have economic repercussions.'

Leach nodded, looking relieved that I had broached the subject. 'Mr Purcell has appointed his brother, Herschel, executor. Herschel lives in New York City, and is a professor of history at New York University. I'll send a telegram immediately after you leave. I imagine it might take him a day or two to extricate himself from his duties before he can come to Fairfield. Until that time, provisions have been made to grant Mr Purcell's lawyer, Ambrose Johnstone, stewardship over his many concerns, not only in Fairfield, but elsewhere as well. Mr Purcell left his affairs in order, Dr Deacon, of that you can be assured. He was extremely organized when it came to his money.'

EIGHT

I met Stanley at the Sheriff's Office the next morning, early, at seven o'clock.

He planted both elbows on the basswood table and stared at me stoically when he found out he had a third murder to solve.

'And has the stepdaughter been informed?' he asked.

The Henry bullet found at the scene sat upended like a little gold rocket before him.

I shook my head. 'Marigold is still in hospital in Buffalo.'

'Should we send a telegram?'

'Her condition will still be delicate this early in her recovery. We should wait until she's been discharged.'

'And so Billy had some fighting words about Purcell the afternoon before he got shot?'

I nodded. 'I've been up since five this morning looking for him, but I can't find him.'

'You were over at the smithy?'

'I was. He wasn't there.'

Stanley ruminated. 'I'll tell the other deputies to keep a lookout for him. And I'll saddle up and have a ride-about myself.'

I again couldn't help thinking how tired the sheriff looked. 'Stanley, I know you're busy with your other cases right now. Plus with Christmas coming you've got your family to think about. Since I've already started this one, why don't you let me handle it? You don't have to go looking for Billy. I'll do it.'

He raised his hand. 'Now, Clyde, I don't want you offering your services when Jeremiah's coming home.'

'He's not due for another few weeks, Stanley. You let me take care of Purcell. You need to be with your family at this time of the year.'

And in fact, my old friend looked relieved. Without too much more fussing, he said, 'All right. I'm mighty grateful.' He raised his finger. 'But let me know if you need help.'

'I will.'

'As to the murder itself, what exactly happened?'

I recounted what I knew for the sheriff: that there had been one, possibly two shots; that the shots had most probably originated from the back alley next to the Grand Hotel, but also possibly from a rooftop or upper window; and that a whisky flask appeared to have been taken from the victim.

'A witness says the shot came from the alley,' I said. 'But the evidence suggests a rooftop or window origin for the shot.'

'What witness?' asked the sheriff.

'Albert Swinford.'

Stanley tapped the table. 'Swinford's a good man. Regular army, retired. If he heard it, he heard it.'

'I'm not so sure about that. There was something odd about his manner when he came forward to tell me about the shot. He was too eager. And he was nervous. I could tell he had a mission.'

'And what mission was that?'

'To make me believe, come what may, that the shot came from the back alley.'

'What are you suggesting? That he had something to do with it?'

'His actions were odd, and they've left me suspicious.'

'I don't see Swinford involved in something like this.'

'Then why, if the evidence points a rooftop or window position, was he so eager to tell me that the shot came from the alley?'

'What evidence?'

I explained to him about the gunshot wound angle. 'If Purcell was shot from the back alley, the wound angle would have been parallel to the ground. It's not. It's at a forty-five-degree angle to the ground.'

'Maybe the wound angle can be accounted for by the way Purcell had his body positioned at the time of the shooting.

'Likely forward and down?'

'Yes.'

I remained unconvinced. 'Purcell would pretty well have to be on his hands and knees crawling toward his assailant to account for the wound angle, and that just doesn't make sense to me.'

'Maybe there was a fight first, and he got knocked to the ground.'

'There's no evidence of contusions or bruises.'

Stanley shook his head. 'What about the flask?'

I paused. 'What do you mean?'

'If the robber shot Purcell from a rooftop or window, do you think he would have time to get down to the street to rob him of the flask before other people came along?'

My shoulders sank. 'No. He wouldn't.'

He motioned at the Henry round standing on the table in front of him. 'And you found this bullet in the back alley.'

'I did.'

'So Swinford is right.'

'Not necessarily. Not with the wound angle the way it is. It just means we don't have the proper explanation for the flask or the bullet yet.'

We both puzzled over these discrepancies for a few moments.

Then the sheriff asked, 'Anything else taken from the victim?'

'No. Just the flask.'

'Not his watch? Not his card case?'

'No. Nothing.'

Stanley's brow rose. 'Ain't that peculiar?' He tapped the basswood table, thinking. 'Maybe I'll send Ray around to the Purcell place, and over to the club as well, to see if Purcell left his flask in either of them two places. Maybe Purcell left it somewhere. And if he did, it would make things a lot simpler. Might as well try to eliminate the possibility of a robbery so we can get a better idea of where the shot really came from.'

'I can see why they made you sheriff.'

We lapsed into silence for a few seconds.

Then I shifted the conversation back to Billy. 'You've lived in Fairfield a lot longer than I have, Stanley. You wouldn't happen to know if Billy Fray owns a Henry, would you?'

'So you're really thinking Billy?'

'Right now I am.'

'Good. Because I really don't think Albert Swinford has anything to do with it. As for Billy, I'm not rightly sure what kind of rifle he owns. I know his grandfather fought in the Civil War, and that Henry rifles were popular with Union soldiers back then, and that Isaiah Fray left a lot of junk in the smithy when he died. He could have left a Henry.' The sheriff glanced at me. 'You checked the smithy for it earlier this morning when you went looking for Billy?'

'I did. No rifle, no ammo.'

Stanley lifted the bullet and pondered. 'Maybe he's keeping it at the Fairfield Shooters Club.' The sheriff rubbed his mustache a few times and put the bullet back down. 'If you can't find Billy to ask, why not talk to Perry Nolan, the president of the Shooters Club? I know Billy goes to the range a lot. Perry might know what rifle Billy uses. He might even have Billy's rifle in the gun locker there.'

I felt some optimism. 'I'll do that, Stanley. You wouldn't happen to know if anybody else might be angry at Ephraim Purcell, would you?'

Stanley thought. 'I wouldn't think so. He employs just about half the town, and most of them are grateful for their jobs.' His eyes narrowed. 'But now that I think of it, there was one incident back in October. Something I was directly involved with. Mind you, I don't believe for a minute it has anything to do with this here shooting.'

'What is it?'

'Do you know Daisy Pond?'

I searched my memory. 'Any relation to Orville Pond, the cement works owner?'

'His daughter. She also happens to be good friends with Marigold Reynolds. She was up visiting Marigold on Cherry Hill Road back in October, and I guess there was some kind of dispute with the old man, and the upshot was, he hit the girl.'

'Hit Daisy?'

'Yes. And hit her hard. Right in the mouth. She was bleeding. She came down here and was madder than all get-out. I'd never seen an angrier young woman. She wanted to press charges. She didn't care how rich he was. She said he couldn't go around hitting defenseless young women. And she's got a point.'

'What came of it?'

Stanley raised his brow. 'I was getting ready to ride up to arrest the man when he comes down to the Sheriff's Office, and he's got his lawyer, Ambrose Johnstone. Mr Pond is with them, and he's brought his daughter back down. Orville Pond is nervous, and he tells me how Daisy doesn't want to press charges after all. Course, I've got to do something, so I talk to Judge Norris, and he's nervous about it, too, and we finally decide to throw Purcell in jail for five days. He makes bail in a day. Later on I learn Orville Pond was in negotiations with Purcell to provide concrete for the warehouse Purcell plans to build on North Railway. I also learn that Purcell is the judge's number-one campaign contributor. Both the judge and Mr Pond wanted to bury the matter. It sure did make Daisy mad.'

Before riding back to the surgery, I stopped by the funeral home.

Edmund Wilson had recovered the bullet for me, and had it ready in an old embalming fluid jar.

'It's in fairly good shape, doc. I can see the lands and grooves well.' He held up the jar and had a closer look at the slug. 'That's a mighty big piece of lead.'

He handed the jar to me and I had a look. 'Definitely a rifle.'

I made one more early-morning stop before returning to the surgery, the *Fairfield Newspacket*, where I spoke to Ira Connelly, the editor-in-chief.

He was an eager young man in grey flannels, a grey vest, and a white shirt. His hair was slicked back with pomade, and his face was clean-shaven in the modern way.

His eyes became hungry, and he quickly snatched his notebook and pencil from his desk as I gave him the preliminary details about the Purcell murder case.

'I've been waiting for you, doc. I knew either you or the sheriff would show up sooner or later. And thanks for coming early. We've been holding the morning edition. I think we're going to sell a lot of papers today.'

'Just make sure you let the town know Mr Purcell's business concerns won't be affected.'

After I finished at the paper, I rode over to the Grand Hotel and had another look around.

I climbed the stairs to the fifth floor, then the final set of iron steps to the roof. I pushed the door open and went outside.

I found myself on a broad flat roof with a tar base and pebble surface. The brick walls of the façade went up to my hip, a perfect spot to lean a rifle against. The big electric hotel sign rose above that.

I walked to the edge and looked down at Fairfield. The river meandered past the Cattaraugus Cemetery out beyond the Green. The silver steeple of Fairfield Congregationalist Church rose off to the left, a cross on top, taller than any other structure in town. I heard a train rumbling through Hoopertown, the town's poorer section, and saw a plume of black smoke racing along behind the buildings along North Railway, the locomotive unseen until it crossed Tonawanda Road to the south.

Certainly the angle was right.

But Stanley had a point about the flask robbery.

How could a man intent on robbing Purcell of his flask get all the way down to the street from here before other people got to the scene first?

The flask was turning into a big puzzle.

Especially because it was a law of the universe, according to Edmund Wilson, that Purcell always carried it about with him.

When I got back to the surgery a little before eight, Miss Gregsby, in uniform for her first full day of work, was waiting for me on the side stoop, a shawl around her shoulders and a scarf over her head.

'Good morning, Dr Deacon,' she called.

'Good morning, Miss Gregsby,' I called back, doffing my hat as I rode up on Pythagoras.

We spent a little time discussing the events of the previous evening.

'I was so sorry I couldn't do more for Mr Purcell,' she said.

I showed her around the surgery and told her what she might expect during a typical day of practice on Culver Street.

'As for remaining at the hotel, I insist you come here until you find a place of your own. I've got plenty of room in this big old house, and you could save yourself some money.'

'I couldn't possibly impose, doctor.'

'Yes, you could.' For I couldn't stand the thought of her having to live alone in a hotel another minute longer, maybe because she reminded me so much of Emily. 'There's a spare room at the front. I'll have Munroe lay a fire and make the bed. And I'll send for your things at the Grand.'

She looked at me closely. 'Are you sure?'

'Of course I'm sure. We're professional colleagues, and I'm extending a professional courtesy.'

I spent a pleasant morning with Miss Gregsby seeing patients, and by lunch I wondered why I hadn't hired a nurse sooner. I was relieved to see she knew everything about basic – and advanced – examination, and that she was a scrupulous note-taker. Also, whenever either of my two exam rooms displayed the least untidiness, she was in them with a quick step to set things right. In addition, having not had a woman in the house since Emily had died, I found myself susceptible to her female presence. As a nurse she was courteous, professional, cheerful, pleasant, and thorough. As a woman, she was captivating.

Yet every so often I saw melancholy in her eyes. I knew she was thinking of the friend she had lost. It put me in mind of my own Emily, and made me feel closer to Miss Gregsby, and as if we had made the same sad journey, and had completed the same sorrowful passage.

It being cold and flu season, we were busy all day and had a full schedule of patients until well into the afternoon.

When we were finished, Miss Gregsby said, 'Let me do your charting.'

As I discovered that her handwriting was much neater than mine, I surrendered the job to her willingly and let her record the medical happenstances of the day in a script that was so square and regular it was close to what a typesetter might find in his upper and lower cases.

Freed up in this way for the last few hours of the afternoon, I pinned my deputy's badge back to my chest and once again turned my attention to the Ephraim Purcell murder case.

NINE

On my way to the Fairfield Shooters Club to ask Perry Nolan about Billy's Henry rifle, I saw that work had been finished on Flannigan's Stationery Shop, and that any miscreant tacks had now been removed from the thoroughfare. At least I didn't have to worry about getting a painful poke in my toe again.

I rode over to the west end of town and soon reached my destination.

The Shooters Club was a long narrow building on Riverside Drive and Allegheny Avenue, sound-proofed, with seven ranges. I tied Pythagoras to the hitching post and went inside. Rifle and gun reports assaulted my ears the moment I opened the door. It reminded me of San Juan Hill, one of the more harrowing moments of action I'd seen in Cuba a number of years back. At the far end, I saw the main office, where Perry Nolan, the club president, sat in a derby and vest receiving dues from a member, a ledger-book in front of him. He looked up and gave me a nod, then continued with his transaction.

As I waited, I looked at various trophies in glass cabinets along the wall, and at group photographs, one showing the women's contingent of the Fairfield Shooters Club, damsels in shirtwaists, skirts, and beribboned boaters, posing like a gang of powdered and perfumed ruffians with rifles, shotguns, and pistols. In this group photograph I was interested to see Marigold Reynolds wielding a rifle. As she was close to the deceased, it was of course a detail I couldn't ignore, and so took out my notebook and jotted the discovery down.

Mr Nolan finally completed his business and came out to greet me.

He was roughly my own age, forty-one-or-two, with a neatly trimmed mustache, mild blue eyes, and an engaging helpful smile. 'Howdy, doc. I see Stanley's got you wearing that star again.'

I nodded. 'And in fact, I'm here in my capacity as deputy to ask a few questions, Mr Nolan. In regard to the Purcell murder case.'

He grew appropriately solemn. 'I read about the murder in the morning edition of the *Newspacket* today. I'll do whatever I can to help. Mr Purcell was a generous member of this club.'

'Thank you, Mr Nolan. Your cooperation is much appreciated.' I came to my chief point of inquiry. 'I understand that Billy Fray is a member of the club.'

The club president corrected me. 'An associate member. He's never had the money to pay the full annual fee. In fact, he's never paid any fee. But he's such a good shot we let him use the range. In return, he teaches the ladies how to shoot.'

This was interesting news, considering the long-range dynamics of the shooting last night. 'A good shot, was he? How good?'

'One of the best we have.'

'And did he own his own rifle, Mr Nolan? Or did he rent one from the range?'

He gave me a cautious look. 'Say, doc, is Billy a suspect?'

I circumlocuted. 'The young Mr Fray had his differences with Mr Purcell. We have to look into them. I'm counting on your discretion, Mr Nolan.'

He considered this, then said, 'Of course, doc.'

'So did he rent?'

Nolan shook his head. 'He hardly had the money to rent. He and his pa were in pretty bad straits. He actually used his grandfather's old rifle whenever he came to the range. A Henry. He kept it in the gun locker here.'

I was thunderstruck by my apparent luck. 'And is the weapon in the locker now?' For if it was, I could subject it to the relatively new science of ballistics and test-fire it on the spot to see if I had a match to the bullet recovered from Mr Purcell's corpse, and be done with the case in less than twenty-four hours.

But it turned out it wasn't going to be that easy.

A furrow came to Mr Nolan's smooth brow. 'I'm afraid the rifle's not here, doc. Billy came yesterday to get it. Must have been around four o'clock. He said he was so broke he was going to have to sell it at King's Emporium. Only thing was, when he headed out, he didn't head toward King's. He went the other way. Strange. Because I know he's always anxious to get his hand on another dollar or two. Didn't see him come back this way till this morning. He passed by while I was opening the range. I'm out at the door and I say howdy to him, and he's got the rifle in his hand, only it's in a bag, and he never carries it in a bag.'

'And he was going to King's this time?'

'That's what he said. Guess last night he couldn't bear to part with it. Your grandfather's rifle has got to have some sentimental value.'

Or maybe Billy just needed it to kill Purcell last night.

As King's Emporium of New and Used Merchandise was only three blocks away from the range on Hooper Avenue, I deferred my visit to the Welland Street Club and headed over there instead.

The emporium was in the heart of Fairfield's poorer section, a district known as Hoopertown. No fine carriages or pretty women with parasols here. That was for Cherry Hill. In Hoopertown, one found a more unornamented species of humanity. A woman in rags was selling chestnuts from an open brazier. A man lay passed out in a doorway, his bowler having fallen from his head, an empty whisky bottle by his side. Two children picked through a midden down a back alley.

Inside King's Emporium, I walked past old musical instruments, jewellery, racks of used clothing, farm implements, and leather goods, all of it crammed together in such chaos it was a wonder the owner and proprietor, Anthony King, could find anything at all. Amid all this junk I was surprised that I could even find Anthony King.

But find him I did, at the rear of the shop.

He was a man with a bald pate and a rim of thin brown hair running from ear to ear around the back of his head. He was sitting on a stool behind a sales counter. His stomach, despite his relatively thin frame, was substantially rounded and solid. He wore a jewel-ler's loupe in his left eye and was holding a man's ring up for inspection. He was mumbling to himself. He had a cup of tea and a piece of pound cake at his elbow. As I approached, a mouse came out from under some papers, darted on to the plate, absconded with a choice crumb, and ran back under the papers, all without Mr King's notice.

I cleared my throat to get his attention.

He looked up, the loupe still in his eye. He removed it, the optical device leaving a red circle, and blinked. He looked at the tarnished brass badge on my lapel with a sudden drooping of his lips, as if he found unannounced visits by the local constabulary a source of acute dyspepsia.

'Afternoon, doc. I wasn't expecting any more customers this late in the day. What's your pleasure? Back for more glassware?'

'As a matter of fact, Mr King, I'm here on sheriff's business. You may have heard there was a murder in front of the Grand Hotel last night.'

He nodded. 'Poor Mr Purcell. He was such an able businessman.'

I leaned my hands against the counter. 'Right now, our suspicions point toward Billy Fray, the blacksmith's son.'

This gave him reason to pause for several seconds. At last he said, 'Billy Fray, Billy Fray,' as if he wasn't sure who I was talking about.

'We have it on reasonable authority that he visited your establish-ment, most probably this morning.'

Mr King looked away, his eyes alighting on a dented sousaphone on the floor. With some equivocation, he said, 'You have to under-stand, doc, I don't keep an official log of who actually comes in and out of my shop. I wish I could recall. I surely do. It being so close to Christmas, I've had so many customers lately. I can't keep track of them all. We literally have throngs of them.'

I glanced around the emporium – not a throng in sight – and turned back to Mr King. 'I fully understand that the emporium is a dynamo of commerce, Mr King, but if you could carefully examine your memory, I'm sure you'll recall if Billy Fray was here or not. In aid of your recall, I can tell you that the young man may have brought in a rifle.'

King's head jerked upward as if he had just been poked in the ribs. 'A rifle, you say.' He shook his head and sighed. 'We get so many rifles, doc. I've got enough rifles to arm a militia. By the way, if you ever want to trade up your Army Colt, let me know.'

'The weapon in question was a Civil War era Henry.'

He jerked again. 'A Henry!' He seemed astonished by the notion. 'Now that's a rifle I don't see too often. And when I do, doc, it's really not up to me to verify where the seller got it from, or what he used it for. I can't be going into the origin – or previous use, mind! – of every weapon I hawk, so if you're wearing that star to start asking me questions like that, then I must confess, I don't keep a record of specific details. I'm in the business of making money, not keeping a whole heap of records about where I get things and what they've been used for.'

'I'm the first to realize that, Mr King, and exonerate you of all culpability should the matters of use or origin ever find their way to Judge Norris. Of course, if you find you can't be of any help to me at all, I may have to get my junior deputies in here to start helping you with your record-keeping.'

He thought long and hard about the matter of record-keeping, his eyes bulging so much I doubt a loupe would have fit in the left one at present. He inspected his pound cake. His eyes narrowed, as if he now discerned that it was a crumb short. He then looked at me, and offered some parsimonious cooperation.

'I can tell you that he was here, then, doc, and that he did bring a rifle to sell – not hawk, mind, but sell – and that it was his grand-father's Henry rifle. I gave him thirty dollars for it. I know its worth. I paid him top dollar. No point in bringing your deputies in for that. Everybody knows I pay top dollar.'

I now felt some encouragement, despite Mr King's continuing habit of hucksterism. 'I'm afraid I'm going to have to borrow that rifle, Mr King. I have to test-fire it. I assure you, I'll take good care of it.'

He sucked at his lower lip. 'Problem is, I already sold it.'

Here was another obstacle I hadn't counted on. 'Already?'

'People are always looking for Henrys, doc. They're a special weapon.'

Not to be thwarted, I asked, 'And who did you sell it to?'

'Jerome Highcloud, an Indian fella from the reserve. Paid forty-five dollars for it, cash down. He's been looking a long time.'

I took out my notebook and penned in this information.

'Billy didn't happen to sell a whisky flask, did he?

King looked surprised. 'No, sir, he didn't. But if you've a mind to purchase one, I've got many fine examples in the next room.'

As I rode to the Welland Street Club after leaving King's Emporium to make my final stop of the day, I pondered what I might do about the rifle. I took the Court Street bridge over the river, turned right on Cattaraugus Avenue, and headed over to Welland Street. I decided I was going to have to go out to the Oneida Reserve at Silver Lake and ask Jerome Highcloud to let me test-fire his new weapon, a few extra steps, to be sure, but apparently the only way I was going to obtain a useful ballistics result.

The Welland Street Club was housed in a neo-Romanesque building, one of the few brick edifices in the town, the masonry a sooty red, several chimneys billowing dark smoke, and the windows orange and inviting with lamplight as gentlemen gathered for an evening of cards, drinks, and quiet newspaper reading. The stable boy took Pythagoras from me. I went into the club and ordered supper – for it now occurred to me that I hadn't eaten since break-fast. As I dug into a well-done strip-loin, I caught sight of the club's chief butler, Robert McGlen, passing by in the corridor.

'Mr McGlen, a word, please.'

'Good evening, doctor. I thought you might show up.' McGlen was exceedingly lank, tall, off-the-boat Scots, and spoke with a

Glaswegian accent of singular resonance. He made his way over to my table. 'We've all read the terrible news. Every member is greatly distressed by Mr Purcell's passing. We're rather a fraternity here. No man is an island, and all that.'

I nodded. 'He's a great loss to the club, Mr McGlen, as well as the town. I've been deputized by Sheriff Armstrong to investigate his murder.'

'Yes, Deputy Putsey was in here earlier inquiring about Mr Purcell's flask, and he let us know.'

'Ah. And was Deputy Putsey able to determine if Mr Purcell had left his flask here?'

'No, sir. It wasn't here. Nor, if I understand correctly, was it found up at the mansion.' The butler raised his tufted eyebrows. 'I take it Mr Purcell's flask has some pertinence to your case?'

I equivocated. 'We're not yet sure.' Yet with the information that the flask had not been found by Putsey either here or up at the mansion, I was now confronted with a more real possibility that the flask had indeed been taken from my victim in Tonawanda Road. Which of course complicated a rooftop origin for the shot, as a robber wouldn't have been able to get down in time to take the flask.

'Right now, I'm trying to determine Mr Purcell's movements in the hours before he was killed, and that's one of the reasons, other than this delicious strip-loin, that I've come to visit. I've learned from Mr Purcell's man, Leach, that he was here at the club last night before he went to the hotel.'

'Yes, sir, he was. He spent the entire evening in the Algonquin Room playing cards with some friends. I was in the room all night serving them. He left the club around eight thirty to go to the hotel. I understand from the *Newspacket* story that he met his end around nine?'

I nodded. 'I heard the rifle-fire myself from my bedroom window. I'm not sure if you could hear it from the club.'

'We heard nothing.'

'Anything unusual happen at the club before he left?

'As a matter of fact, yes. A most unseemly display by a non-member.'

'A non-member?'

'Yes. Billy Fray arrived and asked that Mr Purcell come outside. He wanted to fight him. He was in a most frightful state. Stuporous

with drink. I had to summon Lonnie Moses to help me escort him
from the grounds.'

Here was yet more evidence against the young smithy. 'Do you
recall the time of the disturbance, Mr McGlen?'

The tall man thought for a moment. 'It must have been around
eight o'clock, maybe a little after.'

'And did you see which way Mr Fray went when you and Mr
Moses escorted him from the property?'

'I did. He crossed the river at the Court Street bridge. I actually
followed him as far as the south side of the church to make sure
he wouldn't come back. I could tell by then that he was on his way
to the smithy.'

On his way to the smithy to get the Henry, I wondered, stowed
there after fetching it from the Shooters Club? 'Was he carrying
anything at all?'

'Only a whisky bottle. Rare is the time you'll catch Mr Fray
without a whisky bottle.'

I thought about this, then asked, 'Have you ever seen Mr Purcell's
whisky flask? I'm trying to get a good description of it.'

'To be honest with you, doctor, I didn't even know he owned
one. When he imbibes at the club, he drinks the house spirits. Why
should he do otherwise?'

TEN

The following day, Miss Gregsby and I saw patients all
morning and closed early at one o'clock. Fresh snow had
fallen overnight. Out on the roads and byways, carts and
wagons had been replaced by sleighs and sledges. Culver Street,
known for its blue spruces, was taking on a Christmastime look,
now that all the spruce boughs were glazed with a layer of white.

As it was such a pretty day, and as Miss Gregsby was new to
the area, I asked her if she would like to accompany me to the
Oneida Reserve at Silver Lake.

'It will give you a chance to see some of the surrounding area.
Plus I have some business relating to the Purcell murder investigation I must attend to.'

Her eyes brightened with excitement. 'I would love to, Dr Deacon.'

Soon, Miss Gregsby and I were heading out of town on Erie Boulevard in my sleigh-and-two.

Farms were under snow. We saw a dozen local children sledding down a hill on three toboggans one right after the other, the boy in front mimicking the toot of a locomotive whistle. I got to know Miss Gregsby a little better, and she got to know me.

She said, 'I saw a picture of a woman on the mantelpiece in the parlor.'

'That,' I said, 'is my wife.'

She seemed to assimilate this news with some disappointment. 'And is she away at present?'

'I'm afraid Mrs Deacon died in 1888.' With sober stoicism, I added, 'I'm a widower.'

Her pretty lips came together. 'I'm sorry. I didn't realize. You seem awfully young to be a widower.' For a moment, the only sounds were the whish of the sleigh and the snow-muffled hoof-falls of Pythagoras and Archimedes. 'And the photograph of the boy? He's your son?'

'Yes. Jeremiah. He's at school in Boston right now but will be coming home for the holidays. And speaking of holidays, I suppose you'll be going to Sodus Point?'

She looked away. 'Alas, no. I have no one left there. Both my parents are dead and I have no brothers or sisters.' She took a moment, then turned back to me. 'I'm not exactly sure what I'll be doing for Christmas, doctor.'

'What about Rochester?'

'Now that Martin's gone, I have nobody in Rochester either.'

I glanced at her – I had a sense of a delicate vessel brimming too full of sorrow. 'Martin, then,' I said. 'He's this friend you lost?'

She gave me a solemn nod. 'Actually, he was my fiancé. This will be my first Christmas without him.'

This immediately changed for me the quality and character of her grief, and gave it greater commonality with the grief I felt for Emily.

'Can I be of any comfort to you?' I asked.

Even though I saw that her lashes were now wet, dampened by momentary tears, she had a broad and deprecating smile on her face.

'Would you mind if we didn't talk about it? Unless you want to spoil a perfectly lovely day.'

I could do nothing but acquiesce.

She said, 'You were really President McKinley's personal physician?'

What a hapless pair we were, each inadvertently focusing on the other's source of pain. 'I was more than his physician. I was his friend.' That horrible moment at the Pan-American Exposition in Buffalo came back to me, the president shot by the misguided Czolgosz. 'I did what I could to save him. But I failed.'

She was a sensitive girl. She didn't pursue the subject.

Rather, we touched on my great friendship with the current president, Theodore Roosevelt, and how I had been with his Rough Riders in Cuba, a medic, but also a soldier, and how these days I spent a month every summer with him at Sagamore Hill, his Long Island retreat.

'I understand he likes to hunt,' she said.

'He loves anything to do with the great outdoors.'

'And have you ever gone hunting with him? Martin so loved to hunt.'

'I once went elk hunting with him. I can tell you, it was an adventure. After he's done being president, he wants me to come to South America with him. He has rather a fascination for the uncharted tributaries of the Amazon.'

From there, we diverged to even lighter topics – the Christmas parties and balls she might expect to attend in Fairfield.

'I do love dancing,' she said. 'Do you know any of the newer steps, doctor?'

'I haven't danced since Emily died. I've mastered some of the older steps but none of the new ones.'

'Then I will have to teach you.'

An hour later, the reserve came into view. By this time, as the temperature had dropped, we were snug under my buffalo skin – the cured pelt of a bison I had shot outside Cross Plains back when a great number of the creatures still roamed those parts.

The Oneida Reserve at Silver Lake was a hodgepodge of old and new: some homes built recently, others more time-honoured, constructed according to the old ways. As we entered, a woman pounding grain looked up at us. Two boys appeared from behind a nearby pine and watched us pass. Furs had been stretched here and there, and fish caught from Silver Lake lay on a rack smoking over a fire. A geriatric dog with grey chin whiskers and an arthritic hip chased the horses for a short stretch, but soon grew tired and hobbled away.

We reached the Oneida band hall a few minutes later.

Foster Stands-Over-Pool, the reserve's sixty-year-old band leader, was on a ladder removing snow-burden from the roof with a push broom. Except for a single crow's feather in his hatband, he was dressed entirely in American clothes.

When he saw me, a welcoming smile came to his face. 'Doctor. Hello!'

'Hello, Foster.'

He came down. I reined in my horses, and the sleigh came to a stop. I got down, helped Miss Gregsby to the ground, and introduced her to the band leader.

Foster said, 'We know the doctor well, miss. He comes out every other week. Talbert Two-Arrows, our own practitioner, is helping the doctor learn traditional medicine.'

Foster soon had us sitting inside comfortably by the pot-belly stove. We exchanged a few further pleasantries. I inquired after the health of his wife, sons, daughters, and grandchildren.

I then commenced with my official business.

'Foster, there's been a murder in town, and Sheriff Armstrong has deputized me to look into it.' I gave him the details, including what I knew about the Henry rifle, and how I believed the previous owner might have used it in the commission of the crime. 'It now appears Jerome Highcloud has purchased that rifle, and I'm hoping I might impose upon Mr Highcloud, with your kind permission as band chief, to borrow the weapon in order to test-fire it.'

Foster shook his head with some concern. 'But Clyde, I'm afraid Jerome Highcloud isn't here. He's gone to the Adirondacks on a hunting expedition and won't be back for a number of weeks. He took the Henry with him.'

I sighed. It seemed I was going to be thwarted with this rifle at every turn.

'Very well, then, Foster. Could you please tell him to come see me when he returns. We've recovered a bullet from our victim and we're hoping to determine – and eventually prove – that the Henry is indeed our murder weapon. We need to test-fire the rifle in order to do that.'

*   *   *

On the way back, the weather grew colder as winds from Canada blasted down from Lake Ontario.

'Are you disappointed?' asked Miss Gregsby.

'About what?'

'About not getting the rifle.'

'Not at all. We've had a lovely day. You've gotten to see some of the country. And heaven knows when you'll be asked to make a house call out this way. You need to know your way around.'

Over the next mile, the wind grew particularly fierce and Miss Gregsby began to shiver. The bison pelt was only partially effective against the frigid onslaught.

I lifted my arm. 'Come close. You'll freeze if you don't.'

Being a sensible girl, she did as she was told. 'That's better.'

'Can you feel your fingers and toes?'

'Barely.'

'We'll be home soon. You can warm them by the fire.'

I must confess, I enjoyed her closeness. It had been over a decade since I'd ridden in a sleigh with a woman, and it alleviated, at least for a little while, the loneliness I'd carried with me ever since Emily's passing fourteen years ago.

Miss Gregsby and I were in this state of weather-enforced intimacy when, turning up the surgery drive, who should I see waiting for me on the front porch but Olive Wade. When she spotted us, she rose from the bench slowly and studied us with mounting interest. I don't know why I felt guilty. I had no reason to feel guilty. I wasn't doing anything wrong. But I knew I had that look on my face that Olive herself had had after she had come home from her summer with Everett Howse.

She was covered from head to foot in ermine, her wisps of golden hair coming out from under the rim of her fur hat. Her blue eyes widened until they were like large sapphires within the confines of her cream-colored face. She surveyed the two of us with momentary alarm. This emotion was quickly camouflaged with cool appraisal. Munroe came out the side door. He gestured nervously toward the front porch and shook his head in warning. Miss Gregsby and I disengaged and I yanked on the reins to stop Pythagoras and Archimedes.

I rose from my seat as we came to a stop. 'Miss Wade,' I called, 'why didn't you wait by the fire? George could have made you comfortable.'

She looked first at me, then at Miss Gregsby, then back at me, her golden brow knitting, a pinch coming to her lips. Though after her initial seconds of alarm she was now her usual picture of calm, an iciness had come to her eyes, and it betrayed an ungenerous conclusion about what she was seeing.

At last she managed to say with reserve as proper as a church pew, 'It's such a bright day.' Her voice, well-bred in its vowels, was now devoid of the intimate inflection she had used with me since September. 'I thought I would enjoy the air.' Her smile was as stiff as a pine plank left out in the sun for a year. 'And the wind's not so bad on the porch.' She glanced at Miss Gregsby without expression, then turned back to me, her lower lip shifting once – enough to tell me, in this woman who customarily guarded her emotions like a high-stakes poker player, that she was indeed badly misinterpreting what she was seeing.

'Please do stay,' I said.

'That would be impossible, Dr Deacon. I just wanted a quick word.'

'About what?'

She gave Miss Gregsby another blank look.

I rushed with the proper forms. 'Miss Wade, this is my new nurse, Miss Henrietta Gregsby, from Rochester. Miss Gregsby, this is Miss Olive Wade, our town midwife and local heiress.'

Miss Gregsby rose from her seat and inclined her head. 'A pleasure to make your acquaintance, Miss Wade.' Miss Gregsby appeared wholly terrified by Miss Wade, who was standing so regally in her furs, her beauty otherworldly.

Miss Wade said with curt politeness, 'How do you do?'

After a few more awkward moments, I took the initiative. 'Miss Gregsby, go inside and sit by the fire.' I hopped to the drive and offered her my hand. 'You've been freezing out here long enough.'

'Yes, doctor.'

I safely conveyed my nurse from the sleigh.

She gave Miss Wade one last nod, then hurried up the drive and disappeared through the side door.

Munroe took the sleigh and horses.

Miss Wade came down from the front porch and joined me on the drive.

Her face was now like a fortress. 'I had no idea you had hired a nurse, Dr Deacon.'

And I had no idea how to proceed, and feared that whatever I said might make matters worse. So I again extended my hospitality while I stalled for time. 'Would you like to come in and sit by the fire?'

'I shouldn't want to trouble you. You've had a long ride in the country, by the look of it, and you need to rest. In fact, I must be off.'

'But you said you wanted a word with me.'

'I'm thinking it can wait. You look tired. And cold.'

'I should like to know why you've come.'

She stared at me, and it was as if all the warm feeling she had ever felt for me had drained away. It was a most daunting spectacle, and I wondered if I had any true knowledge of the woman who was standing before me, or if she possessed an unguessed-at submerged personality I knew nothing about. The only thing I knew for sure was that she wasn't amused.

'Very well, then,' she said. 'I'm here to talk about Marigold Reynolds.'

I stared some more. Baffled, I steered a neutral course. 'You've heard from Sisters of Charity, then, Olive?'

'Not Sisters of Charity, no. But Daisy Pond came to speak to me about her. Do you know the Ponds, Dr Deacon? Of Finch Street?'

'Must you call me by my surname? I thought we were on intimate terms.'

'I'd prefer proper forms right now.'

'Olive, please.'

Her voice became insistent. 'Do you know the Ponds of Finch Street, Dr Deacon?'

I of course remembered what Stanley had told me about Daisy Pond, how she had been hit by Mr Purcell back in October and had come to the Sheriff's Office to press charges against the man. 'Yes. I know the Ponds.'

'Daisy is their daughter. She and Marigold are best friends. Daisy's one of my piano pupils.'

Then Olive caught sight of Munroe and Miss Gregsby going about the business of making a fire through the parlor window. Having construed my nurse in a sleigh with me as perhaps the most nefarious act in human history since John Booth shot Abe Lincoln, Miss Gregsby, in my parlor by my fire, appeared to strike Miss Wade as an even more heinous sin.

She turned back to me with renewed frostiness. 'It turns out

Marigold was with child after all. Miss Pond took me into her confidence about the whole matter at her piano lesson yesterday, and I thought as Marigold's physician you should like to know. Miss Pond tells me Billy Fray is the father.'

'Miss Wade, won't you come in for a few moments? Perhaps you would like a brandy.'

'It would also seem your hypothesis about an Oneida practitioner's involvement in the termination of Marigold's pregnancy is correct as well. Mr Purcell, when he found out about the baby, sent for Talbert Two-Arrows. The child meant more than anything in the world to Marigold. And to Billy. They were both terribly angry at Mr Purcell.'

While my professional side acknowledged that this was yet more evidence against Billy, personal impulses drove me to place my hand upon Miss Wade's arm. 'Olive, please come in.'

She removed her arm. 'I'm afraid I can't stay, Dr Deacon. My attentions are presently divided.' She glanced in the parlor window, where Miss Gregsby had just taken off her hat and was shaking out her hair. 'As yours seem to be.'

She then turned and walked away before I could speak to her further.

As she left, I felt two things.

First, I yearned for her. I wanted to take her in my arms and crush her to my chest, and tell her everything was going to be all right.

My second feeling was something approaching a lover's irritation.

What right did she have to question me after her summer away with Everett Howse?

Marigold Reynolds was at her stepfather's funeral in a wheelchair. She wore black. She had a veil over her face, and all I could see were her grimly set lips. I saw no tears. The handkerchief in her hand remained unused.

As much as I wanted to question her about Billy Fray, Talbert Two-Arrows, and their lamentably lost baby, I left her alone. And as much as I wanted to confront her on how, because of the whole Talbert Two-Arrows episode, Billy had more than enough motive to kill her stepfather, I knew it simply wasn't the appropriate time or place.

Stanley was there with me. Billy Fray was nowhere in sight. No one had seen him since the night of the murder, which of course was yet more evidence against him.

To Marigold's left stood a man in his mid-fifties. He wore a black overcoat, pince-nez spectacles, and bore a striking resemblance to Mr Purcell, only thinner. I had to conclude that this was Herschel Purcell, Ephraim's history professor brother from New York University, my victim's chief executor, now arrived in Fairfield after extricating himself from his academic duties. Though not shedding any tears, the professor looked truly grief-struck.

Behind these two stood Sidney Leach and the household staff, seven altogether, including Flora Winters, Marigold's maid, all looking appropriately solemn. And behind these were a great many townspeople – friends, employees, probably a few enemies, and the just plainly curious.

One mourner stood apart from the crowd, a young man, seventeen or eighteen, tall, long-limbed, in an old blue farm coat, no gloves, and a felt farm hat. He had positioned himself by the cemetery fence, and was the only one in all that large group who cried.

He now took off his hat. He clutched it and twisted it, as if he wanted to squeeze blood from it, then held it in front of him, up to his face to wipe tears away. Why should he be the only one in this whole graveside group besides Professor Herschel Purcell who was genuinely grieving for the old man's passing?

I leaned toward Stanley. 'Who's that young man over there?'
Stanley looked.

After a moment's hesitation, he said, 'Clarence Swinford.' His eyes narrowed. 'Albert Swinford's son.'

'The man who told me the shot came from the back alley?'
'Yes.'

I began to smell cayenne pepper again. 'Strange.'
'I'll say.'

It seemed as if Stanley was starting to smell cayenne pepper too.

'So I understand. But Clarence Swinford crying at Mr Purcell's funeral – and he was the only one – needs looking into.'

Fletcher thought about it and finally shrugged. 'As I say, I can't help you there. But I was thinking about the murder just last night and there's something you might want to know about it.'

'What's that?'

'You may have noticed how Isaac Jensen has a big going-out-of-business sign in his hat shop window across the street.'

'I have.'

Fletcher paused, as if he felt he had to give me a moment to appreciate and prepare myself for the gravity of what he was about to say. 'It's Ephraim Purcell who's driving him out of business.' The yard boss now seemed keen on proving his worth as a top-flight supplier of town information and gossip. 'He and Purcell go way back. All the way back to business school in New York City, as a matter of fact. If anybody has a bone to pick with Mr Purcell, Isaac Jensen does.'

My brow rose – a new lead after all, just not the Swinford one I had been hoping for. 'And how is Mr Purcell driving Mr Jensen out of business?'

'The usual way. By undercutting him. Taking a loss to drive him under. Heard it from Rufus Hankins.'

'Rufus Hankins?'

'The bar-keep at the Grand Hotel.'

'Oh.'

'Who heard it from Eugene Lapinance.'

I nodded, catching on. 'The hotel manager?'

Fletcher gave his own nod. 'And I guess Eugene got it straight from Mr Purcell.' Mr Fletcher offered explanation. 'Eugene and Mr Purcell are thick.'

'I see. And Mr Purcell was driving Jensen under any way he could?'

'Yes.'

'I take it you refer to the hat sales the New York Emporium is constantly having?'

'I am.'

'Why do you suppose Mr Purcell wants to drive Mr Jensen out of business?'

Fletcher thought about it. 'Purcell and Jensen were good friends at one time. Now they ain't. Eugene says a woman drove them apart.'

ELEVEN

The following day, clouds thickened over Fairfield, and weather grew milder.

Miss Gregsby and I saw patients in the morning.

At lunch, I walked over to the Corn Mercantile Building a spoke to Mr Erwin Fletcher, the yard boss. He wasn't particular tall, but he was rangy in his movements, swaggering from side side as he approached me, his arms moving as if to clutch and pic an invisible cotton crop, his toes, in cowboy boots, pointed outward

'Howdy, doc.'

'Morning, Erwin.'

After a brief discussion about the change in weather, I came to the matter at hand. 'In your line of work, I guess you run into farm-folk of all kinds.'

'That's true, doc, I do.'

'I'm just wondering how well you know the Swinfords.'

He hesitated, then nodded. 'They buy their livestock here. They buy their feed here. And we buy all kinds of things from them. Mrs Swinford's preserves can't be beat.'

'What about Mr Swinford? What kind of man is he?'

'I don't think you'll find a harder-working farmer anywhere in Genesee County.'

'And his boy, Clarence?'

'As hard-working as his father. And smart. He'll be going to college next year, if everything works out.'

'He was crying at Mr Purcell's funeral. Does he know Mr Purcell?'

Fletcher's brow rose. 'Not in any special way, I wouldn't suppose. Though I believe he worked for the man one summer at the Grand.'

'Is there any connection between Mr Swinford and Mr Purcell?'

Fletcher's eyes narrowed and he cocked his head to one side. 'Say, doc, Mr Swinford ain't under suspicion for this here murder, is he?'

For the sake of discretion, I told a white lie. 'Of course not.'

'And Clarence neither? Because they was both right up there on them bleachers when the shot went off.'

'A woman?'

Fletcher nodded. 'Mr Purcell has always been partial to the ladies. And I guess to this one lady in particular.'

'I see. Any idea which lady it was?'

'Can't say as I do. Some lady they knew back in their business-school days together in New York, after they came home from the war.'

I thanked Mr Fletcher for his information, exited the Corn Mercantile Building, and stood on its front steps to survey the Jensen Hat Shop across the street, my curiosity piqued, my investigational appetite whetted.

Of wood-frame construction, the shop had a pretty façade, pink and green, such as its primarily female customers might like, was three stories tall, and was fenestrated with two windows on the second floor and two on the top. I studied these upper windows. Any of them would have made a perfect perch for a rifleman.

I tried to remember what I knew about the Jensen family. Because they were patients of Dr Olaf Thorensen, the town's other doctor, I had never had much occasion to converse with them. The little information I did have came from Jensen's older sister, a spinster, Belva Jensen, my own patient. And all I could recall her telling me was that she liked to spoil her eight-year-old nephew, Alvin, every chance she got.

I moseyed over to find out what I could.

Inside, two young shop girls, presided over by another more matronly woman I recognized as Tilda Jensen, Mr Jensen's wife, stood behind the counter. The two young ladies, if the resemblance was any indication, were Mrs Jensen's daughters. Sitting in the back doorway playing with a toy horse was a much younger member of the family, the eight-year-old son, Alvin, a delicate and intelligent-looking tow-headed boy.

The shop was crowded, mostly with women. The going-out-of-business sign in the front window was having its desired effect, that of drumming up custom.

When Mrs Jensen saw me, her face became welcoming and pleasant. 'Dr Deacon, so nice to see you. Belva was in here just the other day telling me the wonders you've done for her bunions.'

'Good day, Mrs Jensen. Yes, her bunions. The special shoes are helping.' I pointed with curiosity to the sign in the front window. 'You're going out of business?'

Her smile lessened. 'Alas, Dr Deacon, yes. We must fish in other waters now.'

'That's a shame. I'm told you've been a fixture on Tonawanda Road for many years.'

'We have. But we now have high expectations for a new business opportunity in Elmira. We're hoping customers there will recognize craftsmanship and quality, and will choose to buy their headgear not because of price, such as at the New York Emporium, but because of style and durability.'

'Yes, yes, it seems Mr Purcell has a hat sale every week, doesn't he?'

Her expression darkened. 'He buys his hats by the gross in Philadelphia and sells them at a loss. I hardly understand his business methods but he sure has made life unpleasant for the Jensen family.'

I glanced to the back of the shop. 'Is Mr Jensen about? I thought I'd say hello and wish him well.'

'As a matter of fact, Mr Jensen is at present in Elmira looking at suitable properties. If things go well, we will be removing ourselves from Fairfield in the opening days of the New Year. I'll be sad to leave our comfortable home here, and to pull the children out of school, but I'm sure we'll land on our feet.'

'And will Mr Jensen be coming back to Fairfield before the move?'

'He'll be back in a few days.'

I paused, then motioned at the street. 'You of course know of the tragic events of last Saturday evening?'

She grew animated. 'Oh, yes, doctor. It's given us all a scare. I don't think I shall rest easy till you and Sheriff Armstrong catch the culprit. Imagine! And Fairfield such a respectable town.'

'Did anybody in the family see anything? I understand Deputy Putsey spoke to you.'

'No. The girls and I were by the fire in the back and Alvin was asleep. My husband was in his study with the blinds drawn.'

'And did you hear one shot or two?'

'Two shots, doctor. Distinctly two.'

I shook my head. 'It's such a sad business. I'm sorry to disturb you with it. I've actually come on a much happier mission. I would like to buy a hat.'

'For yourself, doctor?'

'No.' I glanced around at the various samples on the shelves, then turned back to Mrs Jensen. 'For Miss Wade. Can you help me choose something that might make her blonde person radiant?'

Mrs Jensen helped me pick out a hat, a Jean Nedra design from Paris, a shimmering specimen, blue brushed velvet, fabulous ribbons, a velvet neck strap, exquisite net detailing, and a lovely red flower made of an ingenious textile. Mrs Jensen boxed my purchase, gift-wrapped it, and away I went, hoping to prove to Miss Wade that my attention was in fact undivided.

Evidence mounted against Isaac Jensen the next day when Lonnie Moses, the Oak Room butler at the Welland Street Club, came to my surgery with some incriminating information about the hatter. Mr Moses was a negro gentleman of some advanced years, from the South, like me, wearing a dark suit and vest.

He behaved in an anxious manner.

'Dr Deacon, it's a dangerous thing for a negro like myself to go accusing a white man, but my conscience can't take it no more, so I decided I had to come and talk to you about it.'

'You can count on my discretion, Mr Moses.'

He nodded deferentially, then looked around the room as if he wasn't used to being in a white man's parlor, gripping the brim of his old-fashioned top-hat and turning it again and again like a steering wheel. 'The night Mr Purcell was killed, I was serving Mr Jensen in the Oak Room. He was sitting by himself. I was serving him drink after drink, and I was getting scared.'

'Why were you getting scared, Mr Moses?'

A crease came to his brow. 'I was afraid because he was stewing about something. The other gents in the room sensed it, too. None of them would sit with him. Even when he asked them to come over, they refused. So finally he asked me to sit with him.' Lonnie shook his head as great dismay settled in his eyes. 'A coloured man generally don't sit with a white man, Dr Deacon. As Southerners, you and I both know that.'

'But this is the North.'

He objected by raising an index finger. 'It ain't so far North it ain't part South.'

I conceded the point. 'I suppose Jim Crow finds his friends in New York State as well.'

He stopped turning his hat and shook his head woefully.

'Mr Jensen started yelling at me, Dr Deacon. Right there in the club. In front of all those other gentlemen.'

'It must have been embarrassing to you, Mr Moses.'

'I don't like it when a white man starts yelling at me. It generally means trouble.'

'He put you in an awkward position.'

'I couldn't sit with him. He knew I couldn't. I been around a while. I know what's good for me. I says to him, "Mr Jensen, I can't sit with you. It ain't right."'

'And I take it this made him angry?'

'He was as riled up as a bear in a bear trap. So I poured him a drink, and then I poured him another, and I said to him, "Mr Jensen, why don't I stand next to you instead. It ain't proper for coloured folk to sit with white folk, you know it ain't. I'll stand here, and you say your say, and I'll be more than happy to listen. Last thing we want is to get these other club members all mad at me for sitting with you." After that, he just stared awhile. Then he says, "Lonnie, if you got to stand, you got to stand." So that's what I did. Just stood there with my silver tray under my arm hoping none of the other gents would need me any time soon. But all the other gents are glancing at me, like I didn't have no right to even stand next to Mr Jensen. Just as I'm feeling like a long-tailed cat in a room full of rockin' chairs, Mr Jensen starts talking to me about Mr Purcell.'

I momentarily sympathized with the poor man's dilemma, then, for the sake of my case, pursued the matter of Mr Purcell. 'And what did Jensen have to say about my victim?'

'He said that thanks to Mr Purcell, the bank was asking him to leave his shop that very day. He then told me it wasn't the first time Mr Purcell's tried to ruin him. "Lonnie," he says to me, "if you knew the half of it." Then Mr Jensen says to me, "Lonnie, I'm going to put a stop to it. I'm not going to let him walk all over me anymore. Before the evening's out, Ephraim's never going to ruin anybody ever again." And then he left by the back door, Dr Deacon, something he's never done before. It made me real nervous. Even more nervous than Billy Fray coming to the front door and doing all that hollerin' earlier on.'

TWELVE

I called on Miss Wade.

I was admitted to the front hall by her maid, Freda. I had brought the Jean Nedra hat. I heard Miss Wade playing her grand piano in the music room at the back, one of Frédéric Chopin's saddest pieces, the Prelude in E minor, Opus 28, Number 4, the so-called 'Suffocation' prelude, a disturbingly emotional piece. Even more disturbing was the pathos she injected into her performance.

Freda, a sturdy woman of fifty in a black and white maid's uniform, retreated to the music room to announce my arrival. After a few moments, the prelude stopped halfway down its descending series of chromatic chords, a strangled dissonance clutching Olive's Steinway. I studied the potted palm in the front hall, in suspense as I waited for the housemaid to return.

When Freda came back, she had a distressed expression on her face. 'Miss Wade is presently not at home.'

I grew still. 'Not at home? But I just heard her playing the piano.'

The corners of Freda's lips drew back and she glanced with worried eyes at the brass umbrella stand. 'Sir, she told me to tell you that she's not at home. And I suppose we must accept her word on the subject.'

I felt disheartened, and also confounded. 'Could you at least give her this present?' I said, offering the hatbox.

'I'm afraid she's asked me not to accept anything from you, doctor.'

I pretended thick-headedness because I couldn't think of what else to do. 'How could she ask you that if she's not at home?'

Shifting with suppressed agitation, Freda said, 'Because, as you know, Dr Deacon, she's a woman of remarkable talents.'

I stared. Then I said, 'Thank you, Freda.' And turned to go.

As I rode Pythagoras down the hill at a slow walk, I couldn't help thinking that the connection between myself and Miss Wade was like a web being stretched thinner and thinner. A part of me wanted to rush back, barge in, and explain that there was nothing between myself and Miss Gregsby, and that she was a fool for ever doubting me, or for ever thinking I would be untrue to her. Another part desisted. What right did she have after Everett Howse? And after the man from Boston? And so I didn't turn back. I kept on, the clip-clop of Pythagoras's hooves muffled by the snow on the ground, the Jean Nedra hat still under my arm, and the connection between myself and Miss Wade growing more tenuous by the moment.

I found Isaac Jensen at home on the appointed day of his return. He was a small man in his late fifties, with a pale Nordic complexion that seemed frosted with tones of talc. He had white-blond hair, and wore wired-rimmed spectacles. He was singularly cheerless. As we shook hands, he gazed at me with bereft blue eyes – I had the impression he was grieving for Ephraim Purcell, despite their troubled past together.

'Come to my office, doctor. We'll be more comfortable there.'

On the way to his office, we exchanged a few words about Purcell.

'We were good friends at one time, doctor,' he explained. 'But not so much anymore. We've had our differences.'

What surprised me most about his office were the twenty-five rifles he had under lock and key in a glass case against the far wall. He saw me scrutinizing the weapons, and a tight grin flickered to his thin lips.

'I'm an avid collector, doctor. But I'm afraid I'm going to have to sell these weapons now. The New York Emporium has driven me out of business and I need to raise capital to start a new venture.' He shook his head, his cheerlessness intensifying. 'It's taken me my whole life to put this collection together.'

'And have you sold any of these weapons lately?'

'Please, doctor. Sit. Make yourself comfortable.' I took a seat on a rocking chair that looked as if it had been around since the Grant Administration. 'Scotch?'

'No, thank you.'

'Not a drinking man?'

'Not at this time of the day.'

'Do you mind if I go ahead?'

'Suit yourself.'

He fixed a scotch. As he opened the large liquor cabinet, I noted, as if fate were conspiring to convict the man any way it could, an extensive collection of whisky flasks, twenty-five or thirty standing shoulder to shoulder.

Rifles and flasks. I hadn't even properly started my questions, and I was ready to indict Isaac Jensen as my murderer.

He finished pouring a drink for himself, closed the cabinet, and turned to me. 'You were asking?'

'If you've sold any weapons recently.'

He frowned. 'Doctor, why don't you get to your point? You might lead Tilda around like a Jersey cow, but I'm a man of education. So please don't tip-toe.'

I paused to reassess. 'Very well, Mr Jensen. I've come about Mr Purcell's murder. As you say, you and Mr Purcell were at one time great friends but that as of late you've had a falling out.'

He nodded over the rim of his scotch glass. 'We fought in the Civil War together.' He grinned, and in that grin there was a lot of heartache. 'That's a bond most men don't break. But he broke it.'

'And the reason I ask about rifles is because I see you're a collector. The weapon used in Mr Purcell's murder appears to have been a collector's item. Do you by any chance own a Civil War era Henry?'

He grew reflective. 'I owned a Henry once. Not anymore. Nothing like a Henry for accuracy and rapid fire. It's a great weapon. I particularly like the distinctive butt, with the brass trim at the back.'

'What happened to your Henry?'

'I lost it. In a bet. Years ago.'

I honed in. 'I also understand that on the night of the murder you told Lonnie Moses you were going to make sure Mr Purcell never ruined anybody ever again.'

For several seconds he didn't answer. Then some colour climbed into his otherwise ghostlike complexion. 'I was upset. I got word from my creditors that morning that we had to leave the hat shop. Then at the club I drank more than I should have. My tongue got loose with Mr Moses.' With a great deal of deliberateness – too much, I should think – he added, 'For all that, I would never take Ephraim's life. Not after I risked my own saving it.'

I was puzzled. 'You saved his life?'

He nodded. 'We were under sniper attack. This was in Georgia, May of sixty-three. Ephraim was wounded, in the open, and a sniper was taking pot-shots at him. I killed the sniper and dragged Ephraim to cover.'

I paused to assimilate this information, then continued with my interview. 'A whisky flask of considerable value seems have been taken from Mr Purcell's person after he was murdered. I look into your spirits cabinet and I see you have an extensive flask collection.'

He shook his head. 'You're right, Dr Deacon, I collect flasks. But that doesn't mean I killed Ephraim Purcell just to rob his corpse of one. I have plenty.'

'If you killed a sniper during the Civil War you must be a crack shot, easily capable of hitting what appears to have been a target of at least modest difficulty out on Tonawanda Road. Can you see why I must be diligent in following this up?'

In a clear unperturbed voice, he said, 'It's true that I'm an expert marksman. But it's also true that I was passed out in this chair when Ephraim was murdered, so there's no way I could have killed him.' Jensen took a sip from his scotch glass. He then tried sprinkling some of his own cayenne pepper. 'But if you're looking for suspects, maybe you should talk to Albert Swinford.'

With the mention of Albert Swinford, our exchange came to a halt. After not getting a Swinford lead from Erwin Fletcher, it seemed I was now going to get one from Jensen. 'I would be much obliged, Mr Jensen, if you would kindly tell me why you think I should talk to Mr Swinford.'

He looked out the window where on the street I saw the north-bound tram of the Tonawanda Road Electric Tram Car Service heading up the hill toward Hoopertown.

'Ephraim had an affair with Melissa Swinford, is all.'

I paused to orient myself. 'Mr Swinford's wife?'

Jensen nodded. 'It happened back in the eighties. She wasn't the first woman, either. Oh, no, there've been others. Some stretching all the way back to his New York City days.' He grew lost in thought. I remembered Erwin Fletcher telling me about a woman driving Purcell and Jensen apart. Jensen looked up at me, his pale blue eyes now helpful. 'It was a bad business with Mrs Swinford, Dr Deacon.' He took one last sip of his scotch and put the glass on the table. 'And I know Albert Swinford's never forgiven Ephraim.'

'Bad in what way?'

'I don't know the precise details. But I know Ephraim used his usual heavy-handed tactics. By the time it happened we were already on the outs with each other, so he never gave me the whole story but he sure let me know how he was having his way with one of the county's prettiest women, and that there wasn't anything she or her husband could do about it. The way I figure, everything that happened was completely against Melissa Swinford's will. And against Albert's, too. And if that doesn't make a husband want to kill someone, I don't know what does.'

THIRTEEN

I stopped by the Sheriff's Office later that afternoon to talk to Stanley Armstrong about the case.

I first started by asking him if he or the junior deputies had seen any sign of Billy Fray.

'Not a hair,' he said. He clucked his tongue, then gave me his opinion. 'The way I see it, Billy killed Purcell, then sold his rifle so he could raise money to run on. Robert McGlen tells us he was at the club the night of the murder wanting Purcell to come out and fight. Everyone knows Purcell makes a regular stop at the hotel on Saturday after he has dinner at the club. Billy walked round to the smithy after going to the club, retrieved his rifle, which he got earlier in the day from his gun locker at the Shooters Club, then got himself to the hotel to wait for Purcell. That's about as premeditated as it gets. And the fact that no one can find Billy makes him look even guiltier.'

We discussed Billy for a while. Once we were done, I revealed to Stanley my new suspect, Isaac Jensen, outlining all the damning details of the enmity between Purcell and Jensen. I finished by saying, 'And the man's a flask collector.'

The sheriff shook his head. 'I hardly think Jensen's going to shoot a man to rob him of his flask. And what about this here wound angle you're concerned about? It's not possible a man would shoot him from the roof or an upper window, then come down and rob him. He wouldn't have the time.'

'That only means we're missing something. It doesn't mean Isaac couldn't have taken the flask.'

'I don't think he would shoot him for his flask when he has a whole collection of them.'

'Stanley, in Cross Plains, men shot each other for their boots. You know that. Just because we're in the civilized East doesn't mean men are any different. Maybe the flask had some special significance. Maybe it was a point of contention between them. Or maybe Jensen shot him over this here woman Erwin Fletcher told me about, or for driving him under, or maybe for some other insult we don't know anything about yet, and then took the flask as an afterthought. And though I'm still concerned about the wound angle in a robbery scenario, it doesn't necessarily rule it out. I'm going to see Judge Norris about the flask. I'll ask him to sign a court order to search the hat shop and the upstairs rooms. Maybe we'll find it.'

I then explained to Stanley what I knew about Albert Swinford. 'Jensen told me Purcell had an affair with Melissa Swinford years ago. It happened back in the eighties. If it happened back in the eighties, and we know that Clarence, the son, is in his mid-teens, then it just might be possible that he's not Albert Swinford's son at all. He could be Purcell's son, and that's why he was crying at the funeral. And if he's Purcell's son, and Swinford knows it, maybe it galls Swinford every day of his life, and it finally just got too much for him.'

Stanley gave the matter some thought, leaning back in his chair, rubbing one side of his mustache with two fingers, then the other. 'I would tread lightly, here, Clyde. Right now, you don't have proof that Swinford's involved in this at all. And making assumptions about who Clarence Swinford's pa is might cause more problems than it solves. As for Jensen, the wound angle and the flask robbery are like opposite ends of the same magnet. They repel. And until you can get them to attract, I think they just confuse each other, which means I think they're going to confuse the whole investigation if we don't watch out.'

Later, I rode south on Fredonia Street. I crossed Fifth County Road and left the town behind, climbing the gentle and well-settled slopes of the Tonawanda River Valley. I then traveled, over the course of the next hour, to the more isolated and sparsely populated farmland tracts of the southern counties. The land evened out, and the wind came barrelling down from the north, unchecked by any protective topography or trees.

It had been snowing for most of the trip – thick, heavy flakes that stuck to man and horse alike. Pythagoras, as usual, was tireless, and made her way through the worsening conditions with only modest difficulty. The ride was long and hard. I was glad when the Swinford farmstead finally came into view.

I turned up the drive to the farmhouse. The log construction abode was a pretty red one with white shutters, two chimneys, and a broad front porch.

By this time the snow had stopped. As I rounded the back, I saw young Clarence clearing snow from the farmyard with a horse-drawn plough. He heard me coming and turned. He shook on the reins to stop his horse.

He observed me for a few seconds. 'Morning, sir. It's Dr Deacon, isn't it?'

'It is.' I brought Pythagoras to a halt. 'And you're Clarence?'

'Yes, sir.'

'Is your pa about? I'd like a word with him.'

The corners of his lips tightened and his eyes narrowed; it was as if at the mention of his father something changed – all his initial civility disappeared and he now looked as blank as the snow around him. 'He's out in the wood-lot, fellin' trees. I can show you the way, if you like. Lots of paths back there. You could take a wrong turn somewhere and get yourself lost.'

'I'd be much obliged. You want to ride that plough horse, or do you want to climb on the back of mine?'

'Thunder, here, he don't take kindly to people riding him. Let me just tie him up.'

After unhitching Thunder from the plough and tying him to a nearby maple, Clarence came over to Pythagoras. I took my boot out of my stirrup so he could get a foothold, and with one athletic jump he was up and over the animal, and sitting behind me.

I spurred her to a walk and we soon followed a trail out past the barn and across a field.

A line of brown trees fringing the bottom of some hills drew closer.

'What brings you to Reese's Corners, sir?' asked Clarence. He spoke in a cautious tone. 'We don't get many visitors out this way. Someone we know in town sick? Maybe Mrs Wiley?'

'I heard you know the Wileys.'

'We do, sir. Ma's good friends with Mrs Wiley. I sure hope she ain't sick. She tends to get the ague this time of year.'

'No one's sick, Clarence. I've come to talk to your pa about Mr Purcell's murder. I want to verify that he heard just the single shot, and that it came from the back alley behind the Corn Mercantile Building.'

I could feel him tightening behind me.

He didn't speak until we were nearly at the trees. 'Pa's never wrong about things like that, sir. He was in the army, so knows a thing or two about gunfire and how to track it. And I was there with him. I heard the shot. So I think maybe you wasted a lot of horse flesh coming all this way.'

'There's a three-pronged fork up here. Which way do I go?'

'Keep straight. Through those cedars.'

I kept straight. Dark cedars bordered the path on either side, the branches thick overhead, arching above us like joined green hands. 'So you heard the shot, too?'

'Yes, sir.'

'And did you hear one shot or two?'

'One shot. I know some people say they heard two, but there was only one.'

'And it came from the back alley?'

'Yes, sir.'

'Your father and you are certainly insistent on that point.'

Some irritation crept into his voice. 'We know what we heard.'

'And were the two of you in town by yourselves, or was your mother with you?'

'She was with us.'

'And did she hear the shot as well?'

'She was visiting Mrs Wiley at the time. They were practicing Christmas carols for the church Christmas Concert so she didn't hear much of anything.'

'I understand you once worked for Mr Purcell.'

He hesitated again. 'Back when I was fifteen. At the hotel for the summer. He taught me accounting. Or at least some of the basics.'

'I saw you at Mr Purcell's funeral. You were crying.'

He didn't say anything for a long time. As we emerged from the cedars and climbed the hill out of the trees, I sensed a slackening of his body behind me. We entered a snow-covered meadow that sloped upward. A hand-pump from an old well rose out of dead fallow, its iron handle and spout rusted from years of disuse.

He said, 'Don't funerals make you sad? Like I say, he taught me a lot that summer. He knows a great deal about business, and I plan on going to business school.'

I let it go at that.

We found Mr Swinford a short while later. He was felling a pine tree with a broadaxe. An ox in a harness with drag chains stood nearby, ready to haul the tree back to the farmstead. Despite the cold, Swinford had removed his coat and shirt, and was bare from the waist up. For a man his age, he had a Herculean physique. He had his back to us as we approached.

He was just lifting his axe to take another swing at the tree when he must have heard us. He stopped, turned, saw us, and lowered the axe. His breath steamed over in the cold, his face was red, and his mustache had some frost clinging to it. His bare skin steamed as well, so that I had the passing fancy he was a creature from the underworld. He made no move to greet me, or attempted anything even remotely approaching social grace, but just stood there, as uncivil and uninviting as a tombstone, looking like he was getting ready to run me off his land with his axe.

Clarence got off Pythagoras. I followed suit.

'Morning, doc,' the farmer called at last. 'Son, you'd best run back to the house and finish with that snow ploughing.'

The two stared at each other for a few moments. Something passed between them, I wasn't sure what.

Clarence finally said, 'Yes, pa.'

The boy turned around and headed back.

We watched him go.

Then I glanced at Swinford. Here was a man with no chinks in his armour.

He swivelled toward me with all the friendliness of a Comanche warrior on the warpath. 'You've come to talk to me about Purcell. Ain't no other reason you'd ride all this way. But I already told you all I know.'

He lifted his axe and got ready to chop again, like we were done.

So I used an axe of a different kind. 'Is it true Purcell took advantage of your wife?'

He stopped, the axe poised high above his head. After a long pause, he took a swing at the tree and lodged the axe deep into its white meat with considerable force. He dropped his hands away from the axe handle, turned to me, his face now as ruddy as a piece of smoked ham. 'Is that why you're here? Because of some old rumour you heard in town?'

'I thought I would come to you first, Mr Swinford.'

In a more snappish voice, he asked, 'Come to me for what?'

'To find out how you feel about Mr Purcell. And to learn how the members of the Swinford family connect to Mr Purcell.'

'Ain't no connection at all, doc. You wasted your time.'

I tapped the badge on my coat. 'I've been entrusted by the county to solve Mr Purcell's murder.'

'I've already cooperated with the county. I heard the shot. It came from the alley between the Grand Hotel and the Corn Mercantile Building. That's all I got for you, doc. Do what you want with it. But I'd be careful about the rumours you hear in town. They're usually lies. There was never anything between my wife and Purcell. Melissa and me have been married in the Lord for twenty-two years, and we've shown no dishonour to each other since our wedding day.'

'Do you own a Henry rifle, Mr Swinford?'

He frowned. 'I'm a Winchester man, myself.'

'Do you mind if I check the house, the barn, and the outbuildings for weapons?'

His frown deepened, got a hacked look to it, like the tree he was chopping. In words as cold as the day, he said, 'You're not welcome here, doc. I'd appreciate it if you got off my land. I'll give you five minutes. After that, I'm setting my dogs on you.'

As I had no legal authority to stay, I nodded a brief goodbye, got back on my horse, and headed out of the woods back to the farm.

In the farmyard, I found Clarence ploughing away. He looked at me. He didn't say anything. He didn't even wave.

I continued on.

In the kitchen window, I saw a woman peering out at me – Melissa Swinford, in an apron, a shirtwaist with puff sleeves, her hair up. When she caught sight of me, she quickly closed the curtains, as if she didn't want me to see the tortured look in her eyes.

Far in the forest, Swinford's tree crashed to the ground, scaring a few grouse into the air.

They flew away in a panic, like lost souls fleeing the gates of Hades.

PART TWO
An Invitation to the White House

FOURTEEN

Ambrose Johnstone, Purcell's lawyer, came to the surgery for an appointment. Though ostensibly his complaint was one of an ingrown toenail, I soon came to realize he was here for more than just this small affliction, and that he had in fact come to talk to me about his client's murder.

He sat with his bare foot in front of me. I had my examination lamp turned against the offending toe. The nail had curved into his skin, and the epidermis was inflamed. I glanced at his shoes – expensive dongolas with an opera toe – then at the patient himself. He was in his late fifties, had a rim of argent-tinted hair around his bald pink pate, and possessed the fleshy face and generous mid-section of a man who enjoyed a fine meal more often than was good for him.

'I usually see this condition in younger men, Mr Johnstone. Those who are more active on their feet.'

He shook his head stoically. 'I've been suffering with it for a while now, doc. I've had to take a good shot of whisky now and again to dull the pain.' With glum consolation, he added, 'At least I've got an excuse for Edna now.'

'You should get rid of those fancy dongolas and wear something more sensible. Something with a London toe, perhaps. That's your long-term solution. Short-term, you should be soaking the injury four times a day in warm water. I know you're a busy man, but it will help. Stick a roll of cotton batting under the offending nail. This will train it to grow properly. And if you notice even the slightest sign of infection, come to me immediately.'

'I will, doc.'

I then set about treating the toenail.

While I was doing this, he talked about the Purcell estate, and by this circuitous route, the Purcell murder.

'Mr Wilfred Hurren at the Exchange Bank gave Professor Purcell and me access to the accounts this morning, and I've learned that more than half of Mr Purcell's assets are owned by Marigold, and that fully sixty percent of the estate is from her mother's side. The profits generated by those assets are supposed to be deposited in a trust fund for Marigold, available to her when she turns twenty-five. But it now appears a substantial portion of them have been funnelled into a private bank account in Switzerland. The account holder is Ephraim.' He shook his head. 'I hate to admit this, Clyde, but it looks as though Ephraim has been robbing his own stepdaughter. Before I came here, I drove up to Cherry Hill Road and had a word with young Miss Marigold about it. She says she's known of the scheme for a number of years but has been too afraid to do anything. From what she tells me, she's lived in a state of terror ever since poor Francine died. She's been powerless to stop her stepfather's robbery.'

This was indeed interesting news. I sniffed the first faint scent of a new motive and a possible new suspect in my case – just because Marigold was in hospital the night it happened didn't mean she couldn't have been involved in Purcell's murder. Perhaps she and Billy were in it together?

'Marigold never told you anything about this before?'

'No.'

'Has she told anybody?'

Johnstone flinched as I snipped off a piece of nail. 'Just her friend, Daisy Pond, and more recently, Billy Fray. They urged her to go to the sheriff, or even Judge Norris, but she was too afraid.'

'What have you advised now?'

The lawyer shrugged. 'Her stepfather's dead, so the point's moot. I only raise the matter because it pertains to Ephraim's murder. His wholesale robbery of his stepdaughter would certainly be a motive.'

'I was just thinking the same thing.'

But it turned out Johnstone was having a different train of thought in regard to motive than me.

'Not that I think Marigold herself had anything to do with the crime. Heavens, no. But as Professor Purcell is understandably anxious to see someone prosecuted for the slaying of his brother, he felt it my duty to bring to your attention Billy Fray's particularly angry reaction to Mr Purcell's piracy of Miss Marigold's monthly dividends. Herschel can't help thinking Billy may have taken things into his own hands on her behalf. When you add it to everything else you have against him, it's certainly worth looking at. Professor Purcell would be greatly obliged if you would pursue it vigorously.'

Once again, things were mounting up against the poor young

blacksmith, and the evidence might have been definitive if it hadn't been for the growing number of suspects in my case.

'Thank you, Johnstone. I'll most definitely look into it.'

'And please try not to bother Marigold too much about it. She's terribly upset as it is, and her condition is still delicate. Yes, yes, she's had to admit to Herschel and me what's happened, and we know all about her pregnancy. I always thought the girl had more sense than that.'

Munroe brought my mail to me on a tray at lunch time.

I hadn't received my consult note on Marigold from the doctors at Sisters of Charity yet, and with this new information about the pirated dividends Johnstone had brought me, I was now growing suspicious in regard to its tardiness. I searched for a consult note on the tray, but it still hadn't arrived.

Yes, it was extremely late.

Why hadn't it come?

There were two possible explanations.

Either the transcriptionists at the hospital were backed up.

Or Marigold hadn't gone to the hospital in the first place and had been here in town on the night her stepfather had been murdered.

Which meant she could have had a direct hand in the crime, and not just colluded in it.

Though no consult note from Buffalo came, I did find an envelope from the White House, the dimensions of which told me it was my annual invitation to the president's Christmas party.

I slit the envelope and had a look. At the end of the formal printed part of the invitation, Theodore had written a personal note. 'I do hope you can attend, Clyde. We had such a jolly time at Sagamore Hill in August. And please bring Olive Wade. After all the belly-aching you did about her on Long Island, Edith and I feel we almost know her. And of course bring Jeremiah if he's back from Boston at that time. Kermit would so love to see him.'

Alas, my son wouldn't be home from Boston until later in the month. What had me more disturbed was the president's insistence I bring Olive Wade. How could Theodore expect me to bring Miss Wade to Pennsylvania Avenue when she wasn't even accepting my calls at Poplar Avenue? His request seemed more daunting than his standing invitation to explore the uncharted tributaries of the Amazon after he was done being president.

I ruminated on the problem until Munroe interrupted me a second time.

'The sheriff's come to see you, doctor.'

I at first feared the sheriff had driven himself so hard that he had precipitated a fatiguing illness, and had come to see me as his doctor, not as his deputy.

But it turned out there had been a development in the murder case.

'Clyde, we caught Billy Fray. He was holed up in the Pleasant Hotel. Putsey and Mulroy went up the front while I went around the back.'

I inspected my old friend. 'And judging from your condition, Stanley, I take it he came out the back?'

The sheriff touched a gash on his left eyebrow. 'He put up quite a fight.'

It appeared Stanley needed me as his doctor after all. 'Let me clean you up and get you bandaged.'

He dutifully followed me into the examining room.

Once I had him sitting on the table, and was dabbing at his one-inch laceration with hydrogen peroxide, he said, 'I do believe Billy Fray's your man, Clyde. He wouldn't have put up such a fight if he wasn't. Also, we now have an eyewitness.'

I paused in my ministrations. 'An eyewitness? Who?'

'Alvin Jensen, Isaac Jensen's eight-year-old son. It turns out he saw Billy on the night of the murder. He was looking out his bedroom window. He says Billy was behind those garbage cans with a rifle.'

I grew immediately suspicious. 'Yes, but Isaac Jensen is a suspect in our case, Stanley. Now you're telling me his eight-year-old son saw Billy Fray murder Ephraim Purcell? Jensen might be coaching his son to deflect blame. And by the way, it looks like you're going to need a stitch or two.'

An irritated knit came to the sheriff's brow, making the gash bleed even more. 'Question the boy yourself, Clyde. Isaac Jensen has him down at the Sheriff's Office. He was looking out his bedroom window at the whole thing.'

'Stanley, you know children make unreliable witnesses. The three times we had child witnesses in Cross Plains, we always had one or two jury members not willing to trust their word. Killers and horse thieves went free because of our child witnesses. Now you want to try again?'

With some sourness, Stanley said, 'You come over to the Sheriff's Office and talk to him yourself, Clyde. You know Miss Wharry?'

'The school teacher?'

Stanley nodded. 'She says Alvin's one of the smartest grade-schoolers she's ever taught. I'm telling you, Clyde, I've questioned him every which way, and his story stays the same. Not like those kids in Cross Plains. He says he saw Billy Fray in that back alley behind those trash bins on one knee with the Henry poised ready to fire while Purcell was leaving the Grand Hotel. Putsey and Mulroy questioned him independently, and got the same story. The boy knows what he saw.'

Just like the Swinfords knew what they had heard, I thought, with some scepticism.

'Stanley, you have no suspicion that Mr Jensen is putting his son up to this in order to get us looking at somebody else other than himself?'

'If Alvin's story wasn't so consistent, I might have thought that. But come talk to him yourself. That is, after you sew up this here scratch.'

FIFTEEN

The child was asleep. Isaac Jensen tried to rouse the boy, but when boys that age have a mind to close their eyes, there's little God or anybody else can do to stop them.

'I'll stop by the hat shop later,' I told Jensen.

'He's telling the truth, doc.' There was a pleading tone to the man's voice. 'My little Alvin has never told a lie in his life.'

But Jensen seemed too desperate to convince.

Once Jensen was gone, and because I was already in the jailhouse, I talked to Billy Fray.

He looked as if he had been mauled by a pack of wolves – Stanley had that effect on a man when he decided to put up his dukes.

'Billy,' I said, 'it's looking bad for you. The evidence keeps mounting up. First off, everybody in town knows Purcell was trying to keep you away from his stepdaughter. Then there's the matter of the baby – I heard all about Talbert Two-Arrows and the rest of it

from Daisy Pond. Then there's Mr Purcell stealing Marigold's dividends. Then you blame Purcell for kicking you out of the smithy
and for your pa's suicide. To top it all off, you were over at the
Welland Street Club on the night of the murder causing a ruckus.
This was four hours after you went to the Shooters Club to pick up
your Henry rifle. The next day, after the murder, you sold your
Henry rifle. I find a live round of Henry ammo at the scene. You
hole up in the Pleasant Hotel and hide on us. Now we've got little
Alvin Jensen says he saw you shoot Purcell.'

Billy was flabbergasted by all this. 'That's plain impossible, doc.
I was nowhere near the Grand Hotel when the old man got shot.'

I kept at him for another half hour, but he maintained his story.
'I was at the smithy, sleeping it off. Ask that dang old butler at the
club. He can tell you how drunk I was.'

Because he insisted for the time being on being intransigent, I did
what any self-respecting strategizing lawman would do – scared him
by telling him he was going to fry in the electric chair if he didn't
start telling me the truth soon, then let him stew in jail for awhile.

I decided it was finally time to talk to Marigold Reynolds, the
victim's stepdaughter, even though she might still be in a delicate
state of convalescence.

I got on Pythagoras and rode up Cherry Hill.

Leach let me in. I told him my business, and after a wary look
he said, 'She's by the fire in her studio. I'll have to ask her if she's
fit for visitors. She's still quite weak.'

I nodded. 'Of course, Mr Leach. But as I'm her doctor, I should
examine her in any case. Think of it as a house call.'

Leach retreated to the studio. I sat on the bench in the big front
hall.

I re-examined the full-length painting of Francine Reynolds,
Marigold's mother. The portrait was eight feet high and four feet
wide, and must have cost a fortune to commission. I got up and
was just inspecting the painter's signature, James Tissot, when Leach
came out and told me Marigold would see me.

I followed the butler down the hall and soon came to Marigold's
studio, a room with three large arched French doors that faced north
on to the grounds. Only the nearest had its curtains open, and through
them I saw a turned-off fountain with gold cherubim and a dozen
cherry trees, leafless at this time of year.

'Marigold, how are you, my dear?'

'You needn't have troubled yourself with a visit, doctor. I'm feeling much better.'

'And have you been taking proper nourishment?'

'Yes, doctor.'

'And getting plenty of rest?'

'Yes, doctor. Flora has been ever so careful with me. And so has cook.'

'And how are your spirits? You've had an awful time. And to have it followed so quickly by the murder of your stepfather.'

She was sitting up, her legs covered with a down comforter decorated with blue peacocks and pink fans. On the table was a cup of hot apple cider with a cinnamon stick. The fireplace, twice as large as any in my house, smoldered with indolent flames, casting shifting light over her pale complexion.

Unexpectedly, her face quivered with emotion, and her eyes, mint and cream, glimmered with tears. 'They say in town that Billy Fray killed my stepfather. My Uncle Herschel has kept me informed.'

I was still concerned about her condition and, as she appeared to have true feeling for Billy, tried to minimize whatever she had heard. 'We've yet to conclude our investigation, my dear. Billy hasn't been formally charged.'

With sudden urgency, she said, 'Please don't execute Billy. I'm sure he had nothing to do with it.'

'My dear, as your doctor, I'm asking you not to trouble yourself with that just now. You look pale. The physicians at Sisters of Charity looked after you well?'

'They did.'

'And are you now prepared to give me the medical history behind it all?'

She fidgeted. I glanced around the room where I saw an easel with a half-finished painting of snow-covered cherry trees. I waited for her to tell me about Talbert Two-Arrows and the botched abortion, but she remained mute. I waited for her to admit she had been pregnant with Billy's child, but she said nothing.

Then I saw a rifle rack on the wall, and stopped waiting for much of anything because, much to my growing interest, I saw a Henry rifle up there.

Feigning a casualness I did not feel, I strolled over to the rack and got a closer look at the rifle. It was the only weapon there.

In the guise of making conversation, I said, 'Ah. A Henry.' I
turned around. 'I understand you shoot, Miss Reynolds? I chanced
upon your photograph at the Shooters Club.'

'I do, doctor.'

'A most enjoyable pastime.' Realizing I was going to have to
sacrifice, at least for a few minutes, my own treatment plan in regard
to the delicate state of Miss Reynolds's convalescence, I said, 'Did
I tell you I recovered a Henry bullet at the scene of your stepfather's
murder?'

Soon enough, she got my implication. 'But doctor, surely you
don't think I was responsible for my stepfather's murder.'

'I understand that until recently Billy also owed a Henry rifle.'

She sat up, her back straightening with the same rectitude as her
mother's in the full-length Tissot portrait. 'But this is all so ridicu-
lous, doctor. I was at the hospital. And there are several more likely
candidates.' She raised her hands in frustration. 'Isaac Jensen for
one. I don't know what you've heard, or what your investigation's
revealed, but my father did everything he could to drive that poor
man out of business.'

'Yes, I've heard that. And the matter's being looked into.'

'And then there's Albert Swinford.'

I stared. Here again was the farmer from Reese's Corners. 'You
know about Albert Swinford?'

'Yes.'

'How?'

'My mother told me the whole story before she died. Melissa
Swinford told her. They were on the church social committee
together. Mr Swinford has a lot more reason to kill my father than
either Billy or I do.'

'You refer to your stepfather's affair with Melissa Swinford?'

'You've heard?'

'Only the fact of it. I possess none of the details.'

Marigold grew less agitated, her manner more reasonable.

'Mrs Swinford is a picture of rectitude, isn't she? Her father was
reverend before Eric Porteous took over. She's a woman of impec-
cable morals, a God-fearing one, and she lives her life by the Lord.
So when my stepfather grew interested, she of course refused. But
that wasn't going to stop my stepfather. Back then, he owned Reese's
Corners, and all the properties around it. In fact, the reason it's
called Reese's Corners is because my stepfather's middle name is

Reese. When Mrs Swinford wouldn't give him what he wanted, he raised their rent – the same thing he did to Mr Fray – and said he would run them off their land if she didn't surrender her charms. In order to hang on to the farm, she had no choice. My stepfather didn't care that Mr Swinford should know. In fact, it gave him greater pleasure that he did. At least that's the way my mother told it. In church, Mrs Swinford holds her head up high. But you can tell she thinks she has one foot in hell.'

I digested all this, then probed further. 'So am I to infer that Clarence Swinford knows who his real father is?'

Marigold stared at me, and an admiring grin came to her face. 'Your powers of deduction are indeed remarkable, doctor.' She gave me a nonchalant nod. 'Yes, Clarence knows. And since the reading of the will, we have found out that a provision has been made for Clarence. He will go to college, thanks to the Purcell estate. Isn't that lovely, doctor? At least some good has come of my stepfather's death.'

On the way out, I encountered Flora Winters, Marigold's maid, in the front hall, dusting the frame of the magnificent full-length painting of the late Mrs Reynolds. As Flora had accompanied Marigold to Buffalo, I thought now was my opportunity to verify that Miss Reynolds had actually gone.

'Miss Winters, a word.'

She stopped dusting and turned. 'Sir?'

'I've yet to receive my consult note in regard to Miss Marigold's admission to Sisters of Charity. I assume you were the one who spoke to the admitting physician upon arrival?'

Colour climbed into her face. 'Yes, sir, I was.'

'And you let them know I was her doctor, and that I have my mailing address on Culver Street?'

'I did, sir.'

'Because I haven't received my consult note yet.'

'I gave them your address, sir.'

'Good girl. What did the doctors say once they assessed her?'

She paused again. 'Only that my mistress was in stable condition and that she would pull through with proper rest and nourishment.'

I left the Purcell mansion thinking that if I did not get my consult note the next day I would have Henny – for that's what I called

Henrietta Gregsby now – telephone the hospital to see if it had gone astray.

I took the Cherry Hill Road bridge back into town.

I hitched my horse in front of Jensen's Hat Shop and went inside. Tilda Jensen gave me a worried look from behind the high mahogany counter – I surmised she was now fully aware of her husband's place in my case.

In a lowered voice, she said, 'Alvie's awake now. He's in the back room waiting with his father.' A pinch now coming to her brow, she said, 'Dr Deacon, I know my Isaac didn't do this. I know he didn't. Please. We've lost our business. I don't want us to lose Isaac, too. I know he's had his troubles with Ephraim, but he would never kill the man.'

'Madam, we're by no means close to making an arrest just yet, so I implore you not to worry. Your husband is just one of many possible suspects the sheriff and I are looking at, and by no means at the top of our list.'

I found Alvin in the back room with his father playing with a toy Indian and a toy cowboy. Oddly, he wasn't making them fight, as most boys would. He was making them talk, a conversation about fishing spots in the river. As I came in, he stopped and looked at me.

Mr Jensen came forward and put his hand on his son's shoulder. 'Alvie, this is Dr Deacon. He's come to talk to you about what happened out front. Remember you told the sheriff? About the man with the rifle behind the garbage cans? Now the doctor wants to hear it.'

The boy looked at me, then at his father, then back at me. He waited with wide expressionless eyes. I moved forward and knelt next to him.

'Can you tell me about the man with the rifle, Alvin?' I asked.

He looked at his father again, then back at me. 'I saw the man shoot the other man.'

'And do you know who the men were?'

He nodded. 'Mr Purcell. He's the one who got shot.'

I nodded. 'And who was the man with the rifle?'

'I don't know his name. He puts shoes on horses.'

This, then, amply identified Billy Fray, because that's all he did at the smithy, shoe horses, his father looking after more finicky forge business.

'And what exactly did the man with the rifle do? How did he go about shooting Mr Purcell?'

'He got down on his knee behind the garbage cans beside the hotel, and he shot Mr Purcell.'

Yes, all very well, but I still couldn't help thinking his father had coached him. If I was to trust the veracity of the claim, I needed further specifics. 'And did he do anything else besides shoot Mr Purcell?'

The child grew still. 'He drunk some whisky before Mr Purcell come out of the hotel.'

'Anything else?'

The boy thought some more. 'He dropped a bullet to the ground.'

Unaware that he had delivered to me a critical piece of evidence, something only a true eyewitness could know, he went back to playing with his figures. Taken in conjunction with the Henry bullet I had found at the scene, I now knew I had an even stronger case against Billy Fray.

'Mr Jensen, may I use your telephone?'

'Of course, doctor.'

On the phone, I told Stanley about the additional evidence. 'Did Alvin say anything about the bullet to you?'

'Nope. But I told you he wasn't lying, and this just proves I'm right.' My old partner sounded transcendent with glee.

I always felt I had to do something about Stanley's glee. 'I only wish the wound angle wasn't so wrong.'

I could sense the sheriff fuming with sudden consternation. He then tried to explain it away like a carpenter building a house with rubber nails. 'Purcell must have been coming at him from the ground, or crawling at him, like we talked.'

'Miss Gregsby said she saw him crawling away from the alley, not toward it.'

Thus ended Stanley's glee, his more characteristic orneriness taking its place. 'Dang it, Clyde, the boy saw Billy drop a bullet. Only a real witness would know that. Ambrose Johnstone's been calling me. Professor Purcell wants Billy to go on trial.'

'Johnstone's been calling you?'

'Professor Purcell is apparently mad with grief and wants to see Billy go to the electric chair, the sooner the better.'

I now felt some of my own orneriness. 'And are you thinking of taking what we have to Judge Norris before we've explained away all the other conflicting evidence? What about the wound angle? What about the flask?'

'Clyde, the evidence is now overwhelming against Billy, and the town is growing restless.'

'We're not going to have mob justice, Stanley.'

'And you're the sheriff, now?'

I sighed. 'Just give me a chance to rule out our other suspects before you go taking anything over to Judge Norris. And by the way, I'm beginning to think we're going to have to add Marigold Reynolds to our suspect list.'

Taken off guard by this, he said, 'Marigold Reynolds?' More than taken off guard; stunned. 'You've got to be pullin' my leg. And my arm. I thought she was in the hospital the night it happened?'

'I still haven't got my consult note from Buffalo. And, until I do, we can't be sure she went. Which means she could have been in town. She also owns a Henry. And if Billy was in the alley, and the wound angle is wrong, I can't help thinking she might have been somewhere else, maybe up on the hotel roof, where the wound angle is right, and that the two of them acted together. Two shooters might explain two shots.'

SIXTEEN

The next day, Dr Charles Pritchard, the town dentist, arrived on my doorstep to deliver personally an invitation to his Christmas party.

'I'm terribly sorry about the oversight, Clyde, but because you're so new in town, you weren't on our standing list, and Martha never prepared one for you.' I sensed Henny in the corridor behind me. 'Once we discovered our mistake, I came straight over. I'm afraid it's tomorrow night, awfully short notice, I know, but I certainly hope you can attend.'

I took the invitation, smiling. 'I'd be delighted, Charles.'

'Oh, good. Martha will be so relieved. We've hired some musicians from Buffalo, and there'll be a lot of dancing and jollity, and I'm sure it will turn out to be a capital evening.'

'Splendid.'

'We'll see you at seven, then?'

'I'll be there.'

When Dr Pritchard was gone, I turned around and saw that Henny had disappeared.

I looked for her in the parlor, then the office, then the kitchen, but couldn't find her.

I finally spotted her out the back window walking up and down the drive, no coat on, hugging her arms, her skirt dragging in the snow, her lips pursed, her eyes focused intently – and with great distress – on absolutely nothing.

I walked around to the side door, descended the stairs, and stepped on to the drive. 'Henny, what on earth are you doing out here?'

She looked up. 'Just catching a breath of fresh air, doctor. No need to be alarmed. Do we have a patient?'

I could see there was much need to be alarmed. 'No. I suppose we should take lunch now.' I paused. 'Are you sure you're all right?'

This time she couldn't answer. She turned away from me. Oh, dear. Christmas was often hard for a person if they'd just lost someone. I hurried to assist her. She looked around and saw me coming. Her face creased with anguish and tears welled in her eyes.

I went up to her and put my arm around her. 'Henny, what is the matter?'

At first she couldn't answer, had to struggle to regain her composure, but at last got herself under control.

'I have nowhere to go for Christmas, doctor. I thought I would be fine. I thought I would be happy. But then your friend came with his Christmas invitation, and it brought home to me how lonely I was.'

So. Just as I suspected. Christmas, one of the chief misery-makers of the world, had stirred up things again.

'Come. Sit in the parlor.'

I ushered her along the drive, in the side door, and up the steps to the corridor.

In the parlor I got her sitting in the tabouret chair and built up the fire. I then fetched a linen handkerchief, knelt next to her, and gave it to her.

She dabbed her tears and said, 'It's Martin, you see. My fiancé.'

I remembered my own Emily. 'Yes, dear, I know. It's hard.'

For several seconds she was too overcome to continue. I let her sit for a full minute. Finally she looked at me and said, 'I'm sorry, doctor. It's just that this is the first Christmas I shall be without him.'

'I know, I know.'

She stared at her hands for several seconds.

'His family's in Wisconsin. We were to go for the holidays.'

'My dear, if you need time off to go to Wisconsin, by all means, you can have it.'

This just exacerbated her tears.

'But they don't want me now!' she said with sudden emotion.

I was puzzled. Her future but never-to-be in-laws didn't want her, even though they knew she didn't have a soul in the world?

'Why ever shouldn't they want you, dear? You're one of the most agreeable creatures I've ever met.'

Her emotional condition grew even more volatile.

'Because the Booths blame me for Martin's death!'

Here was a statement that needed some amplification.

'And why should they blame you for their son's death?'

She struggled to regain control. In a calmer tone, she said, 'I was only trying to help him. He was a good doctor, but prone to bouts of melancholia.'

I could see she was too upset to give me instant clarification. So I simply cooed in the most commiserative fashion I could. 'I see.'

'I would go to his room and force him to come to work. I would have to get him to look after himself and to take an interest in things. I would sometimes sing and dance just to get him to smile. As a nurse, I recognized his condition. On the ward, I've dealt with melancholia often, and so I easily recognized it in Martin, even though he always denied it to me. All I was trying to do was help him. All I was trying to do was make him better. And so I thought a change of scene might be beneficial.'

'I prescribe the exact same thing for my patients with like conditions.'

She looked at her hands, thinking, then turned her attention to the fire. In a friable voice, she said, 'I thought a stay in Sodus Point might cheer him up. So I booked a room at the Bright's Cove Hotel, with a view of the lake. A weekend at the beach was all I intended. I thought it would make him happy. And I thought he would be interested to see where I grew up. But then he went for a swim one day and didn't come back.' She looked at me, her eyes bereft, guilty. 'They found him a mile down the beach the next morning. His

parents have never forgiven me. They believe I gave him the means.'
She shook her head, more tears coming. 'When I met them last
spring in Wisconsin, before Martin's death, they treated me like a
daughter. I was so happy. I felt I had found another family. We were
going to spend Christmas with them, Martin and I, but now they
don't want me because they think I'm responsible. They say I never
should have taken him to the water.' Her voice tightened and climbed
into a higher, softer register. 'I'll have to spend Christmas alone.
And no one will invite me anywhere because no one in Fairfield
knows me. You'll go to your party tomorrow night, and I'll have
nothing better to do than darn my socks.'

She wept quietly.

I leaned forward and put my hand on her shoulder. 'My dear, you
don't have to worry about spending Christmas alone. You can spend
it with Jeremiah and me. Put off finding new lodgings until the New
Year. I can't stand the thought of you in a dreary boarding house on
Christmas morning. Not only that, I want you to come to Dr
Pritchard's Christmas party tomorrow night. A young woman such
as yourself should have the chance to dance whenever the opportunity
arises. And weren't you going to teach me some new steps anyway?'

Later, when we had finished with an afternoon of patients, and
Henny was in the surgery restocking dressings, bandages, exam-table
paper, and the like, I went upstairs to the spare room where she was
staying, spied her address book on the secretary, opened it, found
the Wisconsin address of Mr and Mrs Booth, scribbled it down, and
returned to the surgery before my nurse knew I had committed this
small burglary. For I had decided that I was going to have to write
a letter of advocacy to the Booths on the poor girl's behalf.

When I went back downstairs, Henny came up to me with a
puzzled look on her face. 'I phoned the Sisters of Charity Hospital
in Buffalo in regard to the Marigold Reynolds consult note? The
clerk told me she couldn't immediately place her hand on the chart,
but would call us when she had. They're in the middle of reorgan-
izing their filing system.'

'But they have a record of Marigold's admission, don't they?'

'She was going to put in a call to Admitting and get back to me.'

I sighed.

Why not send my consult note off on a hunting expedition to the
Adirondacks for all the difficulty I was having in obtaining it.

* * *

Before Miss Gregsby and I set off for Dr Pritchard's Christmas party the next evening, Munroe pulled me aside while Henny was getting dressed.

My man looked at me with earnest blue eyes and said, 'Is Miss Wade going to be at the party?'

'I imagine she is.'

Munroe shifted with sudden agitation. 'Mind you, it's not my place to give you advice. I'm just happy to be part of a doctor's household.'

I paused. 'And I'm happy to have you as my man, George. You've been an invaluable help.'

He peered at me cautiously, assessing my words.

'So if I gave you any advice, you wouldn't think I was overstepping? Especially because you know Miss Wade a lot better than I do? You'd think I was just trying to help you, like I always do?'

I could see that he was working himself up to something, but that he wanted to test the waters first. 'George, if you have some advice to give me, or something you wish to say in regard to Miss Wade, you're more than welcome to say it. You might be an employee in my household, but that doesn't mean you don't have the right to speak.'

'Well, sir, I'm just wondering about you bringing Miss Gregsby to this here Christmas dance. I hope you don't think I'm being bold.'

'You object to it?'

'I don't object, sir. But a man brings a woman to a dance and it usually means something. If Miss Wade is there, and she sees you coming through the door with Miss Gregsby, she's going to be thinking it means something, too.'

Though I could see his point, I raised what I thought was my chief problem. 'So you think I should just leave Miss Gregsby here at home when we both know how she has her heart set on going, how lonely she is, and how she doesn't have any family in the whole world but us?'

Munroe took a moment to recast his argument. 'Miss Wade's going to see you coming to that party with Miss Gregsby, and after the sleigh-ride incident, it won't matter what you tell her. She's going to see what she's going to see. No amount of explaining's going to change that. And things are going to go from bad to worse as far as you and Miss Wade are concerned.'

He was, of course, raising a legitimate concern, one I had

considered myself; and while I found Munroe's earnest advice touching, I now explained the moral dilemma I faced so that he would better understand my present course of action.

'As a doctor, George, I'm every day faced with the same unalterable equation whenever I prescribe treatment. I must measure risk against benefit. I know I'm taking a risk bringing Miss Gregsby to Dr Pritchard's party. I know I might even jeopardize any future chance I have at an intimate alliance between myself and Miss Wade. But Miss Gregsby has recently lost somebody who was extremely dear to her. Over and above that, her poor late fiancé's family has rejected her for reasons that are tragically misguided. The girl needs kindness. And it's my duty – nay, my moral obligation – to be kind to her. I know what it's like to lose someone. I know what it's like to spend your first Christmas alone. And as much as I've grown to love Miss Wade, and even hope to marry her one day, I can't abandon Miss Gregsby in her hour of need. It would be wrong of me, no matter how much I personally stand to lose.'

Yet as I had Munroe bring the sleigh around, I couldn't help thinking I was being obstinate on purpose. Was it because I wanted to teach Miss Wade a lesson? Maybe it was. After all, what right did she have to doubt me after Everett Howse? And after the man from Boston? I was going to be kind to Miss Gregsby. And Miss Wade was just going to have to accept – and trust – that there was nothing more to it than that.

SEVENTEEN

Miss Gregsby's dress was of considerably greater sophistication than the dresses I saw on many of the local Fairfield damsels later on at the party – she was, after all, from the much larger metropolis of Rochester, where shopping was better by a factor of ten.

As we entered Pritchard's ballroom, I saw that the only woman who might possibly outshine Henrietta Gregsby was Olive Wade.

Olive spotted us as we entered, her large blue eyes like sapphires in her fair face, her red satin ball gown wonderfully set off by the

Christmas tree she was standing next to. She held my gaze for several moments, then turned to Henny. I suppose Caesar seeing Brutus with a knife would have had a friendlier expression. Then she grew upset. She turned from us, knocking a present wrapped in silver tinsel with her toe, and made her way to the dining room without giving us so much as a trace of a greeting.

I again felt a lover's irritation with her. She shouldn't be behaving this way. I had done nothing to induce her mistrust. I thought it was unfair of her to so badly misinterpret appearances. Furthermore, I felt it wasn't up to me to explain. After all, I had never asked her to explain her summer away with the assemblyman or her history with the married man from Boston. So I let her be. She could learn her lesson in peace somewhere.

I broached the whole miserable matter with Stanley fifteen minutes later.

He wasn't in a tuxedo, just his Sunday best. He said, 'It's a woman's God-given right to misunderstand, Clyde, so let her misunderstand awhile. A man can have his diploma in rhetoric. He can even be the president of the best debating club in the country. But if a woman has her mind set on misunderstanding, she's like a mule set on not budging.'

'She ran away. Like I had yellow fever.'

'If that's the case, you should ignore her and do what you came here to do. Make Henrietta Gregsby happy.' He motioned across the ballroom floor. 'Look at her standing there. Everybody's dancing. Not her. She's waiting for you. She doesn't know a soul. Maybe you better go over.'

'What if Olive comes back?'

'You're going to leave Miss Gregsby a wallflower all night just because you're afraid Olive's going to come back? Show the girl a good time, Clyde. After what she's been through, it's the least you can do.'

He had a point. It was my Christmas duty to take a beautiful young woman in my arms and dance her off her feet, no matter how miserable it made me.

Accordingly, as the band finished their current number and struck up 'The Sidewalks of New York,' I walked over to Henny, took her in my arms, and swung her around the dance floor, determined to give her happy memories despite the way I kept a lookout for Miss Wade.

'You're rather good, aren't you?' said Henny.

'With these older dances, yes. My mother made sure I learned how to dance when I was a boy. It's what southern gentlemen do.'

I danced the next three numbers with her, then introduced her to a young sport, Harvey Hamish, son of Marvin Hamish, the county chairman.

Soon the pair were inseparable on the dance floor.

With this Christmas mercy accomplished, I found myself relenting toward Miss Wade. Maybe it wasn't fair I let her learn her lesson in peace. Maybe I should seek her out, even if she hadn't accepted the Jean Nedra hat from me.

With my sentiments softening, I set off like an icebreaker in search of the Northwest Passage.

I knew there was going to be a lot of ice to get through.

I was about to check the study at the front of the house when Mr Purcell's lawyer, Ambrose Johnstone – he of the ingrown toenail – approached out of the throng with another gentleman, one I recognized as my victim's brother, Professor Herschel Purcell.

'Dr Deacon. Can we have a word?'

I stopped my search for Miss Wade, even though I realized I was now becoming exceedingly anxious to find her. 'Of course, Johnstone. Merry Christmas.' I looked inquiringly at his companion. 'This, I take it, is Professor Purcell. I saw you at the funeral, sir. Unfortunately, I couldn't attend the wake, as I had surgery business to attend to, and so I don't believe we were formally introduced.'

'Merry Christmas, sir,' said the professor. 'A pleasure to meet you.'

'The pleasure's mine. My deepest condolences about your brother. I'm doing everything I can to apprehend his killer.'

Sorrow flashed through his eyes. 'Yes . . . well. I'm glad to have a man of your stature – a presidential physician, no less – looking after the case.' Herschel was younger than Ephraim by about ten years, and a lot thinner. He wore a clubhouse tie, an eccentric Persian-design bosom-shirt, and a brown twilled Melton suit. He had a scholarly look, as one might expect from a professor of history, especially with the pince-nez eyeglasses poised over his nose. 'And in fact, it's on this subject Ambrose and I wish to speak to you, doctor. We understand you've captured my brother's killer. This is most splendid news!'

The corners of my lips tightened. I looked at the younger Purcell brother, then at Johnstone, then turned back to the professor. 'If you're referring to the arrest of William Fray, he's currently being detained for assaulting a police officer, not for the murder of your brother. No murder charges have been laid.'

This intelligence produced some disappointment in Professor Purcell, a reaction I could readily discern in the drooping of his Franz Josef-style mustache. 'But I understand he was seen at the Grand Hotel on the night of the murder with a rifle.'

Blast! I had to wonder who had leaked the details of my investigation, and who, particularly, had told him about Alvin Jensen's witness account. I couldn't help thinking it was Jensen himself.

'I admit that certain facts point to Billy Fray's possible involvement in the crime, but there are a number of other suspects I still have to exclude, as well as some discrepancies of a physical nature that need to be addressed.'

Professor Purcell's disappointment turned to distress. Grief, raw and spontaneous, shone from his eyes. Underneath his mustache, his lips trembled. Having lost my own brother, Wyatt, in 1880, to typhoid fever, I knew exactly what he was going through.

Professor Purcell finally got himself under control. 'Mr Johnstone assured me that your other suspects were tangential at best, and the proof against them fragmentary and confused. I've urged him to immediately launch criminal proceedings against Mr Fray. I don't understand why we should delay. I'm hoping to get the matter settled before Christmas, especially now that we have an eye witness.'

'If you're referring to Alvin Jensen, please remember that he is an eight-year-old boy, and that his father is also a suspect in this case.'

This startled him. 'Isaac is a suspect?' Professor Purcell's familiarity with Mr Jensen's Christian name told me that they must know each other.

'He is under investigation.'

The professor turned to Johnstone. 'You didn't tell me about Isaac.'

The lawyer hesitated. 'Yes . . . well . . . he was your brother's good friend for many years. And yours.'

'Oh, dear, I had no idea. We all used to be such great chums together back in New York.'

I cocked my brow and confirmed. 'So you know Isaac Jensen?'

'Heavens, yes. We were a tight little circle back in our Manhattan days. Me, him, my brother. Ben Whitmore. Hattie Whitmore. Oh, dear, this is terrible news.'

I turned to the lawyer. 'Mr Johnstone, if you're acting for Professor Purcell in this matter, I urge you to have him defer criminal proceedings.'

Mr Johnstone motioned at the academic. 'Yes, but Dr Deacon, Professor Purcell isn't the only one in town who wants to see swift justice. Ira Connelly of the *Newspacket* was talking to me just yesterday about the case, and he says that much of Fairfield would like to see Billy Fray executed for the crime. Mr Connelly can't understand what the hold-up is. And I was also talking to Judge Norris, and he admits he's mystified by your current restraint. Mr Purcell was an important man.'

Infernal town! How was a deputy to maintain the integrity of his case if prejudice was allowed to fester?

Calming myself, I said, 'I would hate to see justice done to the wrong man, that's all, Johnstone.' Then I hit upon an idea. 'Maybe I could take Professor Purcell away from you for a few moments. Why don't you allow me the opportunity to give him some perspective on the case?' I patted my breast pocket and took out my cigar case. I turned to the professor. 'I invite you, Herschel, to take a seat with me in the smoking room and have a cigar. I've got a couple fine Imperators here. And Dr Pritchard has a wide range of spirits.' I spied Ira Connelly looming nearby. 'We could talk there more privately.' I motioned toward the smoking room. 'If you'd be so kind.'

The professor and Johnstone looked at each other.

After a moment, Johnstone said, 'I should say hello to Dr Pritchard and his wife anyway. You two gentleman run along. Herschel, we'll speak later.'

The lawyer left us.

I ushered the bereft brother toward the smoking room, getting him away from Ira Connelly as quickly as I could.

EIGHTEEN

'I understand you're a professor of history, Herschel.'
'I am.'
'In any specific field or discipline?'
'Antiquities.'

'How fascinating. Do you ever do field work?'

'Yes. Most recently in Egypt. I was on a three-month dig.'

'So I'm sure you understand how history and murder investigation have many things in common.'

He didn't respond immediately. In the interval, we successfully
navigated our way into the smoking room, where a number of other
gents were pursuing the pleasures of strong spirits and cured tobacco.
We found comfortable chairs in the corner. I went to the bar, got
two bourbons, returned to our pleasant bivouac, and set the drinks
on the table.

Professor Purcell said, 'I perhaps see how history and murder
investigation might have a little in common, sir. But enlighten me
further.'

I nodded, 'In history, you piece the facts together using clues,
either in the form of recorded witness accounts or physical artefacts.
In a murder investigation, you do much the same. I'm sure in Egypt
you had to analyze fragments, and correlate them to other fragments,
and put them in their proper historical context, and measure them
against everything else you've learned about Egypt. That's what I'm
doing with your brother's murder case. What I have now are a lot
of clues, and some of the clues point in one direction, and some in
another. Until I'm confident the clues point to an ascertainable fact,
I continue to analyze, just as I'm sure you do with the material you
unearthed in Egypt. One of the clues I'm curious about, and which
has given me a sleepless night or two, and which may be the thing
that either exonerates or indicts poor Billy Fray, is your brother's
whisky flask.'

His eyes widened over his pince-nez. 'My brother's whisky flask?'

I nodded. 'I'm wondering if you know anything about it.'

His brow rose. 'What on Earth would Ephraim's flask have to
do with his murder?'

'So you know of his flask?'

'Yes, of course. He won it in a bet from Isaac Jensen. He was
proud of it, and of the bet. He said it was proof of how shrewd he
could be.'

Won it in a bet from Jensen? I gave myself some time to process
this new and possibly vital piece of information.

The professor apparently took a moment to consider it as well,
for he presently said, 'Oh, dear. Isaac Jensen. Again.'

'You see?'

I took the Imperators out and used my cutter to snip off the ends. I handed one to Herschel, put one in my mouth, offered a light, then took one for myself.

Once we had puffed for a few seconds, I said, 'I understand your brother carried the flask around with him at all times. Yet it wasn't on his person when we found him deceased in Tonawanda Road. We're now beginning to think the murderer may have taken it from him. Perhaps as an afterthought. Yet he didn't take anything else. Odd, isn't it? Now you tell me your brother won it in a bet from Isaac Jensen. If the flask had originally belonged to Isaac, and it was not on your brother's person when we found him, maybe Isaac wanted it back. If that's the case, you might see why I'm reluctant to go ahead with further prosecutorial action against Billy Fray. Perhaps Isaac took it from your brother. Even though there are certain mitigating facts that confuse the issue of the flask, it certainly makes Isaac Jensen a stronger suspect in the case. Can you tell me about the flask at all?'

The professor cast around. 'The flask . . . the flask.' His expression grew more certain and he nodded. 'By the time my brother won it, he and Isaac were trying to best each other any way they could. So they made a bet. On the 1896 Presidential election, of all things. Ephraim was convinced McKinley would win. Jensen was a staunch Bryan supporter. You wouldn't take Jensen for a fool, but everybody knew Bryan didn't stand a chance. Isaac just gets so pig-headed when it comes to my brother. My brother goaded him. The flask was extremely important to Jensen. I don't know why he wagered it.'

'And why was it important?'

'Because it was presented to him by Theodore Roosevelt.'

'It was?' Usually Theodore had a story about everything, but I didn't recall a story about him giving this flask away to Isaac Jensen. 'When was this?'

The professor screwed up his eyes, remembering. '1895. Roosevelt was still the President of the Board of New York City Police Commissioners. My brother and Jensen attended a reunion of their old regiment at GAR Post Number 327, in Brooklyn, the Grant Post, as it's known. Roosevelt was handing out medals and other presentation pieces. Jensen was awarded not only a medal but also the flask for his brave actions at Monckton, Georgia, when he heroically neutralized a sniper at great risk to his own life to save Ephraim's.'

'Ah, yes. Isaac mentioned this to me.'

Herschel nodded and took another pull on his cigar. 'Isaac was never recognized for those actions at the time. So when Roosevelt presented the medal and flask back in ninety-five, he was terribly moved. And proud. I was there myself. I saw his tears. He particularly liked the flask. Which is why I never understood why he would foolishly wager it in a bet the following year.'

This was all extremely telling. 'You see, Professor Purcell? This is why we don't want to make a headlong rush to judgment on Billy Fray. The flask was missing. Mr Jensen is a flask fancier, and has a whole collection of them. This particular flask now seems to be of special importance to him. Also, Jensen practically lives on top of the crime scene. Add to that the fact that your brother drove Mr Jensen's hat shop out of business, and that they were apparently in a tangle over a woman earlier in their lives, and you can see why I'm concerned. Now Mr Jensen's son is telling us he saw Billy Fray in the alley. Why? Is Jensen coaching him to cast blame away? That makes Jensen look guiltier. Also, Jensen's a sharpshooter. He took out that sniper. The evidence suggests that the shot that killed your brother was a long-range shot. So we really must be careful about who we pick as a defendant in your brother's murder.'

Professor Purcell thought about all this and finally nodded. 'I see your point, Dr Deacon. In the history field, it would be the equivalent of publishing too soon.'

'Precisely. And so we have to gather more facts. I've just now gathered further facts about the flask. But I'm still relatively factless about this woman they fought over. Tell me, do you know anything about her?'

'I already mentioned her. Hattie Whitmore. She and her brother, Ben, were part of our little circle.'

'Ah.'

'Isaac and my brother fought over her when they were school chums in New York City together. Just after the war. Ephraim stole her away from Jensen. My brother couldn't stand the thought of Jensen having someone as exquisitely beautiful as Hattie all to himself. Rather an awful business, really. First my brother stole her away from Isaac, then led her on until he was sure Isaac was married to Tilda, then he ruined her, and left her penniless. I'm glad her brother, Ben, stepped in. He's doing what he can for her but I'm afraid her lodgings in Manhattan aren't the best.' He shook his head.

'My brother's done some awful things in his time, and I don't condone the way he treated Hattie, or Isaac for that matter, but he's still my brother, after all.'

'He ruined Miss Whitmore?'

'Yes.'

'The poor woman.'

'Hattie was heartbroken. And so was Isaac.'

'You see? Motive. Perhaps an even stronger one than the flask.'

Herschel puffed meditatively on his cigar for a few seconds. 'Perhaps.'

'Do you have any idea what the flask looks like?'

Herschel thought for several moments. 'I only ever saw it once. I believe there was an engraving of Ulysses S. Grant on it.'

This didn't coincide with the description Edmund Wilson, the undertaker, had given me. 'You're sure it wasn't Abraham Lincoln?'

The professor considered. 'Maybe it was? I can't be sure. Like I say, I only ever saw it once.'

'Out of curiosity, what did your brother bet in return?'

'His Henry rifle.'

My heart seemed to thud an extra beat. 'A Henry?'

Herschel nodded. 'The one he used as a soldier in the Civil War. My brother actually gave it to Jensen because Jensen kicked up such a fuss about losing his flask. So it's not as if Jensen didn't get anything in return for it. He got the Henry. Which proves my brother isn't that bad after all.'

Having cooled Herschel Purcell's ardour about electrocuting Billy Fray at the earliest possible convenience, and succeeded in gaining critical evidence about Isaac Jensen's flask and his affair with Hattie Whitmore, I went to Dr Pritchard's private study and jotted a few notes down about it all.

I then put the murder investigation firmly from my mind and again focused my attention on finding Miss Wade. I decided I would be a fool not to put aside my uneasiness about Everett Howse. And what should I care about her married man in Boston if he was consigned to her past?

I searched the first floor, but couldn't find her.

So I climbed the stairs, a switchback affair, the first set rising to a capacious landing where a large bunch of mistletoe hung from a chandelier in front of a stained-glass window. I was rounding the banister to go up the next run when I saw Miss Wade coming toward me along the second-floor corridor.

Her brow was pinched and her eyes were intent on the floor, so she didn't at first see me. From her expression, I understood she was upset about something, most probably me. Before I could warn her of my presence, she was already at the step, lifting her resplendent crimson skirt so that I caught a glimpse of her Trilby shoes, her white lisle hosiery, and her taffeta lace underskirt, a decidedly intimate view that stunned me into silence for a few seconds.

When she looked up, she was already on the landing. 'Oh! Dr Deacon!'

'Forgive me, madam. I didn't mean to startle you.'

She lifted her head and peered upward, her eyes like two pieces of sky come to earth. Wondering what she was looking at, I cast my own curious glance and realized we were standing beneath the mistletoe. I looked at her, and she looked at me, and never had I seen her face turn a brighter shade of pink. Her eyes swam in panicked confusion. I, too, felt extremely discomfited. The strain of what the mistletoe implied, and how its silent and traditional command couldn't possibly be obeyed, was nearly too much for us. And thus, we were both relieved when Chester, Dr Pritchard's bulldog, no more than an overgrown pup, rocketed along the corridor like a runaway motorcar, leapt down the stairs, barrelled past us, lost his footing on the hardwood floor, and slid into the metal radiator, limbs akimbo like a circus contortionist practicing a new act.

I went to attend to the dog, helping it up. 'There's a boy. I think you need new tires.'

Miss Wade took the opportunity to move herself out from under the mistletoe.

I knew I shouldn't have taken it as a rebuff, but I did, and I felt my stance against Miss Wade hardening again.

Chester went on his way downstairs, his cheerful mood not at all diminished by his mishap.

I turned to my female companion with a serious and perhaps too careful manner. 'Are you well, Miss Wade?'

Her eyes widened with a degree of churlishness I wouldn't have expected. 'Agreeably so, Dr Deacon. Merry Christmas. I have to go. The best to you for the holiday.'

She tried to pass but I physically blocked her way. 'Let me rephrase. Are you *well*, Miss Wade?'

She paused. The stiff smile on her face faded. 'Quite. Now if you'll excuse me.'

'I would like to extend an invitation to you, Miss Wade.'

The coldness in her eyes was nearly too much to bear. 'Oh?'

'The president has invited me to the White House for his annual Christmas party. I should like you to come with me.'

The corners of her lips tightened, producing two enchanting though dismissive dimples. 'I think not, Dr Deacon. Thank you for asking.'

I became bolder. 'Come, Miss Wade. It's a wonderful opportunity. The nation's best society will be there. I spoke to the president extensively about you during my visit to Long Island this summer and he's extremely anxious to make your acquaintance. So is the First Lady. I'm sure you would enjoy yourself immensely. I do so wish you'd come. And I desperately want to mend whatever fissure has come between us. I find it intolerable that you should think ill of me. I thought we were getting along so nicely.'

She looked away, her dimples gone like momentary jewels, her chin dipping, and her shoulders sinking. 'I believe I once told you about a man I knew in Boston.' So, it was going to be about the man in Boston after all. 'When we first met last June?'

My chest tightened. 'The married one?'

'Yes. Edgar Keenan is his name.'

I was now fearful that this Keenan fellow had finished things with his wife once and for all and was getting ready to take Olive away from me. 'He was a cad for treating you so cavalierly. But what does he have to do with my invitation to Washington?'

'Nothing. Except that you and Edgar share some of the same characteristics.'

I felt my face grow warm. 'I refuse to be compared to that mugwump of a philanderer!'

'Oh, but you see, doctor, he had an interesting habit, particularly when he took me to a jewellery store. He was entirely distracted in a jewellery store. He couldn't look at just diamonds. And he couldn't look at just emeralds either. Or rubies. He had to look at them all. He was the same way with women. I was often surprised he didn't employ a loupe when there was a room full of women around.'

'Madam, if by your inference you mean the pains I've taken to make my new nurse, Miss Gregsby, feel welcome in Fairfield, then I must inform you that I am offended.'

'Infer what you must, doctor. In any case, the caliber of your attentions to the young woman have assured me that I must bow out as gracefully as I can.'

'Just as yours toward the assemblyman this summer make me have second thoughts. Now you bring up this Boston man?'

She didn't flinch. 'Perhaps we should conclude that your affections belong, and always shall belong, to your poor late wife.'

This left me struggling for words, especially because her eyes were now like the blue core ice found in the middle of glaciers. 'Madam, I hope you understand that my fondness for you remains undiminished.'

Her face remained as immobile as a slab of marble. 'A Merry Christmas to you, doctor. I should be going.' She moved past me and down the stairs before I could do anything to stop her.

I looked at the mistletoe. I frowned at it.

Dr Pritchard might as well have hung a sprig of hemlock up there for all the good it had done me.

NINETEEN

In the Pullman car on the way down to Washington on Tuesday, Henny absently fussed with the gold tassels that hung from the armrest covers. She craned to look out at snow-covered farmland – the rolling hill-country of Pennsylvania. Her eagerness uplifted my soul but did little to moderate the anxiety I felt over Olive. Her youth invigorated me. Her prettiness enchanted me. But I couldn't help wondering what, if anything, I could do about Miss Wade.

I tried to distract myself by reading the day's edition of the *Fairfield Newspacket*. But the *Newspacket* just added to my distress because of a story by Ira Connelly about Alvin Jensen. I read how 'one of the town's innocent lambs, Alvin Jensen, eight years old, witnessed that monstrous fiend of a scoundrel, William Fray, shoot, in cold blood, Fairfield's most beloved and respected benefactor, Ephraim Purcell.' Connelly further wrote that 'it seems only a matter of common sense that Fray should be tried as soon as possible for the murder, but the authorities defer, failing to see the crime as clearly as public opinion does.' And I finally read how 'Deputy Deacon, so astute and sure-footed in his investigation of the Charlotte Scott murder last summer, seems to have lost his way, and this reporter can't help wondering if he should hand the case over to the more experienced Sheriff Armstrong.' I shoved the paper aside, disgusted with Connelly's brand of penny-dreadful journalism, and also convinced that Isaac Jensen had leaked the story to the *Newspacket* as a way to deflect blame from himself.

For several miles on the approach to Philadelphia, I thought I had made a mistake bringing Miss Gregsby to Washington, and that Miss Wade would again interpret it in the wrong way, invoking, as Stanley called it, her God-given right to misunderstand. But, Theodore's personal note notwithstanding, the printed part of the invitation specifically stated I was allowed to bring one guest. And was I to waste this most gracious once-in-a-lifetime summons, or make use of it to broaden a young woman's horizons? Again, it was a moral question for me. I couldn't bring myself to leave Henny all alone in Fairfield at this festive time of the year when, casting myself as her mentor, I could introduce her to the President of the United States.

All that aside, I still felt a lover's irritation with Olive, and knew my motive to bring Miss Gregsby to Washington wasn't as pure as all that.

In Washington the next evening, the White House grounds were covered with snow. A variety of horse-drawn conveyances as well as a handful of new-fangled motorcars stopped in front of the pillared portico where guests were welcomed by butlers, stable-hands, and other White House staff.

'Is he a nice man?' asked Henny.

I had to think about this. 'Can a president ever be nice?'

'But I'll like him, won't I?'

'My dear, you'll hardly have more than a few seconds with him.'

Having been President McKinley's presidential physician for three years, the rooms, corridors, and furniture inside were all familiar to me. It was like coming home. Many staff – old friends – greeted me, and there were several pleasant reunions. No one seemed to hold it against me that I had lost President McKinley, and everybody asked after Jeremiah, and how he was doing at school in Boston.

With a suddenness I wasn't expecting, Henny, unable to contain her excitement, stood on her toes and kissed me on the cheek. 'You look ever so dashing in your tuxedo.'

I turned to her. Inwardly, I cringed. Why hadn't I seen it before? She was smitten with me! It didn't bother her a tick that I was nineteen years older than she was. I realized I was in trouble. If, as Stanley said, women had the right to misunderstand, then men had the right to be hopelessly obtuse. I had fashioned myself her mentor, but I now understood she had taken it in the wrong way.

Instead of the State Dining Room, the East Room was used for dinner – this to accommodate the large number of guests. Men wore black tuxedos and women sumptuous gowns in a bouquet of festive colours. Present were representatives from all departments of government, all branches of the American military, all walks of American life. Several foreign dignitaries had been invited as well. I felt honoured and particularly fortunate to be a close personal friend of the young vigorous president, a leader who embodied the hope and spirit of the new century.

The receiving line moved forward, and soon Henny and I were standing face to face with Roosevelt, his wife, Edith, and their children.

The president said, 'Doctor, I see you've brought a lovely companion. Bully for you! This must be Olive Wade. A pleasure to meet you at last, Miss Wade.'

The president took Miss Gregsby's hand in a rough fashion and kissed it.

Henny, rattled to be mistaken this way, said, 'Oh, no, Mr President. I'm Henrietta Gregsby. The doctor's nurse.'

She turned to me the way a student turns to a tutor, anxious to know if she had followed proper form.

The president looked at me, his silent inquiry penetrating, direct, and complete. 'Clyde, I must have missed your last letter about this.'

I smiled with some embarrassment. 'Mr President, allow me to introduce my nurse, Miss Henrietta Gregsby.'

The president stared at me some more. Then he turned to Henny. 'Well, then! A Merry Christmas to you, Miss Gregsby. And thank you so much for coming to my little gathering. I'm sorry I mistook you for Miss Wade.'

And that was that.

But before we left the receiving line, I said to the president, 'Theodore, if I could have a word with you later on.'

'Of course, Clyde. We'll have drinks in the Red Room.'

'I'm investigating a murder. And you might have been a witness.' I then moved off.

I glanced back at the president. He stared after me through his oval wire-rim spectacles, his walrus mustache drooping, the receiving line forgotten, the chief-of-state looking as bewildered as a hare beaten by a tortoise in a foot race.

When we were seated for dinner, we sang the national anthem then said the Lord's Prayer. The president made a short speech, and soup was served.

Henny used this interlude to make an inquiry. 'Why did the president think I was Olive Wade?'

I felt myself squirming. 'We spoke about her last summer when I visited him at Sagamore Hill, that's all.'

I could see she was disturbed by my revelation. She lifted her linen napkin and dabbed her lips, even though she hadn't eaten a morsel yet. Her former gaiety deserting her, she asked, 'And is Miss Wade a woman of any special importance to you?'

I deflected in the interests of saving the evening. 'Do we have to talk about Miss Wade? I find her a vexatious woman at times.'

She stared at me for several seconds, a knit coming to her brow. Then the corners of her lips lifted upward in a grin. 'Merry Christmas, Clyde.'

My own lips rose. 'Merry Christmas, Henny.'

After soup, the various courses came.

The wine flowed. The noise thickened.

Between the end of the final course and the serving of dessert, the president made another speech, short, jocular, and admirably apolitical.

He then circulated among the tables, shaking hands, giving personal Christmas wishes to many of his distinguished guests, finally working his way to our table.

'Miss Gregsby, you must allow me to take the doctor away for fifteen or twenty minutes. I'm sure if we're not back before the dancing starts, a young woman as pretty as yourself will have no difficulty finding any number of partners.'

She blushed. 'Of course, Mr President.'

Roosevelt gestured toward the East Room entryway. 'Clyde?'

We left.

A servant in a black swallowtail coat followed to attend. We walked down the hall and soon found ourselves in the Red Room.

I could see at a glance that Theodore's architect had moved the mantels from the State Dining Room to the Red Room, and had hung the walls with burgundy wallpaper instead of the more traditional crimson. Nothing stayed the same, I thought. McKinley dead, Theodore president, and the Red Room redecorated. I complimented the president on his improvements, to which he said, 'Edith will have her way with the place.' Then we sat on a red and gold sofa. The servant brought us drinks and retreated to the corridor so we could talk in private.

'You say I saw a murder, Clyde. That's interesting. I've always prided myself on my memory, but I honestly can't say I remember witnessing this particular crime.'

'Theodore, you might recall a flask.'

His eyes narrowed and a more serious set came to his face. 'A flask, you say. I'm not much of a drinking man, but I have to tell you, I remember many flasks. I find they make good presentation articles, especially where the military is concerned.'

I raised my finger. 'And that, Theodore, is precisely the species of flask I'm talking about. You presented this particular flask in 1895, while you were still the President of the Board of New York City Police Commissioners. It was given to a veteran of the Civil War, a Union Army regular by the name of Isaac Jensen, at a Grand Army of the Republic reunion. This would have been at Post 327, in Brooklyn. The Grant Post?'

He thought for several moments. 'Ah, yes. It's coming back to me. I remember the occasion. I've been to that post many times.'

'No one has yet been able to give me a definitive description of the flask. One witness says it has an engraving of Abraham Lincoln on it. Another says it has one of Ulysses S. Grant.' I now went into the details of how and why the flask was important, and how it had become a vital if confusing clue in the murder of Ephraim Purcell. 'I would like to search Jensen's rooms above his hat shop, and I must do so quickly because he and his family will be removing themselves to Elmira soon to start a new business venture. But before I do, I need an accurate description. As you're the one who gave it to him, I'm hoping you might remember what it looked like.'

The president grinned. 'I can remember precisely what it looked like, Clyde. I ordered those flasks by the gross. Except for the personalized inscriptions, they were all the same. On one side was engraved the face of Abraham Lincoln, and on the other was the motto: Where Liberty Dwells, There is My Country.'

I was relieved. At least I had something concrete to go on now.

We discussed the flask and the murder for a few more minutes, me letting Theodore know my intent to have Judge Norris sign a court order so I could search the Jensen premises, the president wistfully longing for his police work days of the mid-1890s.

He then turned his attention to a more delicate matter. 'What happened to Miss Wade? The way you talked about her at Sagamore Hill last summer, I thought you would have been married to her by now.'

I hesitated. 'The pressures of establishing my practice in Fairfield used up a great deal of my time. And it's taken Miss Wade and I a while to bridge our differences since her summer romance with the junior assemblyman from Albany.'

Theodore stared at me. He shook his head as if he were disappointed in me. 'Clyde, there's a special resonance that comes to a man's voice when he's profoundly in love. I know that sound because I heard it in my own voice when I met Edith. And I heard it in your voice when you spoke of Olive Wade last summer. Now you come to my Christmas party with Miss Gregsby?'

'Yes.'

'But you don't have the same tone when you speak of Miss Gregsby. I see that you have no serious intentions toward her.'

'I don't, Theodore. These were special circumstances.' I told him about Henny and the Booths. 'So you see, all I was trying to do was be kind to her. And I thought by bringing her to Washington, it would be an excellent opportunity to broaden her horizons.'

'Yes, but there's a difference between kindness and giving false hope. And so I'm more concerned about Miss Gregsby than I am about Miss Wade.'

I now grew even more sensible to the unasked-for part Henny unwittingly had played in the battle I seemed to be waging with Olive. I felt small, and even ashamed. I cursed myself for my own blindness, and was humbled that, in part, it was the President of the United States who was opening my eyes.

Theodore squinted at me through his oval spectacles. 'Miss Gregsby loves you. I can see it in her eyes. And that's a pity, because love is a terrible thing to disappoint in an American so young. And so is hope. But disappoint them you must. Do you have any idea of the extent of the injury?'

For several seconds, I couldn't speak. 'Theodore, I admit, I've been rather a bumble-brain about the whole thing.' I then explained my confused feelings about Olive Wade, about Everett Howse and the Bostonian, and about my lingering grief for Emily and how it had been exacerbated by Miss Gregsby's arrival in Fairfield. 'I didn't realize what I'd gotten myself into until I was halfway up the hill.'

The president now grew reflective. 'A young woman who's suffered a recent loss is bound to be susceptible, Clyde. She's desperate to belong to someone. And if the way she was looking at you at dinner was any indication, she believes she belongs to you. So now the question arises, what do you do about it?' The president shook his head. 'By Jove, Clyde, I don't think you've done this much damage since you took out that artillery position on San Juan Hill. With that hill, you had to keep going. But with this hill, I think it's time to turn around and come back down. And do it as gently as you can.'

When Henny and I got back to the hotel that night, and I delivered her to her door, she lingered in the soft electric lamp light of the corridor, her hat still on her head, her shawl around her shoulders. She looked up at me with shy eyes. I could see the president was right, that I had foolishly misled her without knowing it. I wanted above all to do the right thing. Her eyes filled with tears. I don't know whether they were happy tears or sad tears; whether she still had hope or if she knew it had to end. One way or the other, they were tears of need.

I cursed myself for allowing this to happen – the last thing I wanted was to hurt Henny. Yet I could see what she needed. To be embraced, if only for tonight. To be shown that she still belonged to the world. And so, as I tried to do the right thing, I opened my arms and did the wrong thing. She came to me. She pressed her cheek against my chest. I closed my arms around her. And I held her near simply to reassure her, and to make her understand that she wasn't by herself.

I could sense that for the first time since Martin Booth had walked into Lake Ontario, she felt safe.

As for myself, I felt like Martin Booth – that I was in too far over my head.

TWENTY

Upon my return to Fairfield, the sheriff and I gathered Deputies Putsey, Donal, and Mulroy, and rode posse-style to Jensen's Hat Shop.

Much to my dismay, I saw that the curtains were shut and that there was a big sign in the window that said, 'CLOSED. WILL REOPEN MONDAY.'

'You reckon he's running?' asked Stanley.

I got off Pythagoras, tied her to the hitching post, climbed the wooden steps to the plank sidewalk, and peered through a crack in the curtains. The shop was dark, but I saw a light on in the back. The sheriff and the other deputies got off their horses and climbed to the boardwalk. I moved away from the window, went to the door, and rapped.

At first nobody came, so I rapped again.

After a minute, I saw the Jensen household maid, Sally Snell, appear. She was one of my patients, a short stocky young woman of twenty-one. My search party ranged themselves behind me. As the maid spied me through the glass, her lips tightened, her eyes widened, and her face flushed. She gathered up her skirt and hurried forward. Reaching the threshold, she turned the bolt, then the knob, and pulled the door open.

'Dr Deacon? Did you not read the sign?'

'Merry Christmas, Sally. Is the family not at home?'

She looked past my shoulder and saw the sheriff and the deputies. 'They're in Elmira. They've settled on a property and they've all gone down to have a look at it.'

'And so they'll be back on Monday?'

'Yes.'

'Even Mr Jensen?'

Her eyes widened, and I could see that she was confused by my distinction. 'Yes.' She glanced at the posse – grim-faced men armed with rifles and shotguns – then turned back to me. 'Is it hats you want?'

I pulled out my court order. 'We have a warrant from Judge Norris to search the premises.'

Two spots of crimson climbed into her cheeks and she looked as surprised as new spring corn after a May snowfall. 'What for?'

'In connection to the murder of Ephraim Purcell.'

Bless her loyal heart, she took the order and read it carefully, a frown coming to her face. At last she looked at me, as feisty as a sparrow protecting a bread crumb. 'Try not to muss the place too much. Mrs Jensen and I spent hours cleaning it for Christmas.'

'Perhaps you might help us, then, Sally?'

Her brow arched. 'How?'

'We're looking for one item in particular. A flask.'

'Oh. Well, now. Mr Jensen has a whole collection of them in his study on the second floor. He must have twenty-five.'

'And are you responsible for dusting those?'

'Oh, no, sir. Mr Jensen's very particular about his flask collection. He dusts them himself.'

'I see.' I thought for a moment. 'Do you recall seeing a silver flask with a portrait of Abraham Lincoln on it?'

She hesitated. 'I've never seen one like that, no, sir.'

'Very well, Sally. If you would let us pass.'

She moved out of the way. 'Mind you wipe your feet.'

We filed in one after the other, dutifully wiping our shoes and tipping our hats in nervous greeting like cowed schoolboys.

I then gave orders. 'Putsey and Donal, you take the third floor. The sheriff and I will search the second. Mulroy, you check the shop.'

We split up.

Stanley and I climbed the stairs and entered Jensen's study at the front of the building. We went through his flask collection.

He had all manner of flasks – silver ones, glass ones, even a specimen fashioned out of an antelope horn. Nowhere could we find a flask with a portrait of Lincoln on it.

We did, however, discover an ornamented pine keepsake box that was of some pertinence to the case.

We opened it and saw the kind of mementoes a woman might bestow upon a favoured gentleman: a garter, a hairpin, and several photographs. The earliest of these photographs was dated 1867, and was of the daguerreotype variety, while the latest was from 1901, courtesy of Eastman Kodak. I looked on the back of the 1901 photograph and saw a name: Hattie Whitmore, the same woman Jensen and Purcell had fought over when they had been in business school in New York years ago. I looked at an 1875 photograph of the same woman. She was beautiful in this one, had a cascade of curly brown hair, skin that was like the light of the moon, and a bewitching grin as hypnotizing as da Vinci's Mona Lisa.

Then there was a stack of letters, some yellowed with age, others as new as last month.

I turned to Stanley. 'Looks like Jensen has remained in contact with Hattie Whitmore.'

We took the box and contents into evidence, then checked the window ledges for any signs of rifle-fire, powder burns, or other ballistics matter; but, as Sally Snell had said, the place had been scrubbed clean for Christmas, and we found no firearms clues.

Just as I was despairing that the whisky flask was nothing but a big red herring sent to mislead us (we still couldn't reconcile the wound angle with the flask robbery), we heard Raymond Putsey calling us from the third floor. 'Sheriff? Deputy? I think I found something.'

We moved out into the corridor.

Ray came clumping down the third-floor stairs. He had in his hand a silver flask. As he came towards us he presented the piece, raising it in his hand, holding it between his thumb and fingers. 'It's got a picture of Abe Lincoln on it. That's the one you're looking for, right?'

The young deputy surrendered the flask to me. Lincoln, intaglio, stared at me with kind steadiness from the sterling silver surface. On the other side I found the words: Where Liberty Dwells, There is My Country. Included also was a personalized inscription: 'To Private Isaac Jensen, presented for bravery in the line of duty, Friday, September 20, 1895, by Theodore Roosevelt, President of the Board of New York Police Commissioners, Grant Post, GAR, Brooklyn, New York.'

I looked at Putsey. 'Where'd you'd find it?'

He pointed up the stairs. 'There's a crawlspace on the third floor.'

I nodded and turned to Stanley. 'I guess we wait till Isaac comes back.'

Stanley was doubtful. 'If he comes back.'

I had my own concerns, and a moment later, the sheriff picked up on them.

'Clyde? You all right?'

'I'm just thinking of the wound angle again.'

Stanley thought about it. 'I know. It doesn't make sense.'

*   *   *

That night, I read through Hattie Whitmore's correspondence to see if I could find clues and background to the unfortunate triangle between herself, Jensen, and Purcell. There was no return address on any of the letters, perhaps for discretion's sake.

Even upon a first reading, I could tell that Hattie was still deeply in love with Isaac. In a letter dated as recently as March of this year, she made a plea, apparently for the hundredth time: leave Tilda and come live with her in Manhattan.

Then I came upon incriminating lines in a letter written just two weeks prior to Purcell's murder, ones that made me grip the missive more tightly and lean forward: 'I don't blame you for wanting to kill Ephraim, dearest Isaac. He is a snake. And after the way he trespassed against me during his recent visit to Manhattan, he certainly deserves to see the dark interior of a penitentiary for many years. Is it right that we take matters into our own hands and mete out the punishment he so justly deserves? Only God can judge.'

I let the letter sink to my lap. Out the window, I heard a group of carollers singing 'Joy to the World' on Culver Street.

I now had a mind to go over to the Sheriff's Office and release Billy Fray from jail, no questions asked, for it seemed the burden of guilt was shifting in significant ways toward other suspects.

TWENTY-ONE

That night, a blizzard moved in, and wind and snow howled around the surgery. The drive got buried deep. The temperature plummeted.

I was just going out to make sure the stove was still lit in the stable so Pythagoras and Archimedes wouldn't freeze, and to make certain that their horse blankets hadn't come off, when, out on Culver Street, I saw a sledge pulled by a team of two turn up my drive, its lantern blurred by the wind-driven snow.

I turned from the stable and walked down the drive, surmising I was faced with a medical emergency.

I raised my kerosene lantern so whoever was driving would see me. 'Hallo, there!'

I now saw young Clarence Swinford and Mrs Cora Wiley, the

druggist's wife, sitting on the driver's box. Mrs Wiley looked distressed, her features drawn, her eyes wide with anxiety. Clarence's face was no better; he was pale with fear.

In a high fretful voice, Cora Wiley said, 'Doctor, Mrs Swinford's been injured in a most horrible way.'

I took a few more steps toward the sledge. 'What's happened?'

'She's been shot!' cried Clarence. 'You gotta help her, doc! She's lost a lot of blood!'

I took a moment to assimilate this information, then left off being a doctor and became a deputy. 'Who shot her?'

Clarence jerked on the reins and brought the horses to a stop. 'I did, doc. I went out hunting rabbit, and when I got back, I guess I forgot I had a round in the chamber. I was putting my rifle on the table, and somehow the dang thing went off and got my ma right in the shoulder while she was sitting there sewing my pa's britches.'

So, an accident. I dismissed the deputy and became fully a doctor again. But it was rather odd that here were the Swinfords again, again involved in a life-and-death situation. The weight of their possible involvement in the Purcell case hovered in my consciousness.

The sledge was of the market-wagon variety, used for heavy winter farm work. I moved to the back where I saw Albert Swinford kneeling over his wife. 'Mr Swinford? Is she all right?'

He turned, his expression grim, a notch away from irritable, and gave me a gruff nod. 'Sorry to trouble you so late, doc, but I'm afraid we've had a shooting accident. We went to Doc Thorensen's place – he's our reg'lar doctor – but it looks like he's going to be gone a spell.'

'How badly hurt is she?'

'She ain't dead yet.' A catch came to his voice. 'But pretty darn close.'

'All right. Let's bring her inside. I'll get the stretcher.'

'Much obliged, doc.'

I quickly had Munroe and Henny out of their beds, and soon had the patient on the exam table.

I then banished everybody but Henny.

I studied Mrs Swinford as Henny first took away the homemade bandages, then snipped away the woman's shirtwaist, and finally her chemise. She was roughly forty, with sandy hair pinned up in a mound on top of her head. She was a pretty woman for her age, with a fine nose and lips, but lines here and there that spoke of a hard life. She looked at me, and tears came. I could see that there was a lot more hurting going on than just the bullet wound to her shoulder. I detected deep shame in her eyes.

'Mrs Swinford, tell me what happened?'

Her face creased, and her lips came together, then pulled back. Her eyes closed, squeezing tears away, the muscles in her throat constricting as she fought to hold back a sob. She took several seconds to get herself under control, and after she had forced herself into a state of relative calm, she said, 'Clarence was out hunting grouse. He came in and I guess he forgot to put the safety on, and he rested the gun in the gun rack, and it went off while I was sitting in the rocking chair knitting.'

I stared. Though the outline of her story was similar to Clarence's, the details were strangely different. In Clarence's story it had been the rifle on the table and ma sewing britches. In ma's story, it was rifle in the gun rack and ma in the rocking chair knitting. Was she confused, or was there something else going on?

As Henny began irrigating the wound, Mrs Swinford winced in pain. I went round and had a look.

The bullet had entered through the anterior deltoid muscle just below the left scapula and had exited through the posterior trapezius muscle, fortunately missing the left pulmonary apparatus, wrecking some muscle, busting some bone, but otherwise leaving the victim with a survivable gunshot wound.

I tried to cheer my patient up. 'You won't be churning butter any time soon, Mrs Swinford, so you can forget about those Christmas butter cookies, but you should pull through all right.'

Then I noticed an odd thing. Her right shoe was on and her left one was off. Had she been wearing slippers, it wouldn't have been so unusual, for the missing slipper could have been easily dislodged in the rush to get her to medical attention. But she was wearing a full shoe, and women's styles being what they were in this modern age of ours, that meant considerable lacing, sixteen sets of eye-holes altogether. In short, it was the kind of shoe a woman would need a shoehorn, possibly dynamite, to get off her foot. Yet here she was, one shoe on, one shoe off.

'Henny, prepare thirty drops of laudanum for Mrs Swinford.'

'Yes, doctor.'

As Henny went to the dispensary to prepare the painkiller, I took another look at the wound. Some coagulation had occurred, though with the irrigation of the injury, the bleeding had partially started again. The story given and the nature of the injury – in through the anterior deltoid and up through the posterior trapezius, a pronounced upward trajectory of forty-five degrees – didn't make sense to me. In both versions of the story, either from the table or the gun rack, I would have expected a level trajectory, if not a downward one. But the trajectory I was seeing suggested the rifle butt had been resting upon the floor, the barrel lifted upward, and the trigger activated with the great toe of Mrs Swinford's bare right foot. Furthermore, I suspected the target had been her head, and because of the awkward mechanism of commission, the barrel had shifted at the last second to spare her life. Put simply, I believed I had before me the victim of a failed suicide attempt.

I lifted Adson forceps from my tray as well as a magnifying glass, and searched for any removable piece of debris, bullet, or powder, but it looked as though the wound was a clean through-and-through.

'Tell me, Mrs Swinford. How did Mrs Wiley come to be with you tonight?'

She struggled a bit with glottis, larynx, and lips. 'She's my very good friend, Dr Deacon.' She spoke in a clutching breathless way, fighting her pain. 'When my husband, son, and I found out Dr Thorensen wasn't home, we went to the drugstore to see if Mr Wiley could do anything. He's a fine chemist but he's also fairly practiced at first-aid. That's when we met up with Cora.'

'So instead of coming to me, the town's only other doctor, you went to a chemist first?'

This definitely sounded like they were trying to hide the suicide attempt.

She looked away. The element of shame on her face was now even more pronounced.

'Yes.'

Henny returned with the laudanum and soon our patient was more comfortable.

I had to use a number of internal stitches to repair the deepest part of the injury, both back and front, then closed the surface area with a strong mattress stitch. As the wound was at the shoulder, the risk of dehiscence was great – the shoulder was, so to speak, a moving part. I told her to keep her limb immobile for the next six weeks, but because the laudanum was now making her mind misty, I judged it best to give this instruction to Mr Swinford as well.

Accordingly, I let Henny sterilize the wound and dress it, and as usual she proved a most able young nurse. I scrubbed down, deposited my bloody apron in the hamper, put on my jacket, and proceeded to the waiting area, where I found father and son – stepson, really – waiting on chairs, craned forward, anxious about their wife and mother.

'Mr Swinford, would you mind coming into my office for a moment? Clarence, if you could wait here.'

Mr Swinford followed me into my office.

Once we were settled, I said to him, 'Has Mrs Swinford been out of sorts lately?'

He lifted his chin. I saw suspicion in his eyes. 'In what way?'

'Has she been tired? Or withdrawn? Or not showing her usual interest in things?'

He frowned. 'She's been fine, doc.'

I wasn't going to put up with any nonsense. 'And has she tried to harm herself in the past?'

His face turned red, and his expression evened out like a pitcher of spilled molasses.

'I don't know what you're talking about.'

'Everything I see points to a self-inflicted gunshot wound, Mr Swinford. This was no accident. This was intentional.'

He fumed.

'You don't have to worry about Melissa, doc. I've got her well in hand.' And that was all, as if we were talking about a bee sting and not a failed suicide attempt. 'Anything I ought to know about this here wound of hers?'

I saw there was no getting past his defences.

'She was extremely lucky, Mr Swinford. A few inches up, and it would have been a head wound. An inch down and it would have been the heart or the lung.' I let the implication sit. 'There's some bone and muscle damage, nothing so serious that it won't eventually heal. But she shouldn't be using that arm for at least six weeks. Come back in ten days and Henny will remove her sutures. You must have her rest, Mr Swinford. And then you should have her return to see Dr Thorensen some time early in the new year just to make sure the wound is healing the way it should. As to the other matter—'

'What other matter?' he asked sharply.

'Watch her, Mr Swinford. Watch her carefully. Her melancholia is more profound than you think. Keep the rifles locked away. Clear the house of poisonous substances.' I remembered Martin Booth. 'And make sure she doesn't go for any walks along the river by herself. I don't know what happened today, but I know it wasn't an accident. This is a serious matter, sir. I know you're worried about public shame. I know you're concerned about this town's infernal rumour mill. But if you don't take care, she might try it again. And then you'll be taking her to Edmund Wilson, not me.'

TWENTY-TWO

Ambrose Johnstone, Mr Purcell's lawyer, came to see me on Monday morning to follow up on his ingrown toenail.

He informed me that he had inserted cotton batting underneath it, as I had advised, with unremitting discipline. 'I seem to have trained the little fellow away from my skin.'

I examined the nail. 'It looks a lot better, Ambrose. But might I again recommend you stay away from an opera toe. Please try a London toe. They have a wider breadth.'

'I might do that, doctor. Especially because I'm run off my feet with the Purcell estate.'

'I trust everything's going smoothly with that? I see it's business as usual at the New York Emporium.'

He nodded. 'Herschel's been a big help. He's been going through his brother's papers. He might be a history professor, but he seems to have a good business sense as well. And he's been a great support to Marigold. Not that she's particularly shaken about her stepfather's death. They were like a rattler and a rooster in the same barnyard. But she's taken to her step-uncle in a way I wouldn't have expected. They're the only family each other has now. By the way, Herschel is at me again to prosecute Billy Fray.'

With a pinch of frustration, I said, 'As I told him at Dr Pritchard's Christmas party, I still have several suspects to rule out.'

'And Jerome Highcloud hasn't yet returned from the Adirondacks?'

'No. He's to come to the surgery when he does.'

Johnstone grew thoughtful. 'I suppose it's the only way we can prove things one way or the other with Billy Fray. I should point out that another name has come to light.'

'Who?'

'Clarence Swinford. Albert Swinford's son.'

Here were the Swinfords once more, insisting on nosing their way into the investigation yet again, despite all the cayenne pepper they had sprinkled around. 'You have some information?'

'From an old friend, Eugene Lapinance.'

'The manager at the Grand Hotel?'

He nodded. 'Eugene was one of Ephraim's closest friends. I take it by this time you know Ephraim had a weakness for the ladies?'

'My investigation has revealed this fact, yes.'

'He used some pretty rough tactics with Mrs Swinford back in the mid-eighties.'

'I'm aware of this.'

Mr Johnstone reached for his sock and put it back on. 'Eugene has informed me that a week before Ephraim was killed he again began making advances toward Mrs Swinford, and that he was using the same kind of strong-arm tactics he used last time. Last time, he held their rent over their head. He couldn't do that this time because the Swinfords now own the place. This time he used other leverage, and it directly impinged on young Clarence's future. This is why I must raise the young man's name.'

'To what leverage do you refer?'

'It seems Ephraim left a provision for Clarence in his will. They grew fond of each other when Clarence worked at the hotel.'

I nodded. 'You speak of Clarence's college trust fund?'

Johnstone raised his brow. 'You know of it?'

'Marigold mentioned it to me when I spoke to her.'

He nodded. 'As a document, it exists on its own. The provision in the will was in case of death, and that's how I came to be aware of it. Clarence is an exceedingly bright boy. The young man did the books at the hotel for a while. Did them better than any grown-up ever did. Eugene had a little office for him in the back. The boy's a whiz at math and arithmetic. Eugene tells me Clarence's chief aim was to go to college.'

'And your deceased client used the college fund to leverage Mrs Swinford?'

Johnstone nodded and said, 'Eugene told me she refused. So Ephraim threatened to terminate the trust, but was killed before it was officially cancelled.'

I grew mildly exasperated. 'Why didn't Mr Lapinance tell me about this sooner?'

Johnstone shrugged. 'To spare Ephraim's reputation, I suppose. Would you like to go to your grave known as the man who killed a young man's dreams? When Clarence worked at the hotel, he spoke to Eugene of college. College means the world to Clarence. He was passionate about obtaining a higher education. To have his trust fund cancelled would have devastated him. So you can see that he has a strong motive, and that he might do anything to stop the abrogation of the fund.'

'Possibly.'

'Herschel Purcell is extremely anxious that I let you know about this. If we can't proceed against Billy Fray, he wants a vigorous investigation of Clarence Swinford. In light of Mr Purcell's recent advances against Melissa Swinford, not only did Clarence have to consider his mother's continued virtue, but here was Ephraim, threatening to take away his entire future, everything he had ever dreamed of, with a single stroke of a pen. And, let's not forget, Clarence was in the vicinity of the murder the evening it happened. It's also common practice for farm-folk to carry rifles in their wagons in case they can bag a rabbit or duck to and from town.'

I stared at Johnstone, then rose and went to the window, parting the curtains a fraction. I glimpsed my neighbours, Mr and Mrs Richard Caine, shovelling snow off their stable roof. I couldn't help contemplating Mrs Swinford's attempted suicide on Saturday night. I speculated that Mr Purcell's renewed attentions may have had something to do with it. How ashamed she must have felt. Perhaps she even blamed herself for nearly ruining her son's future.

Be that as it may, I wasn't yet ready to consider Clarence Purcell guilty of the crime. I turned to Mr Johnstone. 'An eyewitness tells me Clarence was inside the Corn Mercantile Building when the fatal shot was fired.'

'And who was your witness, Dr Deacon?'

'Erwin Fletcher, the yard boss.'

Johnstone showed some confusion, then shook his head. 'I guess you don't know, then.'

'Know what?

He reached for his fancy opera-toe shoes. 'That Erwin Fletcher is

Melissa Swinford's older brother. Naturally he's going to try and protect his sister and her family any way he can.'

TWENTY-THREE

On Monday afternoon, a few hours after I'd finished with Ambrose Johnstone's toenail, Professor Purcell came to my office.

'By God, I found it among Ephraim's most important papers!' He was flushed, excited, barely in control. 'I had to ask myself, why would Ephraim have a signed promissory note from Daniel Hepiner, his shipping man, in the amount of ten thousand dollars? Daniel Hepiner never buys goods and services from Ephraim. And Ephraim always pays Mr Hepiner for freight and shipping up front. He never borrows. Not from anybody. Not ever. I know my brother, and that's just the way he is. Mr Hepiner also has a no-credit policy. It's cash on the barrel-head. A promissory note like this doesn't make sense so I began looking into it.'

'Professor Purcell, calm yourself. I have a waiting room full of patients. Come to my parlor. Perhaps a dram of medicinal brandy might help you.'

'I telephoned Mr Hepiner at the shipping office!'

'Right this way, Professor Purcell. We can speak more confidentially in the parlor.'

He allowed himself to be ushered to the front of the house. I got him seated in a chair by the fire.

'And do you know what Mr Hepiner told me?'

I went to the tray of spirits on the side table and poured some brandy for the professor. 'Go ahead, Herschel. I'm listening.'

'That he never signed such a note! Just to be sure, I had Leach drive me round to the shipping office in the motorcar. I showed the promissory note to Mr Hepiner. He studied the signature closely, and though he was impressed by its accuracy, he pointed out minor differences. We were soon convinced it was a forgery.'

I finished pouring the drink and brought it over. He took a sip.

'Professor Purcell,' I said, 'I'm afraid a forgery like this would

have to be reported to the Sheriff's Office. My current capacity as deputy extends only to your brother's murder case.'

'But that's what I'm here about!' His eyes positively bulged. 'The two are connected. Mr Hepiner and I decided that whoever made the forgery had to have access to a copy of his signature. Ephraim has all kinds of old waybills from Mr Hepiner's shipping business in his home office. They all have Mr Hepiner's signature on them.'

'And how does this connect to your brother's murder?'

'Because, as acquisitive as Ephraim might have been, I know he would never legally endanger himself with a forgery of this kind. Obviously someone else had done it, and obviously my brother had caught the fiend or else he never would have had the promissory note in his possession.' The professor took another sip of brandy, and appeared to gain a measure of composure from it. 'We were stumped as to who the fiend could be, Dr Deacon. So we called Johnstone. He came up with a theory. He said that the only other person who had access to my brother's home office was Marigold – she occasionally works for him as an assistant. He said that in light of my brother's irregularities regarding Marigold's dividends, my step-niece may have perhaps taken advantage of her access and exercised poor judgment. In a fit of malice she may have decided to engage in this risky venture. I daresay, I was at first affronted. Our dear Marigold, having something to do with the likes of this? Well, sir! Mr Johnstone and Mr Hepiner induced me to delicately question my step-niece.' His eyes bulged again and his voice grew louder. 'I did so in Mr Johnstone's presence. And we were staggered by what Marigold told us. She said it wasn't herself who forged the promissory note, but Billy Fray! I was as startled as a pigeon in a pie. He did it in a last-ditch effort to save the Fray smithy.'

I grew still, taking a few seconds to digest this. Then I said, 'So Billy Fray devised a promissory note made out to your brother, presumably because if he made it out to himself, the bank would never cash it because the Fray smithy credit is so bad.'

'Precisely.'

'I don't understand. If it was made out to your brother, how did he ever expect to cash it?'

'He was going to have Marigold cash it for him because she has privileges at the bank for her stepfather. But of course she would have never agreed to the scheme and only found out about the whole

affair from Billy after the fact. So she's entirely innocent, except for not coming forward sooner and telling us about the whole thing. The poor misguided dear was trying to protect Billy.'

'But Billy has access to your brother's home office?'

'Yes, yes. Marigold has given him a key to the house so he can sneak in and out the back door at night to see her.'

'I see.'

'Billy knew of the Hepiner waybills and came over the Thursday evening before my brother's murder. Hepiner is wealthy and definitely has the ten thousand to cover it. Billy apparently knows that Thursdays and Saturdays are my brother's club nights. He went into Ephraim's study when he thought Ephraim was at the club and forged Mr Hepiner's signature on a blank promissory note he had procured from the Exchange Bank. He didn't want to risk taking a waybill from the office because he knows Ephraim keeps them in such precise order.'

'Yes, I've learned from Leach that your brother was very particular about his office.'

'Little did Billy know that my brother was out of sorts that night with his chronic dyspepsia. Ephraim came into his study and caught Billy red-handed. I can assure you, doctor, there was much hullabaloo.'

'I'm sure there was.'

'My brother apparently had Billy surrender the promissory note at gunpoint and vowed to have him in front of Judge Norris before the week was out. An offence like that carries a good many years, up to twenty. That Saturday, my brother was murdered. I believe Billy might have done it in response to the promissory note threat. And if this promissory note evidence isn't enough, there's everything else: the eyewitness, the suicide of Cecil Fray, the shutting down of the smithy, and so forth. I cannot countenance it any longer! We must prosecute Billy immediately! He is our man! I know he is! We shouldn't be waiting for some Indian fellow to return from the wilds of Upstate New York just so we can test-fire his rifle!'

The professor took a third sip of his brandy. He had worked himself up into such a state again that I thought it best to let him sit for a few moments. So I made a pretence of attending the fire, squatting with the poker and adjusting the logs.

I was puzzled by the account. I couldn't see Billy as a man to come up with such a scheme. It would require knowledge of how

the monetary world worked, and Billy came from the world of bellows, forge, and hammer.

Once I had the logs adjusted, I stood up and surveyed Professor Purcell. 'And so Marigold found out after the fact?'

'She did.'

'She loves him.'

'Apparently so.'

'And yet she surrenders him so readily now?'

Herschel's lips tightened and he frowned. 'And by this you infer?'

'If she loved him, you'd think she would have continued to deny everything.'

'Why would she do that? She's a good girl.'

'I don't know. But after keeping it from you so diligently in the first place, why would she so suddenly admit to it now, especially when there's so much to lose? She's essentially sending the man she loves away to prison for twenty years. It doesn't make sense to me, not when she first tried to hide it.'

He seemed to grope for an answer, then said with some uncertainty, 'She realized the error of her ways and came to her senses when Johnstone and I confronted her.'

'Yes, but she was safe. She didn't have to say anything, and the matter would have been dropped. It seems to me she volunteered the information rather too readily.'

He stared at me, jaw now slightly dropped. 'Are you suggesting a plot?'

'Maybe she doesn't love Billy as much as we think she does.'

'Sir, speak plainly.'

'She has access to your brother's office as well. Maybe she herself devised the promissory note.'

'To what end?'

'Perhaps it's as you first suggested.'

'You mean in retaliation for the Swiss bank account matter?'

I nodded. 'And then once she was confronted, she needed a convenient scapegoat so blamed Billy. Or perhaps she devised the note for a more nefarious purpose. Perhaps she's trying to hide her own guilt in her stepfather's murder and was trying to deflect blame elsewhere.'

In other words, more cayenne pepper.

'But that's absurd, sir! She would never do such a thing! She has better breeding than that!'

Yet I couldn't help thinking how I still hadn't received my consult note from the Sisters of Charity Hospital in Buffalo.

TWENTY-FOUR

With this promissory note incident, the matter of Marigold now became pressing.

I put a call in to Sisters of Charity immediately after Professor Purcell had left.

I was told by a different clerk that the original clerk had recently quit and had left her desk in upheaval. 'I'll have to sort through her chart requests and get back to you as fast as I can, doctor.'

Curses! Another Adirondacks hunting expedition.

Not to be put off, I thought it best to question Marigold personally about the Daniel Hepiner forgery episode.

So when the surgery closed for the day, I saddled Archimedes, giving Pythagoras a rest for a change, and rode west on Culver Street until I came to the Cherry Hill Road drawbridge. The drawbridge was up and I had to wait. A small coal barge was passing upriver toward West Shelby. It was either that or ride all the way to the span bridge at Tonawanda. I waved to Wilmer Barner, the bridge-keeper, a hale septuagenarian, and he waved back from the bridge tower. Once the barge had passed and the bridge was down, I crossed the river and headed up to the Purcell mansion on Cherry Hill.

Flora Winters, Marigold's maid, let me in. 'She's in the music room, sir. She's already told me that she's accepting visitors, so you can go right in.'

I found Marigold practicing the recorder, playing 'My Wild Irish Rose.' As I came in, she glanced at me, but didn't stop playing, stumbled a bit as she crossed registers, looked suddenly furious with the instrument, her face reddening, then quietly, and with a great deal of stiff control, put the instrument on the music stand and turned to me.

'I don't know why I try to play that ditty. I *hate* it. I always have. And the *flûte à bec* has such vexatious half-hole fingering.' She glared at the instrument one last time, then turned her attention to me. 'What can I do for you, doctor?'

'How are you feeling, my dear?'

'I'm much better, thank you.' Her fury at the instrument quickly dissipated and I now sensed some nervousness. 'Miss Wade has made house calls to attend to my dressings.'

'Oh. I didn't know that. Henny was not to your liking?'

'I don't know her, do I? And I know Miss Wade.'

'And how is Miss Wade?'

She had to think about this. 'Distracted. Not her usual self.'

As I didn't want to pursue the subject of Miss Wade further, I steered to the matter at hand. 'I was speaking to your uncle earlier in the afternoon, Miss Reynolds. About the promissory note?'

She looked away, her nervousness intensifying. 'And what did he say?'

I gave her a rundown of what I had learned from the professor. She looked pitifully downcast once I had finished. 'It's true, doctor.'

'And you knew of the scheme?'

'Not until after the attempt.'

I observed her. 'Why didn't you divulge this information when I first came to you?'

Tears formed in her eyes. 'I was protecting poor Billy, of course. I now realize I must have broken some law or other.' With more tears, she offered her wrists to me for cuffing. 'And I'll understand if you've come to take me to jail.' She got even more emotional. 'But I was doing it for love.'

I frowned. 'Yes, for love.' Though her manner seemed genuine enough, I couldn't exclude the possibility that she was a skilful actress and so decided I must give her a jolt. 'I find your whole story unlikely, Marigold. The timing is badly off.'

She stiffened. Her arms went down. She seemed hurt by my accusation. 'What's so unlikely about it, doctor?' She peered at me more intently, her eyes as green as fresh sod. 'And why do you doubt the timing?' Her voice had grown tremulous, her nervousness now verging on panic.

'Knowing what I do of Billy, I don't believe he's crafty enough to devise something like this. I'm not even sure he knows what a promissory note is.'

Her lips tightened and her copper-colored brow settled. 'He's a lot smarter than people give him credit for. He was trying to save the smithy any way he could.'

'Perhaps. Only I find it odd that you should initially take pains to hide the business, then be so suddenly forthcoming about it with your uncle and Mr Johnstone. I don't know what you're trying to do here, Marigold, but if I had to guess, I would say you're trying to facilitate Billy Fray's conviction any way you can to save your own skin.'

She was stunned. 'But I love Billy. Don't you understand that?'

'I'm trying to. But I'm having great difficulty.'

She grew even more flustered. 'They had me in tears! They threatened jail!'

'Your uncle said he handled the matter delicately.'

'Hah! If you call browbeating delicate.'

'I believe you orchestrated the whole thing to direct attention away from yourself. I believe you might have been the one to kill your stepfather.'

Her voice grew tremulous, high. 'But I was in the hospital the whole time.'

'That remains to be seen.'

'What do you mean?'

'Hospitals keep records, my dear. They haven't been able to find yours.'

Her shoulders sank, and all nervousness disappeared. In an unexpectedly controlled tone, she said, 'If that's what you think, then please go.'

I frowned. We stared at each other. I could tell that a line had been drawn between us.

'When you're ready to cooperate with me, Marigold – truly cooperate – call me at the surgery. In the meantime, be advised, I have my eye on you. You have every reason to want your stepfather dead. And if you personally didn't do it, you certainly have the womanly wiles to get Billy to do it for you.'

I left her.

I stood in the front hall. No servants were about.

After a moment, I heard Marigold crash her fists against the piano keyboard. A dissonant chord rang through the house. The chord itself was a clue, an unresolved harmony that resonated of Marigold's possible involvement in her stepfather's murder.

I listened to the chord fade, and was about to ring the bell for Flora to bring my hat, gloves, and coat when, on the one-inch heel of Marigold's boot in the boot rack, something caught my eye.

I went over, knelt by the boot rack, and had a look.

I saw a tack. I couldn't be a hundred percent sure, but it looked like the kind of tack I myself had stepped on the day I had passed Flannigan's Stationery Shop on my way to the Grand Hotel to deliver my offer of employment to Miss Gregsby. I lifted the boot. The tack was sunken right into the heel, perhaps not yet discovered because Marigold would never feel it through the one-inch material the heel was made from. And walking in the snow that was all about, she wouldn't hear it tapping on the pavement either.

I worked the tack free and held it to the light of the electrical lamp. Yes, definitely similar, if not downright identical. I pondered the meaning of the tack. I remembered how a day after the murder all the tacks had been cleaned up from the thoroughfare, and how use of the tacks had commenced only on the afternoon before the crime, when Ernest and Oliver Fitzhenry had quickly pinned up the tarpaulin to guard against approaching snow. Which meant if this was indeed a tack from the Flannigan carpentry job, it would have become lodged in Marigold's heel only in and around the time of the murder.

I stood up and rang the bell.

In the music room, Miss Reynolds had gone back to playing the recorder, this time managing to navigate successfully between registers.

Flora appeared from the back in her gray and white uniform. 'I'll bring your coat directly, doctor.'

'Thank you, Flora.'

She retreated, and a moment later came back with my derby, riding gloves, and blue serge cheviot coat. She helped me with my coat. I discreetly slipped the tack into my pocket.

'Flora, could I have a word with you? On the front step? I won't take up much of your time.'

She peered at me from under the frill of her servant's cap, her great and sudden misgiving suspiciously disproportionate to my simple request. 'Of course, doctor.'

We stepped on to the stone stoop.

The snow-covered grounds were arranged prettily around us. Dozens of grackles fussed with the last of the frozen crab-apples in the crab-apple trees on the other side of the drive.

'Miss Winters, you understand that I'm investigating Mr Purcell's murder?'

'I do, sir.'

'And that it's my job to ascertain the truth, and that it's a criminal offence to lie to an officer of the law, and that if the lie is eventually detected, the officer might arrest the offending individual on an obstruction charge?'

Her face now turned pink. 'I must defer to your authority on the subject, doctor.'

I regarded her gravely. 'Then answer me truthfully, Miss Winters. Did you in fact take Miss Reynolds to Sisters of Charity in Buffalo on the night she came to my surgery?'

The young servant looked away, the movement startling the grackles out of the crab-apple trees.

I grew more insistent. 'No one is above the law, Miss Winters.'

She started breathing quickly and I saw that she had now become fairly frantic. 'She sometimes screams at me, sir.' This was indeed a revelation. I could scarcely picture Marigold Reynolds, a woman of better breeding, as her uncle had it, screaming at the help. 'She sometimes hurts me.'

This was even more startling. Here was a secret side of Marigold I hadn't yet seen.

'Was she, or was she not, in Buffalo on the night her stepfather was killed?'

Flora cringed at my sharp tone of voice. She craned, looked through the door, then turned back to me as tears came to her eyes. 'Sir, please, I beg you. She will dismiss me.'

I pressed the matter. 'And I will arrest you.'

After fretting for several moments, the maid finally gave me the truth.

'She insisted we turn around at West Shelby, sir. She wanted to be with Billy. She wanted to be with Daisy Pond. She didn't want to go to Buffalo. I told her she must, that it was doctor's orders.' Flora was now so frightened, she was having a hard time speaking, and her hands were shaking horribly. 'But Miss Marigold threatened to dismiss me on the spot. So I arranged to get the return train in West Shelby. Miss Pond took us in. We went to her house on Finch Street. Miss Pond brought us up the back stairs so that her family wouldn't know. Her house is at least as big as Miss Marigold's, and she has the whole third floor to herself. Her parents never go up there, so it was quite private.'

I turned this over for a few moments. 'And so she stayed at Miss Pond's?' I couldn't help remembering how Miss Pond had been assaulted by Mr Purcell in October.

'Yes. I stayed there with her. Billy stayed with her as well. But then he went to the Pleasant Hotel when he found out you were looking for him.'

'When did Miss Reynolds return to the mansion here on Cherry Hill Road?'

Flora fought to control herself. 'A few days later.'

'Before her stepfather was murdered?'

'I believe it was a day before master was murdered.' She grew frantic again. 'Please don't tell Miss Marigold. I'll lose my position.'

I did what I could to reassure the girl. 'I'll maintain strictest confidence, Miss Winters. Do you know if Marigold was in the house on the night her stepfather was murdered?'

'I retired at eight, doctor. She didn't ring for me after that.'

'Did anybody call?'

'Not until you did to inform Mr Leach of the murder.'

This puzzled me. 'Why didn't Leach tell me your mistress was home?'

She looked at me with desperate eyes. 'We all had strict orders from Miss Marigold about you, doctor. She can be quite a despot when she wants to be. She didn't want you to know she hadn't gone to the hospital. She was afraid she might incur your displeasure. Mr Leach is terrified of her. So am I. Only after you had left did Mr Leach tell her the news of her stepfather's passing.'

'Anything else unusual happen that night?'

She struggled some more. 'There was one thing. The household received a telephone call at eight forty-five. We usually don't receive calls that late.'

'Any idea who it was?'

'No. Only that Miss Marigold must have answered it because all the servants were upstairs by that time, and she was the only one out and about in the house.'

At home, I withdrew the tack I'd found in Miss Marigold's boot from my pocket. I then went to the hallway closet, reached in my clay worsted overcoat, the coat I'd been wearing the day I had passed Flannigan's Stationery Shop, and withdrew the tack I had pulled out of my own boot. I compared the two. They were a match – three-quarter-inch clout tacks made of soft iron.

I went to the Sheriff's Office, where I confronted Billy about the promissory note.

He looked confused by what I was telling him. I had to explain carefully to him exactly what a promissory note was.

'Doc, I sign my name with a' X. My readin' and writin' ain't the best. And I'm not even sure how to spell Mr Hepiner's name.'

'So how do you explain this promissory note?'

'I don't, doc. I don't know nothing about it.'

'Billy, this is an extremely serious matter. If you didn't sign the promissory note, who did?'

'If I had to guess, I'd say Ephraim Purcell. He's such a miser, he'll do anything to get his hands on more money.'

'But that's not the story Marigold gave me. Stanley, tell him the story Marigold gave me.'

Stanley looked up from the mountain of paperwork on his desk. 'Marigold says you forged the note. She says the reason you came into her stepfather's study in the middle of the night was so you could copy Mr Hepiner's signature from one of his shipping office waybills because you wanted to save the smithy. You got caught red-handed by Mr Purcell and he made you surrender the promissory note at gunpoint. He then threatened to turn you in. Herschel Purcell thinks you killed his brother before he could do that.'

This silenced him for several moments.

I finally said to him, 'Here's what I think happened, Billy. She needed a dupe, so she charmed you with her feminine powers. She induced you to do her dirty work. Then, once you were arrested, she got nervous when we were taking so long to indict you, so she came up with this promissory note idea to further incriminate you. She was the one who devised the promissory note. And she's using it as a coffin nail against you.' I shook my head. 'I know you love her, Billy, but start thinking it through. Then ask yourself if you really want to sit in the electric chair for Marigold. We're starting to think she's the one behind it all, even though a witness places you at the scene. Who knows? We might be willing to make a deal with you if you give her up. We could even spare your life.'

TWENTY-FIVE

Deputy Putsey, told to check the hat shop routinely for Jensen's arrival, came to me later that day to tell me that the Civil War veteran's family, if not the actual veteran himself, had returned.

When there was a lull in my patients, I put on my galoshes and walked around the corner to the shop.

Inside, the store now had a bereft look, with less than a third of the shelves now occupied by hats or hat accessories. A few red and green ribbons had been tacked carelessly here and there for Christmas decoration, but they only succeeded in making the place look even more cheerless.

Tilda Jensen and her servant girl, Sally Snell, were behind the counter.

They both gave me cold looks.

I mustered all my southern charm, approached mistress and servant, and doffed my derby.

'Morning, ladies. Merry Christmas.'

Mrs Jensen remained glacial. 'Can I help you, doctor?' She glanced sourly at my derby. 'You don't look as if you need a hat.'

Such a reception could be interpreted in only one way – she knew about my intrusion and search. I dispensed with pleasantries, took out my badge, and placed it on the mahogany sales counter.

'I've come to ask you where your husband is. I understand he didn't return with you.' I glanced to the back. I couldn't help wondering if Jensen had hidden himself back there. 'Is he still in Elmira?'

Mrs Jensen's nostrils dilated and she raised her chin. 'No.'

'Then where is he?'

Her lips stiffened and her face quivered. 'I don't think I'll tell you.' She craned forward like a snapper about to bite. 'And I'll ask you to kindly leave the shop now, Dr Deacon. If you're not going to buy a hat, I see no reason why you should stay. Unless of course you have another order from Judge Norris.'

I stared at her. I could see this was taking a lot out of the poor woman, to stand up to me like this. I wondered if she knew anything about Hattie Whitmore. 'Is he running, Mrs Jensen?'

This apparently shocked her. 'The man's a war hero, Dr Deacon. He doesn't run.'

'I'm going to have to take into evidence every one of his rifles. We must determine if any of them were used in the murder of Ephraim Purcell.'

She grew even more agitated. 'The rifles are gone, Dr Deacon. We had to sell them to make ends meet.'

'And to whom did you sell them?'

'To a dealer in Elmira.'

'So first he runs, and now he destroys the evidence. Mrs Jensen, I don't know what he's told you, but if you aid and abet him, and he turns out to be guilty, you'll be going to prison too.'

'Is this the way you treat innocent mothers in Tennessee, doctor?'

'If you talk to Mr Jensen, I urge you to reason with him.' I nodded toward Sally. 'I'm sure Miss Snell told you about the flask?'

A hint of outrage came to her eyes. 'The one Mr Purcell cheated away from my Isaac?' She was getting more and more riled. 'The one the president himself gave to my husband to honour his heroic actions during the Civil War? The same heroic actions that saved Ephraim's life?'

I tried to get her back on track. 'Mrs Jensen, a man has been murdered.'

'And why is Mr Purcell's death such a bad thing? Have you seen the way his workers live, whole families crammed into a single room in Hoopertown? And do you understand what he has done to us, and also to the poor blacksmith across the canal? So is it truly a great tragedy that such a monster is dead?' She motioned around the shop. 'Look around you, Dr Deacon. We're being forced from our home. Ephraim has crushed my husband, not because he needed to, but simply because he wanted to. Is that the kind of man who should live? I'm sorry, but if you could please leave. I think our business is finished.'

Later on, I said to Stanley, 'I have more than a hunch he's gone to Hattie Whitmore's in Manhattan. Only Manhattan's an awfully big place, and there was no return address on those letters.'

Stanley drummed his long fingers on his desk for several moments. 'Seems to me Herschel Purcell lives in Manhattan. Weren't you

telling me he knows this here Ben Whitmore, Hattie's brother, and
that they all used to chum around together?'

I stared at my friend. 'Thank you, Stanley.'

I met the professor in the Oak Room at the Welland Street Club at
five o'clock that afternoon for a quick eggnog and rum. The
Christmas tree was up, and hollyhock boughs decorated the mantel.

'Oh, yes,' he said. 'I still see Hattie from time to time. As I think
I mentioned, Ben's done his best to give her a home, but he's not
the richest man. She lives in a modest apartment on Hester Street.
She devotes herself to doing charitable work with various orphan-
ages and other philanthropic organizations.'

'So she lives on Hester Street? You wouldn't by any chance have
her exact address, would you?'

He peered over the rim of his eggnog glass. Some of the concoc-
tion had found a home on his Franz Josef-style mustache. 'Doctor,
I believe you have an agenda.'

I told him in strictest confidence about the letters and why I
thought I might find Jensen with Hattie.

Once I was done, I concluded by saying, 'So you see, Professor
Purcell, it's my belief that he might have gone to stay with Hattie
Whitmore, as it appears, based on her correspondence with him,
that they never entirely ended their affair.'

'I see, doctor. Well, then. I have Hattie's address in my address
book. Tell you what. Why don't we pop by the mansion right now
and I'll get it for you?'

TWENTY-SIX

My son, Jeremiah, arrived on the nine o'clock train the next
day.

I watched him descend from the first-class car, and was
surprised by how tall he had gotten, even in just one semester. My
heart expanded with joy. He spotted me and strode toward me, his
brown hair the same shade as Emily's, his face a masculine version
of his mother's. I realized yet again how much I missed my late
wife, and how I longed for her, especially at Christmas, and believed

that Olive might not be too far wrong after all, that my affections belonged, and always would belong, to Emily.

'Pa!' called Jeremiah.

He hurried past the Pullman cars and soon came to me.

While I was a tall man, over six feet, my son was even taller. When he had been a boy, I would scoop him up and hold him close. Now I was lost. Was he a man or still a boy? How should I behave toward him?

'Jeremiah, home at last!' I held out my hand for a handshake.

He looked at it. And then he smiled as if he thought I was an old fool. He came forward and embraced me. 'We're living in the twentieth century, pa.'

There's no greater pleasure a man can enjoy than his son taking him in his arms and embracing him. I felt I had truly ascended to heaven.

Jeremiah pulled away and looked around the platform as the locomotive steamed at the front. 'Where's Miss Wade? I thought she'd be with you. I'm mighty eager to meet her.'

The joy I took in our reunion was now diminished. 'Alas, Jerry, Miss Wade and I seem to have had a falling out.'

He could not hide his disappointment. 'By your letters, I was sure you were going to tell me you were engaged by this time.'

I sighed. 'I might have all the doctor-schooling in the world, son, but that doesn't mean I've figured out women yet.'

Jeremiah was delighted with Henny.

He took me aside once the introductions were complete and said, 'You fixing to marry Miss Gregsby instead, pa? Is that what happened to you and Miss Wade?'

'I have no matrimonial designs on Miss Gregsby at the present time, son, much as she seems to believe to the contrary.'

He nodded. 'Then that's just dandy. Because I'm thinking I'm going to need a wife soon. She's twenty-three. I'm nearly fifteen. That's not too big an age difference. She should be thinking of marrying up soon, before she loses her chance.'

I stared, aghast, again wondering if he was a man or a boy. 'Jerry, you have your studies to think of.'

But he remained smitten with her, and followed her around like a compass following the north pole for the rest of the day.

*   *   *

That afternoon, I had a serendipitous patient, the unmarried sister of Isaac Jensen, Miss Belva Jensen. She was a stout spinster a few years older than Isaac, and though she usually saw me for her bunions, she was here today regarding abdominal complaints. She was entirely without modesty in first shedding her outer garment and then her corset. After listening to the dispirited rumblings of her intestinal tract for close to a minute, I lifted my head.

'I think you should dispense with your corset for the next little while, Miss Jensen. Those old-fashioned whalebone stays might be the source of your present discomfort. As well, I'll prescribe essence of Jamaican ginger, ten drops in the morning, and ten in the evening.'

While I was writing this script, and she was doing up the buttons of her shirtwaist – no easy task now that she was without her corset – I noticed that her hands were trembling.

I lifted my pen. 'Have you had that tremor long, Miss Jensen?'

'Oh, yes, doctor, years. It's nothing to worry about. It doesn't trouble me at all except when I'm trying to darn socks or lift a cup of tea.'

Once I was finished writing her script, I made a note of her new disorder in her chart. I then paused. My eyes narrowed. I stared at her hands as she continued to button her shirtwaist.

I decided I would have to enter the tremor not only into Miss Jensen's chart, but also into the Ephraim Purcell case file.

Later that day, I put on my boots, hat, and scarf, and walked over to the Corn Mercantile Building. Although Deputies Mulroy and Donal had assured me they had by this time spoken to all Corn Mercantile and Grand Hotel employees, I thought a re-canvass couldn't hurt.

They were doing a brisk business in live turkeys – everybody was buying their Christmas bird – and the place was filled with their squawking and stink.

I saw our local butcher, Earl Hadley, haggling with Merle Slack over some turkeys in the commercial dealers' section. Merle Slack was one of the junior yard hands, and I decided he was as good a man as any to start with. I looked around for Erwin Fletcher, Mrs Swinford's brother, and was glad to see he was nowhere about.

I bought my own live turkey, a fourteen-pounder who disapproved robustly when she was transferred from her cage, tied by her wings and legs, and stuffed into a burlap bag.

I then waited for Slack and Hadley to conclude their business. By and by, they were finished.

I went over to the yard hand.

'A Merry Christmas to you, sir,' I called.

Slack looked up from his work. 'Doc. Howdy.' He glanced at my sack. 'You found yourself a nice one?'

The bird was still struggling. 'I wouldn't number niceness as her chief personality trait, Mr Slack, but she's certainly going to be tasty.'

He was a young man of twenty, wore a red thermal undershirt, denim overalls, and big rubber boots. Short in stature and freckled in face, he had riotous uncombed bundles of blond hair protruding from under his brown tweed cap, and a crooked set of teeth.

'Anything else I can help you with, doc?' he asked. 'The girls have made some top-notch mince-meat pie. I had a piece. It can't be beat. Five cents a slice.'

I grinned. 'I may avail myself of that, Mr Slack. But before I do, could I have a word with you about the Purcell murder case? The sheriff has deputized me to look into it.'

His Christmas cheer faded. 'So I heard.' After a moment's thought, he said, 'I never had a problem with Mr Purcell. People call him an old miser, but he was always tipping me nickels and dimes. A miser's supposed to be stingy with his money, and Mr Purcell was never stingy with me.'

'Were you working on the night he was killed?'

'I was.'

'And did you hear the shot?'

'Shots, doc. There were two.'

I nodded – Slack was of the two-shot school, then. 'And where were you when you heard the shots?'

'Right over yonder, at the foot of them there bleachers.'

'So near the window?'

'Yes, sir.'

'And do you have any idea where the shots came from?'

He squinted as he thought about this. 'A lot of people say the back alley between the Grand and the Corn Mercantile. But to be honest, sir, they sounded to me as if they came from an upstairs window somewhere. Or maybe the hotel roof.'

Here at last was a witness account that supported the pronounced angle of the gunshot wound. 'Didn't one of the deputies come to talk to you about this? I had them canvass the whole neighborhood. I thought they had spoken to every employee here.'

'Not me. Just to some of the other fellows. I was in Florida visiting my cousins. I left the day after the murder and didn't get back till last week.'

Hah! Here's where persistence in a criminal investigation paid off.

'So you're certain at least one of the shots came from an elevated position?'

He thought some more, squinting up at the rafters. 'I would have to say both of them came from high ground, sir.'

I cocked my brow. 'Both from the vicinity of the Grand?'

'No, sir. One shot came from across the street. From the drugstore, if I had to guess.'

The drugstore? I paused for a long time after this. Mrs Swinford had been over at Wiley's Drugstore at the time, practicing Christmas Carols, according to her son. 'Do you recall Mr Swinford and his son sitting up on the bleachers at the time of the shooting?'

'Mr Swinford was there. He was bidding on hogs. Clarence was gone, though. There was a bit of a ruckus, you see.'

'A ruckus?'

'Mr Purcell came by and started bothering Mrs Swinford. She got so upset she left. Clarence followed her a few minutes later.'

'How come none of the other workers told my deputies this? All I got from my men was that they had nothing to report.'

'Guess because the rest of the hands were in the stable. It's just me and Mr Fletcher out front on auction night. And the auctioneer, he don't know nobody. He's from Batavia.'

My mind shot over the Swinford family's tragic history with Purcell. And now Clarence hadn't been sitting in the bleachers after all, even though his uncle, Erwin Fletcher, had told me otherwise.

Later on, I discussed these new revelations with Stanley at the Sheriff's Office.

'Clarence worked at the hotel for a while. Eugene Lapinance had him doing the books. He had an office in a back room. I'm sure he had the key to the back door. Stairs back there lead all the way to the roof. I know that. I checked it myself earlier in the investigation. And if not the Grand, then maybe he could have gone over to the Wileys. The way Merle Slack tells it, Clarence left the Corn

Mercantile before the rifle-fire started. Purcell came in and harassed his ma shortly before that. Whether Clarence went to the roof of the Grand Hotel or to an upstairs window above the drugstore, it all has to be looked into.'

Stanley grinned. 'I can see why I make you deputy so much.'

TWENTY-SEVEN

The next day, after a morning of patients, I had lunch with Henny and Jeremiah.

I found it unexpectedly upsetting, sitting with them like that at the kitchen table, eating leftover pork roast and pea soup. It nearly felt like a family. The eager look in Henny's eyes unsettled me. Her over-exerted smiles and too-quick laugh spoke of a woman drowning in grief, desperate to latch on to any flotsam and jetsam passing by. In this case, I was the flotsam and Jeremiah perhaps the jetsam. How miserable it was that I wanted Olive Wade to be sitting in that chair instead of Miss Gregsby.

By the end of lunch I was out of sorts. I decided the only way to improve – or at least distract – my mood was to close the surgery for the rest of the afternoon and throw myself whole-heartedly into the Ephraim Purcell murder case.

I got up abruptly and left without a word.

I felt my son and Henny staring after me.

After a moment, I heard Henny follow me into the corridor. 'Clyde?'

I turned, and realized I was starting to feel unfairly cantankerous toward her. 'I shall be closing the surgery for the afternoon, Henny. There have been some new developments in the Ephraim Purcell murder case, and I will be employed in my capacity as sheriff's deputy for the rest of the day. I'm sure you and Jeremiah can find ways to amuse yourselves.'

Her eyes, brown and large, remained unwavering. 'You're distressed.'

'I'm fine.'

'You say that like a man hanging by thumbscrews.'

For several seconds I didn't respond. Then I took the easiest dodge. 'It's just that at this time of the year, I miss Emily so dearly.'

Her face softened. I saw in her eyes a reflection of my own grief, only keener, the wound fresher, the hurt still bewildering, not smoothed by time to a chronic ache, the way mine was. She put her hands on my forearms, stood on her tiptoes and, much to my alarm, kissed me on the cheek.

'We will have a Merry Christmas, Clyde. I know we will.' She glanced back to Jeremiah, then turned to me and kissed me again. 'Go on, now. Work on your case. And cheer up. I'll be making a special supper tonight. And then perhaps we can sit by the fire together.'

I didn't have the heart to tell her no.

After all, I was a doctor, and commanded by Hippocrates to do no harm.

I stood in Tonawanda Road a short while later. Various horse-drawn conveyances passed by. Mr Woodrow Addison, a patient of mine, puttered by in his Stanley Steamer, the engine hissing and chugging as he manned the tiller beside his fat, goggled wife. They waved a Merry Christmas. I waved back, waited for them to pass, then walked to the middle of the town's main thoroughfare and angled my gaze to the rooms above the drugstore.

I surveyed various possible rifle perches. I did so with ill-humour. My love-life was making me miserable. I turned around and looked up at the hotel roof. The hotel roof irritated me. Everything irritated me at the present moment. Especially the female sex's God-given right to misunderstand.

I shook these troubles from my mind and applied myself to the case.

Given the angle of Mr Purcell's chest wound – down through the lung, stopped by the scapula – the weapon could have certainly been fired from the upper reaches of the drugstore or from the hotel. Though the flask was still confusing me, I was growing more and more convinced that the shot, or shots, had indeed come from – to use Merle Slack's terminology – high ground after all.

What bothered me now was his account of the way one shot had come from the hotel roof and the other from an upstairs window of the drugstore. So much for the theory of Marigold and Billy acting in concert. How could one or the other gain access to an upstairs drugstore window without being discovered? Perhaps it had been members of the Swinford family acting together? Or perhaps two shooters unlinked and ignorant of the other's presence? Yet it hardly seemed possible that two unlinked people had decided to kill Purcell at the exact same time. The coincidental nature of such a happenstance seemed beyond statistical likelihood.

I left the roadway and entered the Grand Hotel.

I found Eugene Lapinance, the hotel manager, polishing glassware in the tavern. He was a dark-haired man of forty in a red and white striped shirt, a black vest, with a healthy dark mustache that joined with his sideburns.

'Dr Deacon! Merry Christmas to you! What can I get you?'

As he seemed intent on dispensing what I saw was a fine Blue Mountain sour mash, I broke my usual five o'clock rule and enjoyed some liquid cheer earlier in the day than was usual for me. After Lapinance had decanted a shot for me, he poured a straight whisky for himself.

I then broached the subject of Purcell's latest transgressions against Mrs Swinford. 'Mr Johnstone told me you were talking to Purcell about his renewed passion for Mrs Swinford shortly before he met his end.'

Mr Lapinance was at first reluctant to speak on the subject. But when I told him it had a direct bearing on the murder case, and might help catch Mr Purcell's killer, he opened up.

'As a married man, I generally didn't approve of Ephraim's habits when it came to women. But Ephraim was a different animal than the rest of us. It was his instinct. You would never ask a coyote why he goes after a rabbit. With Ephraim and the ladies, it was the same thing. Mrs Swinford was his particular favourite. His hankerings go back a long way. He'd been trying to hold them in check, but I guess they finally broke loose again. He was such a lonely man at times, especially after Francine died.'

'I understand Mrs Swinford's son, Clarence, worked here awhile.'

Delight came to the bartender's eyes. 'Yes, sir. A couple years ago. A fine young man, Clarence. Did the books for us. Was fifteen at the time, but smarter than a lot of men twice his age.'

'And he worked in the back?'

'He did.'

I motioned to the lobby. 'Did he come in through the front to get to work? Or did he have a key to the rear entrance?' For to get to the roof undetected Clarence would have had to go through the back.

'He had a key to the rear entrance.' Mr Lapinance stopped to give me a momentary perusal. 'Say, doc, what are you getting at here?'

'When he finished his employment at the Grand Hotel, did he surrender his key?'

A line came to Mr Lapinance's ham-colored brow. 'The assistant manager looked after that for me. Let's see, back then it was Andy Michaelson. He lit out for California eighteen months ago.'

'Do you know if Clarence gave his key back?'

'It was such a long time ago. I'm sure it's mixed up with all the other spares.'

'Can I look at the back door?'

'Of course, doc.' He raised his glass. 'Bottoms up.'

After draining our glasses, we found our way to the rear service entrance.

'On the Saturday night of the murder, was there anybody back here?' I asked.

'Just the kitchen staff bringing garbage to the trash bins in the alley from time to time.'

'Can I take another look around the roof?'

'Be my guest. But if you don't mind, I have to get back to the bar. You think you can find your own way up?'

'Of course.'

Once I was up on the roof I checked it yet again for shell casings and other ballistics evidence, taking extra care this time, going over every square inch, looking into every corner, around all the vents, and even under some flashing. I saw no rifle or gun evidence. I checked the copper that capped the brick walls, turned green from years of weather, but saw nothing that looked even remotely like a powder burn. I inspected lines of fire, focusing on the estimated spot where Mr Purcell had fallen before he had crawled away, and saw that I might have a match. The angle of Mr Purcell's wound seemed to correlate nicely.

But where was the evidence?

Clarence was a bright boy.

Was he bright enough to make sure he left no evidence behind?

TWENTY-EIGHT

Having checked for ballistics evidence in the hat shop during my warrant search of the building to find the flask and discovering none, the only thing left now was to search Wiley's Drugstore.

I left the hotel and headed over.

Though the drugstore was open, the Wileys themselves were visiting relatives in Scranton. I learned from their only store employee, Bruce Farrow, a young man in a green shop apron, that they weren't due back till a day before Christmas.

I told him that I was here not in my capacity as doctor – I often came to the drugstore to purchase routine medical supplies for the surgery – but as the sheriff's deputy, and that I was investigating lines of fire in the Purcell murder case. 'I want to go upstairs to check the windows.' Because I knew Mr Farrow was interested in science, and had aspirations to some day go to college and study in the field, I framed my inquiry as if it were an experiment. 'I need to test a hypothesis, Bruce, and I know you understand all about hypotheses.'

He grew thoughtful after this, put his thumb and forefinger to his clean-shaven chin, and nodded. 'I suppose it would be all right. Who am I to say no to a deputy of the law, especially when he's got some scientific investigating to do?'

He took me to the back and led me upstairs to the private rooms.

I found a lavatory and parlor on the first floor. I checked the two front windows in the parlor, examining closely their sills and drapery for anything like a powder burn from a firearms discharge, but discovered only the dirty handprint of a child.

On the top floor I found three bedrooms. I went into the big one at the front. A quick survey of the furniture and layout told me this was Gordon and Cora Wiley's master bedroom. The green velvet curtains had tassel fringes, and were tied back to reveal lace sheers. I immediately noticed a hole through the north sheer. My heartbeat quickened. I went over and examined the perforation more closely.

In diameter, it was roughly the width of a bullet. A series of fine black dots stippled its outer edge. I decided that the lace sheers could have provided the perfect hunter's blind for my shooter. I took out my Swiss Army knife, retracted the small nail scissors, and snipped the sample away, adding significant margins to optimize my chance at a testable specimen. I deposited the sample in a glassine envelope, then went back downstairs to talk to young Mr Farrow.

'Are you familiar with the Swinfords at all, Bruce?'

'Oh, yes, sir, I am. Clarence and I have become good friends. We play chess together often.'

'Are they frequent visitors here?'

'Mrs Swinford is. She depends on Mrs Wiley when she has her spells.'

'Spells? What kind of spells?'

He thought for a few seconds. 'I guess you'd call them the doldrums, sir. She gets them, and she cries a lot. Mrs Wiley always manages to cheer her up.'

'And how did Mrs Swinford and Mrs Wiley become friends?'

'I believe they were on the church social committee together a number of years back.'

'Is it often that Mrs Swinford comes here in the evening?'

'If the Swinfords are in town late, she'll come over. Especially when the Saturday night auction at the Corn Mercantile drags on.'

'And you board with the Wileys, don't you?'

'I do, sir.'

'And where's your room?'

'In the basement.'

'And were you in your room on the night Mr Purcell was murdered?'

'No, sir. I was out with some chums at the Pleasant Hotel. It was Mickey Hudson's birthday. We were having a fine old time.'

'Tell me, does Mr Wiley own a rifle?'

Young Mr Farrow grew suddenly nervous. 'Don't tell me you think my boss shot Mr Purcell?'

'I wouldn't think that for a minute, Bruce. But as you're a young man who's as sharp as a tack, and has a head on his shoulders, and is aspiring to be a scientist, you admire and understand scientific principles.' Bruce puffed up a bit at this praise. 'You know that in order to arrive at a scientific proof, hypotheses have to be tested and discarded, tested and discarded, until one of them stands. Mr Wiley owning a rifle is a hypothesis. Come now, Mr Farrow, surely as my scientific colleague you can see that I must investigate all rifles within a certain radius of the Grand Hotel.'

He raised his thumb and forefinger to his chin again – a born thinker – screwed up his eyes, and contemplated the soda fountain as if it were a newly discovered planet. 'Radius. I see what you mean. I've been reading up on my geometry, doc. It's a fascinating subject, ain't it?'

'It plays heartily into my investigation.'

'Well, then, I can tell you that Mr Wiley definitely does *not* own a rifle.'

My spirits sank. All that flattery for nothing. 'He doesn't?'

'No, sir, he doesn't. Mrs Wiley and he had a big argument about it recently and she made him sell it.'

My spirits rose, as the fact of anybody getting rid of a rifle in and around the time of my victim's murder was indeed pertinent to my case. 'And when did he sell it, Mr Farrow? Think carefully, now. Science depends on accuracy.'

The young man's eyes focused in appropriately conveyed concentration. 'I would say two days after Mr Purcell met his end out here in the street.'

This timing, then, was even more pertinent. 'And tell me, when Mr Wiley did own his rifle, where did he keep it?'

'In his bedroom closet.'

Ah. The shooter took the rifle from the bedroom closet and shot out the bedroom window. 'And to whom did he sell his rifle?'

'Mr King, over at King's Emporium of New and Used Merchandise.'

My spirits sank again when I visited King's Emporium of New and Used Merchandise.

Anthony King said, 'You mean that old Winchester of his? I don't have it no more.'

'You sold it?'

'Not exactly.'

'Then what did you do with it?'

'I broke it down for parts. It wasn't good for much else.'

So though I had preliminary evidence that a shot had been fired through Gordon and Cora Wiley's bedroom window, and that there had been easy access to a weapon up there on the night of the murder, I had no way to test-fire the rifle in question.

I made a last-ditch try. 'You couldn't have used the barrel as a spare part for another weapon, could you? Because I'm primarily interested in the rifling.'

'The barrel was out of true, so I sold it for scrap to Robson's Metalworks. I'm sure it's gone into the forge by now.'

At home, I went to my small laboratory and took my bullet-hole sample from the glassine envelope with Adson forceps and placed it in a Petri dish. Any kind of lab work acted as a hypnotic on me, and I soon became fixated on my purpose – that of determining whether within this fine piece of lisle fabric there existed minute particles of lead.

I walked as if in a trance to my library and put my hand on Volume 144 of *The American Journal of the Medical Sciences*. After a quick perusal of its table of contents, I turned to page 599 where I found the exact article I was looking for. The title was 'The Chemical Detection of Lead in Gunshot Wounds.' I read it over quickly and returned to my laboratory.

I glanced out my window where I saw Henny and Jeremiah building a snowman. We would get a tree tomorrow. We would decorate it. Henny would look at me with lovelorn eyes and I wouldn't know how to respond.

I put the whole matter from my mind and applied myself to the alchemy of crime.

I selected from my various stoppered bottles some nitric acid, and mixed fifteen drops into a drachm of distilled water. I then dampened my lace sheer in the resulting solution. I chose another bottle, this one containing iodide of potassium crystals, and, using tweezers, placed several of these into an Erlenmeyer flask of distilled water and dissolved them. I then added this solution, by way of an a eye-dropper, to my ballistics specimen, and waited to observe any chemical reaction.

Slowly, over the course of the next five minutes, my sample turned yellow.

Eureka!

I had struck lead!

PART THREE
The Bridge to Eternity

TWENTY-NINE

I had Jeremiah wear a suit. Miss Gregsby wore her green evening gown. I dressed in my black swallowtail tuxedo with black top hat and white gloves.

We were on our way to the event of the season, Dr Olaf Thorensen's annual holiday party.

Once Munroe had hitched Pythagoras and Archimedes to the sleigh, he brought it around to the side of the house. Snow was falling. The three of us got in, and were soon trotting over the span bridge at Tonawanda Road into the rich neighbourhood of Cherry Hill. I glanced up and down the river. Wide enough for various small barge traffic, it was now closed for the season, as ice had begun to form.

Upon our arrival at Dr Thorensen's, the crush was thick. We were swept into the end of the receiving line. Female servants in black uniforms and white aprons plied this line with alcoholic beverages trimmed with sprigs of holly or candy canes. I recognized many people, but several I did not know, and it underlined for me again how I was still a relative newcomer to Fairfield.

Whereas Dr Pritchard, the dentist, had hired a seven-piece band from Buffalo, Dr Thorensen had engaged an eighteen-piece orchestra with female vocalist from New York City. In other words, Olaf had spared no expense to treat the town to Christmas in true Fezziwig style.

I glanced ahead to Dr Thorensen, a substantial man, taller than me, dressed in formal attire, with full shield-front collar and white bowtie. His sandy hair was pomaded back and his golden beard had been trimmed. Mrs Thorensen, beside him, was petite, birdlike, and wore a yellow gown with a diamond tiara. She reminded me of a bejewelled canary.

When we reached him, Thorensen said, 'Ah-hah! We have a fox in the henhouse! Dr Deacon, have you come to poach my patients again?' He chortled heartily; he was always joking with me about stealing his patients, even though there were more than enough to go around. 'A Merry Christmas to you, my fine fellow. And best wishes for the New Year.' His eyes alighted on Henny. 'I see you've brought your lovely new nurse, Miss Gregsby. And bless me! This must be your son.' He turned to his wife. 'Lydia, Dr Deacon has brought his son, Jeremiah. Isn't that marvellous?'

Lydia Thorensen turned. 'My, my, but he's certainly tall enough. They grow like weeds, don't they, Clyde?'

'So true, Mrs Thorensen.'

I made formal introductions.

After we were finished with the receiving line, my son, Miss Gregsby, and I availed ourselves of a buffet-style dinner: cold chicken, jellied oysters, *foie gras*, fruit sauce, mandarins, nuts, and my own favourite, mince-meat pie.

It was during this repast that I saw Olive Wade, arriving late, come through the front door. She was accompanied by a young man I did not recognize. Feeling a pang of jealousy, I immediately lost my appetite. I wondered who this man was. He appeared to be a few years older than Olive. As with all the male guests, he wore a black tuxedo, but he affected a red satin bowtie. The receiving line had by this time dissolved, and so it was left to the butler to greet them. The butler took their coats, and Miss Wade's fox stole and muff, and the pair made their way to the front salon.

Miss Wade spotted the three of us sitting by the fire with plates and champagne. Her face tightened like the first ice on a winter pond, and she quickly turned away. She was resplendent in a mauve gown, and her golden hair was up in a most fetching manner, held there by jewelled combs. I don't think I'd ever seen her lovelier.

Yet she was with this man!

She now turned back to us. Her stiff smile did nothing to hide the troubled cast to her eyes. She said a few words to her companion. He went off to find refreshments, and she came over.

I leaned toward Jeremiah. 'Here comes Miss Wade.'

He turned. His eyes widened – an angel could have entered the room.

The three of us put our plates on the table and rose.

'Good evening, Dr Deacon,' said Miss Wade as she reached us. 'A Merry Christmas to you.' With this salutation out of the way, she now became a little more natural, and gazed at Jeremiah with warm interest. 'You must be Jeremiah.' She extended her hand. 'I'm your father's friend, Olive Wade.'

Jeremiah shook Miss Wade's hand. 'How do you do?' He gazed

at her in stark wonder. Her blonde presence lit up the room the way the electrical star on top of the Christmas tree lit its uppermost boughs. 'Pa's told me about you.'

Miss Wade gave me a glance. She might have been radiant, but I also saw evidence of our current discord in the tension around her lips. 'I hope he was kind.'

I rushed in. 'I believe you've met my nurse.'

More coldly now, she said, 'Yes. Merry Christmas, Miss Gregsby.'

'Merry Christmas, Miss Wade.'

For several seconds none of us said anything.

Then Miss Wade broke the uncomfortable silence. 'I should return to my companion. He's from Boston. He'll be lost in this crowd. So nice to see you, Dr Deacon. And a pleasure to meet you, Jeremiah. Enjoy the party.'

She moved off, as graceful as a summer breeze.

Jeremiah leaned over and murmured, 'Pa, go after her.'

I turned to my son. 'Who's that man she's with?'

'I don't know. But you should do something about it.'

I turned to Henny. Her dark eyes now had a patina of distress. I saw that she was beginning to understand. As much as I wanted her to have a fine Christmas, I knew I had to go after Miss Wade, even though I had no idea what I would say to her.

'Miss Wade, a word, please.'

Olive turned, her expression a picture of self control. 'Of course, Dr Deacon. How can I be of service?'

Her manner remained distant, formal. It pained me greatly. I still had no idea what I was going to say to her. In casting about for a subject, my mind naturally trolled areas of current focus, and I now remembered there was something I had to ask her in regard to the Purcell murder case. 'As you know, I'm still investigating the murder of Ephraim Purcell.'

She nodded with appropriate solemnity. 'Such a sad crime.'

'I've now learned that Miss Reynolds did not admit herself to Sisters of Charity Hospital in Buffalo on the night you so graciously helped me attend her.'

Her golden brow rose. 'She didn't?'

'No. It would appear she came back to Fairfield with her maid after reaching West Shelby. She then sought Miss Pond's hospitality on Finch Street, where she stayed a number of days during her convalescence before returning to her own house.'

Miss Wade thought about this. 'She's a strong-willed girl, sir. If she didn't want to go to the hospital, nothing, not even your order, would induce her. How can I help you in this matter, Dr Deacon?'

My heart sank. 'Olive, please, call me Clyde.'

'No, doctor, your proper title is more appropriate at this point.'

For the next several seconds I couldn't go on. But then I again used the Purcell case as a pretext to talk to her. 'I think you said Miss Pond and Miss Reynolds were friends, did you not?'

'I did. The best of friends.'

'And did Daisy approve of Marigold's liaison with Billy Fray?'

Olive glanced toward the Christmas tree, where two children stared at candy canes with hungry eyes. Her brow knitted and she turned back to me. 'I would have to say that Daisy Pond was as much in love with Billy Fray as Marigold was.'

This unexpected fact gave me reason to pause. 'How interesting.'

'No, doctor, it's quite sad, really. Unrequited love always is.'

I couldn't help thinking she was making an oblique comment on our own situation.

'So in other words, she didn't approve,' I said.

'Only because she loved Billy herself.' Her eyes strayed to the refreshments table. 'I should return to my friend.' She moved off.

I grabbed her by the wrist. 'Olive, please, wait.'

She turned to me. 'Dr Deacon, no.'

'Who is your companion? He's not Edgar Keenan, is he?'

She peered at me. She at last seemed to divine the true depth of my suffering. She looked away. 'He's not Edgar. He's Edgar's cousin, Drake.'

The implication of this panicked me. 'Edgar's cousin?' My heart lurched like a carriage with one wheel smaller than the other. 'Olive, what's going on?'

Her shoulders rose. 'Edgar has sent Drake to talk to me.' With this admission she became a little more relenting in her tone toward me, even if she remained uninformative. 'I should be off. If I can be of further assistance in your investigation, please don't hesitate to call.' She gave me a small bow. 'Good evening, doctor.'

She made off through the crowd. This time I didn't attempt to restrain her.

For several seconds I couldn't move. All my reservations about Olive's summer with Everett Howse now seemed small and pointless compared to the news that Keenan had sent his cousin from Boston.

Perhaps I would have turned to stone on the spot if Stanley Armstrong hadn't made his way through the crowd in an ill-fitting tuxedo that looked as if it belonged in a vaudeville show. He took me by the arm and, without saying a word, ushered me away like a wounded soldier off the battlefield.

A short while later, the sheriff and I stood by the bar having a drink, he a whisky, I my usual bourbon.

'What I can't understand,' I said, 'is why Keenan's cousin is here in the first place. She said he's here to talk to her, but what does she mean by that? And couldn't he have telephoned? Why did he have to come all this way?'

The sheriff took a sip of whisky and pondered. 'Maybe this Keenan feller sent his cousin as an emissary. Last time I checked, you couldn't send an emissary through the telephone.'

I sighed. 'You think Olive's fixing to go back to Boston?'

'Maybe Keenan's called it off with his wife and is trying to win her back.'

I stiffened. 'I won't let that happen.'

'It seems you've been letting it happen all this while.'

I sighed. 'Small things got in the way of bigger things.'

Stanley's voice and manner grew more emphatic. 'Then, Clyde, you have to take a stand. Remember when we had that buffalo herd bearing down on us the time we rode up to Amarillo? Must have been in '89 or '90, one of the last herds that size? We were hunkered down in that hollow, and there was no way out for us because the herd was a half mile across. We thought we were goners. So what did you do? You stood up and did that crazy Comanche war dance. What did the herd do? They parted like the dang Red Sea. You got to do a Comanche war dance for Olive, Clyde, and make her take notice.'

I sighed, confused. 'You want me to do a Comanche war dance at Dr Thorensen's holiday party? That hardly seems appropriate, Stanley.'

'All I know is that if you don't do something soon, you're going to lose whatever chance you have. There she is over there. And it looks like she's fixin' to dance with this here feller from Boston. Are you going to let that happen?'

'What would you have me do, Stanley? She's made it as plain as a pikestaff that she doesn't want to have anything to do with me.

If I cut in on Keenan's cousin, I'll look like a real chump, and that will just make matters worse.'

'Come up with something, Clyde. You know you love her, and you're going to lose her if you don't.'

THIRTY

After mounting the stage and telling the conductor what I needed, he nodded and went over and spoke to the pianist. The pianist, continuing to play, listened, and finally nodded. Then the conductor had a few words with the first violinist. The violinist, in the middle of some pizzicato, nodded as well.

The conductor came back to me. 'The piano player knows the piece,' he told me. 'And Hal says you can use his violin. We're just going to finish this song.'

Hal came over after the song had finished and surrendered his violin and bow. 'My rosin's on my stand if you need some.'

Giving the E-string a few scratches, I was satisfied that the horsehair had sufficient purchase to produce a tone, so didn't bother with the rosin. I thanked Hal and approached the small proscenium arch.

People turned, curious that I was up here.

'Ladies and gentleman, I would like to make a special musical offering to a lady I've grown to know well since coming to Fairfield last spring. She is fair of temperament, generous in spirit, and, I hope, forgiving in nature. I speak of Miss Olive Wade.' I could see her now, stiff in the audience, her mauve gown making her look like an iris bracing against a strong wind. Her companion from Boston stood beside her with a glass of champagne in his hand, a handsome tall rogue with an insufferable smirk on his face. 'Miss Wade, please accept this musical offering as a white flag, and take it as an early Christmas present from a true and ardent admirer.' I turned to the conductor. 'Maestro?'

I played the same piece I had heard Miss Wade herself play the day I had presented myself at her door and had been turned away by her maid, Freda, Chopin's Prelude Number 4 from his Opus 28 collection, now adapted, by ear, for violin and piano.

I poured my soul into each phrase. The pianist followed beautifully. I saw rapture on the faces of many ladies in the audience. I felt my love for Olive Wade as never before – love always finding its truest expression in music.

We were two-thirds the way through when I saw Miss Wade break away from Edgar Keenan's cousin and make for the front door in an agitated manner. My violin went scratch, and I found I was quite incapable of playing another note.

I turned to Hal and gave his instrument back to him. 'Carry on, my good man.'

He took the instrument, found his place, and continued with the Chopin.

To the astonished murmurs of the audience, I rushed down the steps after Miss Wade. I caught a glimpse of Henny looking at me from the far side of the room with the most tragic eyes I'd ever seen.

I saw Olive hurry out the front door, leaving her silver fox stole and muff in the hands of a dumbfounded butler.

As I neared the front door the butler said to me, 'Sir, perhaps you would be so kind as to give Miss Wade her muff and stole.'

I snatched the fur articles from the butler and hurried outside.

Snow still fell, odd because the moon had come out from behind some clouds and the sky was clear. I was confronted with lustrous flakes tumbling gently through moonlight. After a few moments of gazing at this silver-tinted miracle, distracted by the prettiness of it all, I spotted Olive at the end of the drive, her back to me, standing there, staring out at the road. The gas lamps on the street, still not replaced by electrical ones, lit her up so that she glowed as if with platinum-plating.

I descended the steps and approached her with much circumspection.

As I drew near, my feet sinking up to my ankles, I called. 'Miss Wade?' I took a few more steps. 'I say, Olive.'

She swung round. For the first time since my ill-fated sleigh ride with Miss Gregsby, I saw reflected in her expression a true account of the way she felt, tortured, the searching look in her eyes desperate, her lips pulled back at the corners to show the full depth of the way she was suffering. Despite this, she maintained her formal tone.

'I came out for a breath,' she said. 'It's nothing you need concern yourself with, Dr Deacon.'

I reached her. 'Is it Miss Gregsby?'

'Look at this snow. And with moonlight, too.'

'Would it help if I asked her to leave?'

She glanced away, and her sadness became so acute she looked bereft. 'Your playing is so beautiful. I had no idea.'

'Olive, what is it?' I put the fox stole around her neck, the muff upon her right hand, and placed my own hands upon her shoulders. 'What's happened?'

She turned to me. In that infuriatingly proper voice, she said, 'I'm so glad your son has come from Boston to visit for Christmas, Dr Deacon. I myself will be travelling to Boston for the holiday.'

My heart now rushed like the Tonawanda did down near the locks. 'Olive, don't let that cad Keenan entice you a second time.'

'I wouldn't categorize him as a cad, Dr Deacon. I believe he just needs a woman's proper influence. I'm not sure he ever got that from his wife, who, by the way, no longer lives in Boston but has removed herself to Baltimore to be with her parents.'

'Olive, no, please.'

'I'm sure you will have a wonderful Christmas with Miss Gregsby.'

'She means nothing to me. Surely you understand that.'

'I understand only what my eyes tell me to understand.'

'Then your eyes deceive you.'

'I think not.'

Frustrated with her, knowing that in her current state I couldn't talk sense to her, I zeroed in like a hawk on a field mouse and kissed her square on the lips. Her body stiffened, and I could sense she was shocked. But then, after a moment, her muscles eased and she didn't resist, but rather responded. Her lips were soft, like velvet, and the smell of her perfume, mixed with a hint of champagne, was intoxicating. My lids were closed. I opened them, and saw Olive looking up at me, blue eyes wide, studying me as if she were trying to divine the true depth of my soul.

I pulled back. We stared at each other. I detected new significance to the way she looked at me, and I had the curious sensation that my heart was leaving my chest and connecting with hers, and that the two together were joined in flight above us. I felt that the story was already written. We were, in a word, a couple; and, at least for those few moments, as the snow fell around us like flakes from a silversmith's grinding wheel, we shared a deep and unburdened trust, that feeling of union only a husband and wife can share, a permanent and unshakeable belief in one another.

Our lips latched again, this time with greater eagerness, and we kissed with such passion that had there been a hundred violins playing Chopin on the front lawn they wouldn't have achieved the same intensity of our lip-locked embrace. She let her muff slide to the snow, put her arms around me, and drew me near. She began to shake, and I sensed her great need. I remembered how her parents had recently died, and how her Aunt Tabitha had passed away, and how she had been ill-used first by Keenan, then by our junior assemblyman from Albany, Everett Howse. If only I could have had greater understanding of this woman at the outset and not let my reservations guide my behaviour. I saw now that she needed me, but that she was afraid, and unsure – unsure of any man, given her past.

When she finally pulled away, she unexpectedly erected battlements again, and, rather than trust the man who loved her, she encouraged those misconceptions that had been driving us apart since November.

'You would send her away?'

She didn't understand that Henny didn't need sending away, and that she had never needed sending away because she didn't mean anything to me.

Before I could allay her renewed suspicions by professing my undying devotion to her, I heard someone hurry down the front steps. I turned and saw Drake, Keenan's cousin from Boston, now with not just a glass of champagne in his hand but a whole bottle.

He called across the yard. 'Badly done, Miss Wade. Badly done, indeed. What will Edgar think? Especially after he's made so many sacrifices.'

We disengaged. Under her breath, Olive said, 'That was wrong of us.'

'On the contrary, you know just how right it was.'

'It was horribly misguided.'

My throat thickened with anguish. I clasped her hands. 'Search your heart.'

'Leave her alone, mister.' Drake came right up to us, the grin on his face in no way friendly, clutched my elbow, and broke my hold on Olive. 'That is unless you want to find a five-fingered sandwich in your mouth.'

Olive intervened. 'Drake, please. There's no need for that.'

'As Edgar's representative, I think there's every need. Think of me as your personal Border collie.'

'Sir, you insult Miss Wade with your inference.'

Drake's smile disappeared. 'Mister, I don't know who you are, or how you know Miss Wade, but you have no business fooling with her. She's not herself tonight, and you shouldn't be taking advantage of her when she's in this state. She needs a guiding hand just now, and that's why I'm here. If you know what's good for you, you'll leave her alone.' He gripped Miss Wade by the elbow. 'Come on, Olive. I'll have the stable-boy bring the sleigh around. We're going.'

She allowed herself to be led away.

But a quarter way up the drive, she turned and called. 'I'm sorry, Clyde. I've been a fool.'

I said nothing, but I thought to myself: so have I, Olive. So have I.

Later that night, after Jeremiah had gone to bed, Henny came and knocked on my bedroom door. I answered. Her hair was down and she was in her nightgown.

Before either of us could say anything, she pressed her head against my chest. I didn't know what to do. I felt a hot tear fall on my hand. She put her arms around me and held me tightly.

'I can't have you, can I?'

I left my arms at my sides. 'I'm sorry, Henny.'

'Why didn't you stop me?'

I had nothing to say.

She broke away from me and hurried to her room.

Merry miserable Christmas, I thought.

When I was sure she was settled, I got dressed and went down-stairs to my study. I took out writing materials and composed a letter to the Booths, the parents of Henny's dead fiancé. I explained to them how their son's suicide shouldn't be blamed on Henny, gave them many medical details regarding Martin's condition, and told them how Henny was an orphaned young woman in search of a family – a family to come home to for Christmas. I continued by lauding her many wonderful qualities and suggested that though they may never have their son back, a daughter like Henny would be a blessing to any family. I then added a one-dollar bill, asking them that they telegraph an answer as soon as possible, and that, if they were so inclined, I would send Henny to Wisconsin, all expenses paid.

Having taken their address from Henny's desk earlier in the month, I affixed it to an envelope, attached sufficient postage, and put it on Munroe's tray for mailing in the morning.

I was going to miss Henny.

At the same time, I hoped and prayed that this particular Comanche war dance would be enough to convince Olive Wade I had no one but her in my mind.

THIRTY-ONE

My son and I took the noon train to New York City the next day. The sky was sunny and the fields were bright with fresh snow as we headed east.

Reaching the outskirts of the city at dusk, its skyline came into view, many of its buildings over twenty stories tall, twinkling like a festive arrangement of Christmas lights, beckoning us with their promise of bustle and excitement.

Jeremiah said, 'Reminds me of that grass fire we had out in Cross Plains before we came east, the way it's burning so bright.'

We talked about our scheme to flush out Isaac Jensen as we neared East Harlem. 'You're sure you remember what you have to do?'

'Pa, I'm not a child anymore.'

We crossed over into East Harlem through the Bronx and traveled down the Park Avenue tracks until we descended into the Park Avenue Tunnel at 97th Street. Immediately the passenger cars became thick with the smell of locomotive smoke and steam, and, looking out the window, the air was so clouded I wondered how the engineer could see anything at all. I could well understand the big train accident down here that had killed seventeen hapless travelers near Grand Central Depot last January.

The depot itself was under phased demolition, preparatory to the building of the new Grand Central Terminal, and there was much dust, noise, and confusion. I was glad when we finally found our way out to 42nd Street, where we hailed a hansom cab.

Once we were heading away from the depot, I asked my son, 'And you don't mind wearing the hat?'

'If it will help catch a killer, I'll wear a dress, pa.'

We checked into the Hotel Empire, had a couple of porterhouse steaks, then set off for the Lower East Side, Hester Street, Hattie Whitmore's address.

By this time it was dark, but, it being Manhattan, the streets were still fairly well-lit, still with a lot of gas lamps, but with some of the new electrical ones too.

As the professor had suggested, Miss Whitmore's apartment wasn't in the best neighborhood. Garbage and snow were piled high on the curb. Despite the late hour, children ran around in the middle of the street and threw snowballs at any unfortunate horse-drawn conveyance that happened by. Horse manure clogged the gutter, mixing with the slush. We found a drab little row of shops, the masonry begrimed with years of coal soot, their sun awnings drawn up so snow-burden wouldn't rip them apart, their windows showing haphazard arrays of second-hand goods and clothing. Apartments occupied the floors above each shop. It was in one of these that Hattie Whitmore lived.

I took the Western Union Telegraph hat from my bag and gave it to Jeremiah. He put it on. I gave him the fake telegraph. 'If it's Miss Whitmore who comes down, you must say that you're to deliver the telegram personally to Mr Jensen.'

'Yes, pa.'

'I'll be around back to make sure he doesn't leave by the fire escape. Once you're sure he's there, come round and get me and we'll both go in.'

I went around to the back and stood guard there.

Three hoboes sat further down the alleyway, having their own form of Christmas cheer: a gallon jug of wine. A fire burned in a barrel. A small white dog with black markings, one most notably around its left eye, sniffed from the periphery of the group, nervous, jerking back several feet whenever one of them made a sudden or unexpected move.

I looked up and saw the back of the building in the light of their fire. I scanned the iron fire escape for any sign of activity, particularly the third floor, Miss Whitmore's floor, but there was no movement on the landing and the door remained shut.

I soon heard footsteps in the alley behind me. Turning, I saw my son approach, a big smile on his face.

'He's there, pa.'

'And how did he react when you told him the telegram was from Herschel Purcell?'

'Puzzled. And shook up to learn the flask had been left to him in Ephraim's will. And that Herschel knew where to find him.'

A short while later we climbed the stairs to the third floor.

Jensen was shocked to see me standing there when Miss Whitmore opened the door.

'Dr Deacon, what are you doing here?' He looked at my son. 'And why are you with the Western Union boy?'

I explained our ruse. 'I've come to ask you why you've run away from Fairfield at Christmas, Mr Jensen. It doesn't seem like a thing an innocent man would do. I would also like to know how you came to be in possession of Mr Purcell's Lincoln-head whisky flask.'

He fumed a bit, then burst out. 'It's my flask! He cheated me out of it!'

I took his measure coolly. 'Regardless, I think you have some explaining to do. Miss Whitmore, would you mind if we stepped inside for a few moments?'

Miss Whitmore, a graceful if aging woman in clothes that looked a decade old, glanced at Jensen. I could see the hatter thinking furiously.

After Miss Whitmore gave him an encouraging nod, he finally relented. 'Come in, then.' He motioned around the cramped apartment, a guilty look on his face. 'And this isn't what you think it is. Miss Whitmore and I are just friends. Old and good friends. Nothing more.'

'Forgive me, Mr Jensen, but the tone of her letters would seem to suggest otherwise.'

'You're a scoundrel for taking those, by the way.'

'And if your wife knew about them, what harsh epithet would she give you? Scoundrel seems mild.'

This drew alarm. 'You haven't told her, have you? She thinks I'm in Milwaukee with my brother.'

'My only interest is the murder of Ephraim Purcell. That's why I bring up Miss Whitmore's letters. I quote, "I don't blame you for wanting to kill Ephraim, dearest Isaac. He is a snake."'

They both stared.

Miss Whitmore finally mounted a weak defense. 'Dr Deacon, I

hardly think private correspondence intended for an audience of one constitutes lawful evidence.'

'That, Miss Whitmore, is something the court will decide. Come, now. Why don't we have tea and discuss the matter like civilized human beings? Would that be all right?'

'I'll have none of it!' said Jensen. 'You hunt me down like a common criminal and expect me to treat you in a civil manner when I had absolutely nothing to do with Ephraim's murder. I won't hear it!'

I reached in my pocket and pulled out my handcuffs. 'Then you can accompany me back to Fairfield and tell Judge Norris and your wife what you're doing here in Hester Street. I don't believe the adultery statutes in New York State have changed recently.'

Again, stares from both.

Surrendering grudgingly, Jensen turned to Miss Whitmore. 'Hattie, tea, please.'

The woman went to get tea.

Jensen allowed us into the apartment.

It was tiny, consisting of a parlor, a kitchen, a bedroom, and a lavatory. I saw a photograph of Hattie standing with a group of orphans in front of an orphanage. They were all smiling, and she was smiling too. She seemed a good sort. I wondered how she could love a man like Jensen all these years when he apparently had no intention of leaving his wife.

We sat. I contemplated Jensen. His face was set in an expression of angry pride.

In a fit of impatience he looked at me and said, 'Could you ask your questions quickly before you spoil more of our Christmas holiday? And I take it the telegram from Herschel Purcell about the flask was all part of your scheme?'

I ignored this. 'How do your children feel about this?'

'About what?'

'How you've de-camped to Manhattan with Miss Whitmore for Christmas.'

'Like their mother, they think I'm in Milwaukee with my brother.'

'And your brother supports you in this deception?'

'If you knew the entire story, you would understand why matters are the way they are. And do we have to speak about such things in front of your son? He's a little young.'

I turned to Jeremiah. 'Jerry, if you could help Miss Whitmore with tea.'

'Yes, pa.' My son went into the kitchen.

Some of Jensen's feistiness left him and in a more conciliatory tone, he said, 'I don't make excuses for myself, Dr Deacon. I do the best I can with the hand I've been dealt. I don't know how much you know, or what you read in those letters, but at one time, Hattie and I were extremely close. Engaged to be married, as a matter of fact. Hattie was the only woman I ever truly loved. Don't get me wrong. I admire my wife. And I'm fond of her. But I wouldn't have married her if Ephraim hadn't come along and taken Hattie away from me.'

'He seems to have taken a lot away from you.'

He gave me a disgruntled look. 'The minute I married Tilda, Ephraim broke his engagement to Hattie, as if it had all been a lark to him. And so I was married, with my first child on the way, but my heart still belonged to Hattie. After Hattie got over Ephraim, she realized hers still belonged to me. So here we are.' After a few moments, he said, 'I suppose this will just make you think I have yet more reason to kill him.'

'I'm not so much interested in reasons at this point, Mr Jensen, as I am in establishing facts. On the night of the murder, we've established that you left the Welland Street Club after expressing your great displeasure with Mr Purcell to Lonnie Moses. You tell me afterwards you went home and fell asleep in your study. Yet the flask that Mr Purcell was never without went missing from his pocket. I learned that he won the flask from you in a bet, and that originally the flask was presented to you by President Roosevelt for an act of bravery during the Civil War, the same act that saved Ephraim's life. The flask meant the world to you.'

His lips tightened and he looked away. I saw heartache in his eyes. 'He broke the bond.'

'You could have easily made that shot on Tonawanda Road. You neutralized that sniper in Monckton, Georgia.'

His lips quivered and he looked at the table where I saw a dog-eared copy of *Harper's Weekly*. 'We were best friends.' He swallowed against his pain. 'When your best friend becomes your worst enemy, it's the toughest thing in the world for a man. And as much as I could have made any shot whatsoever, I was drunk and passed out in my study when Ephraim was murdered.'

'I don't think you were, Mr Jensen. As I already indicated, you had the flask. I'm sure he didn't just give it to you. So please don't lie. It was hidden in the hat shop's third-floor crawlspace. Why would Ephraim Purcell's flask wind up in your third-floor crawlspace? If you can give me an adequate answer for that, I'll get on the train tonight, go back to Fairfield, and never bother you again.'

Miss Whitmore and my son came out of the kitchen with tea. On a plate I saw shortbread cookies shaped like Christmas trees and stars. She set everything down and poured.

She then said, 'Would you like us to join you, gentlemen? Or would you prefer to continue your discussion in private?'

Jensen gave her a sheepish smile. 'Perhaps the two of you could have tea in the kitchen, Hattie.'

Miss Whitmore turned to my son. 'Come along, Jeremiah. You can help me with the jigsaw puzzle I'm working on.'

The two retreated, leaving me and Jensen to continue our conversation alone.

I waited for him to lift his teacup. All he had to do was raise it to his lips to exclude himself as a suspect in the murder and that would be that. But he now seemed lost in thought, and struggling with himself. 'Maybe I wasn't in my study after all. Maybe that was just a cockamamie story I made up to protect myself. I swear to you, I had nothing to do with his murder. I just stupidly took the flask at probably the most asinine moment I could. Afterward, I figured you might find out the history between us, and start blaming me for his murder. I thought you might come looking for the flask as well. I didn't want to get rid of it so I put it in the crawlspace.'

'How did it all come about, you getting your hands on the flask?'

Much cowed now, he sighed, hesitated, then gave me the story. 'I'd been walking about after my outburst at the club.' He glanced out to the street where a man in a thick coat was leading a mule down the pavement. 'I was trying to calm myself. I finally found myself walking in the back alley out behind my place. I walk there a lot. It's off the beaten track and I find it soothing.' He looked at his hands, then into the fire. 'I was just reaching my place when I heard the shot.'

'You heard only one shot?'

'I'm not sure. I was mighty drunk. I went up along the side of the hat shop to the street, and I saw Ephraim lying there.'

'This was immediately after you heard the shots?'

'Couldn't have been more than ten or fifteen seconds.'

'And you were the first to arrive?'

He nodded. 'I was the only one there at that point.'

'Why didn't you tell me about this?'

'Because of what I did next. This flask business.'

'What happened?'

'I saw him lying there, and the flask had come out of his pocket and was lying next to him. I go up to him, and I see that he's hurt, and I start to panic. At the same time I was angry at him. I'd gotten word from the bank that day that my family and I had to leave the shop.'

'Was he still alive at this point?'

Jensen looked away and nodded woefully.

'And you took no measures to save him?'

'No.' His eyes moistened. His face stiffened and he looked up at me. 'I thought, why should I? After what he's done to me.' His anger left him and he shook his head. 'Then I got just plain scared. I thought, here I am, in the middle of the road with Ephraim, and I'd said those things to Lonnie, and I had every reason to want Ephraim dead, and I was kneeling over him, and if people came and saw me like that, what chance would I have when you and the sheriff came to investigate? I knew I was going to be a suspect. It would have been the last miserable thing he would have done to me. So I figured I had to get out of there. I look up at the hotel and I'm hearing people coming down the front hall. I leave. But as I do, I see the flask lying there. I pick it up, figuring he's not going to need it now. If I hadn't been drunk, I never would have considered the notion. But I did, and it was only afterward I realized my big mistake.'

'It certainly was a big mistake, Mr Jensen.'

Tears now stood in his eyes. 'I reached the corner of the hat shop and I looked back at him. He was crawling toward me.' I remembered how Henny had reported the victim crawling toward the hat shop. 'It was just like that day in Monckton, Georgia. History was repeating itself. But this time around, I just left him there. He deserved it. I figured it was my turn to break the bond.' He shrugged wearily. 'I could have saved him, Dr Deacon. And I should have saved him. But I didn't. Alvin saw the whole thing, but I coached him not to say anything afterward, and to just focus on Billy, as I think Billy's really your man, deputy.'

'Did you see Billy yourself?'

He sighed miserably. 'No.'

'Drink and judgment have never gone hand in hand, Mr Jensen.' But I was thinking how all this explained the flask theft as well as the wound angle. Now that the mechanics behind the flask theft had been revealed, the wound angle most definitely pointed toward an elevated position.

Then Jensen lifted his teacup, and ruled himself out entirely. As it got closer to his lips, his hand shook in a most horrible fashion. I saw that he had what his sister had, benign essential tremor, brought on by exertion, the shake so bad that some of his tea spilled out on his lap, the whole reason I'd included Belva Jensen's hereditary disorder in the Ephraim Purcell case file in the first place.

'Damn this cup!'

'I believe you didn't kill Mr Purcell, Mr Jensen. But not on your say-so. Only because I know you couldn't have made that shot after all.'

He frowned. 'What the devil are you talking about? I'm an ace marksman.'

I shook my head. 'Maybe at one time you were. But these days I doubt you could hit that vase from where you're sitting.'

'Sir, you insult me.'

'Sir, you suffer from benign essential tremor. Your sister has it. It's hereditary. It runs in families. And I'm afraid you have it worse than Belva.'

'President Roosevelt himself recognized my marksman's skills.'

'No one's doubting the sacrifices you've made for your country, Mr Jensen. But I'm a doctor, and I know what's possible and not possible in a patient with benign essential tremor. Plus the circumstances of the flask robbery eliminate you as well.'

He put his cup down, watching his hand shake with dismal alarm. He then glanced at me, looking lost. 'Why does a man have to lose everything he holds most dear, Dr Deacon? Look at that. Sometimes it just won't stop. I've been trying to hide it for the last twenty years. My marksmanship is something I'm proud of. But now I don't have it anymore, and it makes me miserable at times.'

The next day in a Manhattan jewellery shop I did my best not to behave like Edgar Keenan. No wandering eye for me. I focused on Miss Wade, and Miss Wade alone. I needed something pure and rare, a piece that would reflect Olive's character and beauty, untangle all my feelings for her, and set them straight so she would at last understand me, but more importantly, so that I at last would understand her.

I found a necklace of uncultured Japanese pearls. A pink pearl served as pendant. I had the jeweller gift-wrap it for me.

I then bought an engagement ring.

THIRTY-TWO

Upon my return to Fairfield, my original plan had been to go out to the Swinford farm with my ballistics sample, as, of my suspects, only the Swinfords had access to that upstairs drugstore window. But as I was getting ready, I received a call from the Sisters of Charity Hospital in Buffalo. The clerk had damaging news about Marigold Reynolds.

'Dr Deacon, I'm afraid we have no record of this patient, nor of her November admission. She was never an inpatient here.'

With Flora Winters's story about Marigold now confirmed, and confirmed enough so that it would stand up in court, I decided I would concentrate on the victim's stepdaughter instead.

The best method, I thought, given that she and I had drawn a line in our last interview, and that she had told me in no uncertain terms to go away, was to chip around the edges – the edges being the people closest to her.

This meant Billy Fray.

And also Daisy Pond.

With Billy denying everything, and not going anywhere anyway because he was still under arrest and in jail for punching the sheriff in the face, I thought I might first try my luck with Daisy.

So I rode up to Finch Street and interviewed the woman who, according to Olive Wade, was as much in love with Billy Fray as Marigold was, hoping she might have something useful to offer as a witness.

Miss Pond's defining physical attribute was her smallness – she was no more than four feet six inches tall, slim, athletic-looking, with the physique of a petite gymnast. She had curly blonde hair.

We sat in the parlor of her Finch Street home. Her eyes, which were the darkest and strangest blue I'd ever seen, revealed a deep maturity and intelligence, but also a wariness; I understood that she was a young woman who would choose her words carefully.

When I asked about Marigold, she prevaricated politely. 'Is it necessary I speak to you about her, Dr Deacon? Am I obligated by law?'

I paused, surmising in her skilful deflection an intent to protect her friend. I side-stepped with a parry meant to get us beyond that. 'We've learned that Marigold never went to Buffalo for her convalescence back in November, Daisy. We know she came here.' I pulled out my deputy's badge and put it on the table. 'As for the law, I always find it's better to cooperate with a deputy or a sheriff, especially where a murder is concerned.'

She didn't become flustered. Rather she grew extremely pale, and for several moments I thought she might faint. She looked out the window, where servants from the various houses across the street were digging out against the continuing snowfall. I noted an increase in her respiration rate as she struggled to regain herself.

She turned to me. 'I'm desperately frightened of Miss Reynolds, Dr Deacon, that's all. She's not like other girls. We speak of the law. Miss Reynolds has her own laws. I've been subjected to them ever since I've known her.' Her strange blue eyes formed an oblique appeal. 'Must I really utter anything of an indiscreet nature about Miss Reynolds? I'm afraid it might get back to her.'

I saw now that she was asking for my tact. 'Miss Pond, think of this as a confidential *tête-à-tête*.'

She took a deep breath, sighed, and once more looked out the window. Then she stared at me. At last she pulled her sleeve back. I saw a scar, round, and about the diameter of a nickel.

'She did this to me with one of her father's cigars. I love her dearly, but she made me submit to this. As punishment.'

I leaned forward and examined the scar. I grew alarmed. It looked fresh, still had a pink tinge. 'Punishment for what?'

'I deserved it. I crossed her.'

'Goodness gracious. And how did you cross her?'

Her voice became steadier. 'I told her she didn't love Billy Fray the way she should.' A self-effacing grin came to her face. 'And that's all I'm going to say on the subject of Billy Fray. Any more and I'm sure to cry.'

'But you see, Miss Pond, this is exactly what I'm trying to understand. To what degree Miss Reynolds has feelings for Mr Fray.'

Daisy smiled but it was a smile fraught with an effort to contain her emotions. 'You would think they would be strong, wouldn't you, Dr Deacon? After all, she burned me with her father's cigar when I told her they weren't.'

'She doesn't love Mr Fray?'

'She's extremely good at getting people to do the things she wants. She got me to submit to this burn. As for Billy, she needed someone to protect her against her stepfather, that's all. And so she got Billy to do that for her. Mr Purcell's a brute, and quite free with his hands.' I imagined this was an allusion to her own violent episode with Mr Purcell. 'She needed protection. And so she found the biggest, strongest man around, captivated him, and further cemented his loyalty by sharing a bed with him. You of course know about her pregnancy, being her physician, but perhaps what you didn't know was that the last thing Marigold ever wanted was Billy's child.'

Here was a discrepancy I had to clarify. 'Miss Wade tells me that the child was the most important thing in the world to Marigold. Now you're telling me it wasn't. I don't know who I should believe.'

Daisy shook her head, a preoccupied look coming to her eyes. Assuming I had some familiarity with the subject, she said, 'Going out to the reserve to see Talbert Two-Arrows was Marigold's idea, not her father's, much as you might have heard otherwise.'

This indeed was a revelation. 'But I understand you yourself told Miss Wade that her stepfather was responsible for that. Now you're changing your story?'

Her eyelids fluttered. 'Yes. Only because Marigold changed hers.'

I pondered this intelligence. 'Does she change her story often?'

'Not often. Only when it suits her.'

I returned to the previous matter. 'Why would Marigold need protection from her stepfather?'

Daisy arched her brow. 'She's a grown woman now, Dr Deacon. The week before he was murdered, Mr Purcell came to her bedroom on three different occasions. Luckily, Billy was there. Billy has his uses, you see? And so I was quite right in telling her she didn't love him the way she should. He's nothing but a sentinel to her.'

I looked out the window where the snow was mounded up in

drifts on the front lawn, and where a sleigh went by on Finch Street with a Christmas tree bundled on its back.

'I understand you were struck by the old man in October.'

She seemed caught offguard that I should know this. 'Yes.'

'And that you wanted to press charges.'

Anger deepened the porcelain shades of her complexion to a more sanguine hue. 'And I would have gone ahead if my father hadn't stopped me. Mr Purcell was offering the cement works a lucrative contract. He threatened to cancel it if I didn't withdraw.'

I nodded. 'That seems to be his modus operandi, doesn't it?'

But she was back to Billy. 'Billy thinks Marigold loves him. And she cultivates the misconception any way she can.'

I accelerated the interview. 'Mightn't it be possible that Miss Reynolds was the one who killed her stepfather?'

I thought I might entirely unseat her with this last parry. But I didn't. She had to think about it, as if, after all, it wasn't beyond the realm of possibility. But finally, she dismissed the notion. 'I should hardly think my best friend is a murderer.'

'By your account, she heartlessly disposed of an infant child.'

Her eyes filled with pain. 'Billy was crushed.'

It was always back to Billy; I could see she was quite beside herself with love for the man.

'The fatal shot appears to have come from the hotel roof. Does Marigold have a key to the Grand's service entrance?'

Daisy looked up, focused, quickly understood my train of thought, and artlessly offered what she knew. 'Her stepfather has all the keys on hooks in his home office. She wouldn't need her own key. She would just get his.'

'And were you with Miss Reynolds on the night her stepfather was murdered?'

'No, sir. I was here at home by myself.'

'So you really don't know if Marigold murdered her stepfather or not.'

She grew thoughtful. 'No, doctor, I suppose I don't.'

'Miss Winters, you've been lying to me.'

I stood at the servants' entrance behind the Purcell mansion.

Marigold's maid looked at me with wide nervous eyes. 'About what, sir?'

Over in the garage, Leach tinkered with Mr Purcell's motorcar, a Curved Dash Oldsmobile. Though popular, they seemed temperamental contraptions, needing a lot of attention.

'You're afraid of your mistress. I know the way she can be. You listen for her movements. Even when you're in bed, you're so afraid of her that you keep track of her constantly. Tell me what really happened here on the night of your master's murder.' Frightened as she was, I decided I must scare her even more. 'I will put you in jail if you don't.'

Her eyes got even wider, and filled with tears.

I hated to browbeat the poor girl this way, especially as she was as innocent as the fresh-fallen snow around us, but I was desperate to conclude this matter before Christmas so I could commence repairs on perhaps the irreparable mess I had made with Olive Wade.

She looked away, gazing at Mr Leach, her breath frosting over in the cold, then turned back to me, her lips trembling.

'Sir, I will tell you everything. Just don't put me in jail. And please don't let Miss Reynolds find out.'

I softened my tone. 'There, there, Miss Winters. If you cooperate with the Sheriff's Office, you'll have nothing to worry about. But you can't be evasive, or try to protect your mistress. I already know she left the house that night, and that you undoubtedly heard her.' I took the clout tack out of my pocket and showed it to her. 'This tack tells me she was downtown on the night your master was murdered.' I gave her the details in regard to the tack. 'In our last interview, you said she got a telephone call at eight forty-five. Is this true? Or was that a lie too?'

She began to tremble. 'No, sir. I have such a hard time making up stories. You asked me if anything else unusual happened that night and I couldn't think of what to say. So that part is true.'

I took a moment to digest this. 'And at what time after the telephone call did your mistress leave the house?'

She fretted for a few more seconds, looking undecided, then finally said, 'Remember how I told you all the servants had gone to bed, and that Miss Marigold must have answered the telephone call?'

'Yes?'

'I was actually attending to Miss Marigold's bath when the telephone rang.'

'She was in the bath?'

'Yes.'

'Then who answered the telephone?'

'That would have been Miss Pond.'

'Daisy Pond was here?'

'Yes, sir.'

'She told me she was at home.'

'No, sir, she was here.'

'Why didn't you tell me?'

'Because my father is an employee at Mr Pond's cement works. I didn't want to stir things up and maybe cost him his job.'

I paused to puzzle over why Miss Pond would have lied to me about her presence here on the night of the murder. Maybe she was trying to protect Marigold after all. 'And so Daisy answered the phone?'

'Yes.'

'And what did she do once she was finished with the call?'

'She came into the bathroom. She was flustered. She said the call was from Billy Fray, and that he was down at the Grand Hotel.'

At first unsure if the telephone call was significant, I now saw that it constituted a break in the case. 'The call was from Billy?'

'Yes.'

'What happened next?'

'Miss Marigold relieved me of my duties and told me to go to my room. So I left, but I was nervous because I knew something wasn't right.'

'What did you do?'

'I went downstairs to the kitchen, and I listened. And a few minutes later, Miss Pond came running down the stairs. At first I thought she was going to leave but then I heard her cranking the telephone. I thought she was going to call Billy back. But she wasn't. I heard her talking to Viola White, the operator. She was trying to get through to the Sheriff's Office, but Miss White told her the line was in use.'

'The Sheriff's Office?'

'Yes.'

I pondered. Stanley had been in West Shelby that night. I had been at home. Ernie Mulroy had been manning the telephone; I knew he tended to talk to his sweetheart at length. 'And when she couldn't get through to the Sheriff's Office, what did she do?'

'It was strange, really. She went from room to room. Like she was looking for something. I finally heard her leave and ride away on her bicycle. I was in the kitchen by myself when five minutes later I heard Miss Reynolds come down the stairs.'

'And did she leave as well?'

The maid motioned at the tack in my hand. 'Yes.'

I paused as I went through the ramifications of this. 'So first Daisy, then five minutes later, your mistress.'

'Yes.'

'And when did your mistress come home?'

Flora thought for a few seconds. 'Around nine thirty. I went to see if she wanted anything, and she said she was fine, so I retired.' She grew frantic again. 'Please don't tell Miss Marigold I told you anything.'

'And what was Miss Marigold's demeanor upon her return?'

Flora squinted. 'She was . . . agitated, sir. Pacing back and forth, rubbing her hands again and again. I could see she certainly had no immediate plans for getting herself to bed.'

THIRTY-THREE

Armed with accounts by Daisy and Flora, I resolved to speak to Marigold in person, despite our unamicable parting last time.

Flora facilitated this for me, leading me from the servant's entrance in through the kitchen, and finally into the main part of the house.

I soon found myself again admitted to the young woman's painting studio.

Marigold continued to paint her winter scene: snow-covered cherry trees by the fountain. The curtains on the nearest French door were pulled wide open so she could see her subject outside.

I inspected the painting. 'You're quite good.'

She nodded. 'My mother had me study with James Tissot. You've seen the Tissot in the front hall?'

'Of your mother?'

'Yes.'

'I have.'

She nodded, then motioned at her winter scene. 'I plan to paint in the modern style soon. Academy painting hardly reflects our new century, does it, Dr Deacon? This will be the last realistic thing I do. In spring, I move to Paris, where I'll study at École Nationale Supérieure des Beaux-Arts.'

I couldn't help wondering if she would be spending spring in prison. 'Marvellous.'

'I'm free now. My stepfather's dead. I can do whatever I want. And by the way, I apologize if I was abrupt the last time we spoke.'

'No apology necessary.' I edged toward the subject of my inquiry gently. 'I suppose your new life has no place in it for Billy Fray?'

She stopped painting and great sadness came to her eyes. 'I will miss him.'

I took out the clout tack and held it up. 'Do you know what this is, Miss Reynolds?'

She studied the object, still seeming to be partially preoccupied with Billy. 'A nail or a tack.'

'Quite right. But in this particular instance, you'll be more interested to learn what the tack represents.'

Her manner now grew cautious. 'I know it can't pertain to my recent convalescence. So it must have something to do with the other concern you have with me.'

'The carpenters at Flannigan's Stationery nailed up a tarpaulin when they were ripping down the old façade. Snow was on the way and they wanted to protect the interior of the shop. All that paper. All those envelopes. This was the afternoon before your stepfather was murdered. They spilled some tacks on to the road, including this one. We got just a light dusting and it melted by evening. The next morning the carpenters took the tarp down. As for the spilled tacks, some were left for twenty-four hours before they cleaned everything up. But this tack they didn't clean up. That's because someone stepped on it and it got stuck in their boot.'

She put her paintbrush down. In a forlorn tone, she said, 'This must be some new evidence you have against my Billy.'

I took a few steps forward, momentarily confused that she didn't at first understand the implications of what I was saying. 'I'm not here about Billy, Marigold. I'm here about you.' I gave her a moment to orient herself. 'I found this tack in the heel of your own boot. Which means you were in the vicinity of the Grand Hotel on the day – possibly the night – of your stepfather's murder, not in a hospital in Buffalo. You might as well not lie to me anymore. The hospital's confirmed you were never there.'

Her lips shifted and her face reddened as she comprehended what I was getting at. 'Doctor, if you think I had anything to do with my stepfather's murder, then perhaps your powers of deduction aren't as great as I thought they were.'

'Come, now, Miss Reynolds. You have more than ample motivation for wanting your stepfather dead, not only because he swindled your money into a Swiss bank account but also because he had begun coming to your bedroom. I know that you got a telephone call around eight forty-five on the night of the murder, and that Miss Pond was the one who took it for you, and that the call was from Billy, and he was down at the hotel, and that shortly after, Daisy left, then you left.'

'But doctor, I'm confused. If you say I got a call from Billy from down at the hotel, doesn't that answer your question? Billy was down at the hotel. So who else could it be?'

'You lied to me about your admission to Sisters of Charity, and I found this tack in your boot, and yes, I know Billy was there, but the crime scene is a little more complicated than you might think, as it appears you were there too. So I ask you, where did you go once you finished with the telephone call?'

'Who told you I left the house?'

'That, my dear, will remain confidential.'

She stared at me. But then she looked away, and the weight of everything appeared to induce a nullifying, if momentary, pensiveness in my suspect. Then a grin came to her face, but it was a fragile one, and I saw she was on the cusp of a breakdown. When she spoke next, her voice was tremulous.

'It wasn't I who killed my stepfather, much as I would have liked to. You must think that reprehensible, but if you knew of my stepfather's cruelty, and of the way he purposely liked to make people miserable, you might better understand how perfectly ordinary people like my friends and I could begin to talk about murder.' She hesitated; her lips came together as if against a bitter bile. 'In fact, I was the one who tried to stop my stepfather's murder. I don't know why. I hate the man.'

I hadn't been expecting this view of the matter at all. I gave her the benefit of the doubt for the time being. I decided to let her be the playwright, and played my part according to the script she was trying to write.

'How did you try to stop it?'

For if this were a lie, she had a lot of careful fabricating to do, and the slightest false detail would betray her.

She got up from her painting and walked with distracted steps to the first French door, where winter light filtered through in muted tones of silver. 'I won't deny that we all talked about killing my stepfather.' A lone deer appeared through the hedge at the back and we both watched it for a few seconds until it moved off. 'As I say, he was cruel to us. In October he struck Daisy with the back of his hand.' I remembered Stanley's report on this, and how it had put Daisy tentatively on my suspect list. 'In early November he had some ruffians beat Billy down by the railway bridge. As for me, I was constantly afraid of him. Especially lately, when I could tell he was looking at me not as a girl anymore but as a woman. And so, yes, we talked about it. But there was never any firm plan. At least not until my stepfather discovered the promissory note, got Billy to surrender it at gunpoint, and threatened to send him to jail for the forgery.'

'So you're sticking to your story about the promissory note?'

'It happens to be true, doctor.' She turned slowly. 'It's not my fault you chose not to believe me.' She went back to looking out at the grounds. 'Billy wanted to save the Fray smithy.' She grew reflective. 'We all pass that scruffy building on North Railway and we think, who could ever live there, in those three little rooms above the forge? But he was born in the smithy. So was his father. So was his grandfather. It was his home. If you understood Billy's efforts to save not only the smithy but also his father, you might take a more lenient view.'

'A more lenient view of what?'

She got choked up. 'Of Billy. Of the nature of his guilt. And of why he did the things he did.'

'And what did he do?'

Tears formed in her eyes. 'He won't tell you the truth, so I suppose I must, if only to save him from execution.'

'You're telling me he's the killer? I've already told you the scene is a little more complicated than that.'

She grew momentarily indignant. 'I know what I saw, doctor.' She paused for several seconds, then went to the chaise longue and sank upon it, her fingers now fiddling with the cloth of her skirt, her eyes distracted. 'Oh, please, Dr Deacon. Please spare him. Don't send him to the electric chair. I love him so much.'

'Let's start at the beginning, my dear.'

She struggled to control herself. 'There are so many beginnings, doctor. So many things that went wrong. Starting with the way I fell in love with Billy at the Shooters Club when he was teaching me how to shoot.'

'So you love him?'

'Of course I love him.'

'Daisy says otherwise.'

She showed sudden anger. 'Daisy's jealous.'

'She says the only reason you enticed Billy was so that he would protect you from your stepfather.'

'I won't deny that Billy protected me. But that still doesn't mean I don't love him.'

'In fact, she says you burned her with a cigar.'

She was genuinely astonished. 'Why on earth would I do that?'

'As punishment.'

'Punishment for what?'

'For telling you that you didn't love Billy the way you should.'

She thought about this. 'I remember her telling me that I didn't love Billy, but I never burned her with a cigar for it. That's preposterous. What is she playing at? She can be quite devious when she wants to be.'

I took a moment to ponder Daisy. Perhaps the injury was self-inflicted? A stage prop to make her own story more convincing? But why would she need to make her own story more convincing?

'I take it your stepfather didn't approve of Billy.'

'Of course not,' said Marigold. 'They hated each other. And what really escalated the enmity between them was the promissory note episode. Especially when my stepfather took the note at gunpoint from Billy. Did my Uncle Herschel tell you my stepfather fired at Billy, right here in the house?'

I paused. 'No.'

'Billy barely escaped with his life. He bolted off to the woods out back. My stepfather fired after him. I ran down from my room to see what all the noise was. My stepfather was shouting after him. He was saying the next time he saw Billy in the street, he would shoot him down like a dog.'

'So your stepfather threatened Billy?'

She nodded. 'That's what I mean when I say the whole episode escalated the enmity between them. Then around the same time,

Ephraim had Dr Thorensen in to examine me, and that just made matters worse between him and Billy. My stepfather was growing suspicious, you see. He's a shrewd old man. He notices more than you think.'

'He thought you were pregnant?'

'He's familiar with the condition.' With some bitterness, she added, 'Who knows how many bastards he's sired. More than just Clarence Swinford, I'm sure. Before I knew it, he had Talbert Two-Arrows here. Mr Two-Arrows initiated the procedure you so heroically rescued me from.'

'Daisy said you were the one to initiate contact with Mr Two-Arrows, and that you went out to the reserve.'

She grew troubled. 'I don't know why she would say such a thing. My stepfather was behind it all. And I never went out to the reserve. Mr Two-Arrows came here.'

'How do you know for certain that Billy murdered your stepfather?'

With increasing emotional strain, she said, 'Because I know what I saw. I went down the Grand to try and stop it.'

I clarified. 'You witnessed it?'

She nodded. 'It started with the telephone call.' As she put it all together in her mind, she nodded a second time. 'I was in my bath. I usually like to take an hour for my bath. All the servants had retired to the third floor except Flora. She was attending me. So it was Miss Pond who took the telephone call.'

'And after she had taken it, she came and told you?'

'She did.'

'And what did she say?'

Her eyes glimmered with sudden tears. 'That Billy was in a most frantic state, and that he was in the alley outside the Grand Hotel preparing to kill my stepfather. Daisy was so frightened I thought she was going to faint. So I ordered her home and said I would look after it.'

'So Daisy went home?'

'Yes. If she came along, she would have gotten in the way. She's prone to fainting, you see.'

'I see.'

Marigold reached for a handkerchief and dabbed her eyes. 'So I got on my bicycle and rode as fast as I could for the Cherry Hill Road drawbridge. To my great consternation, the drawbridge was up for an evening barge. I had to turn right at Cattaraugus Avenue and ride the three blocks to the Tonawanda Road span bridge. I pedaled madly over the river, but then I heard a shot, and it startled me so much I lost control of my bicycle and fell.' She motioned at the clout tack I held in my hand. 'Right in front of Flannigan's, as a matter of fact, and I guess that's where I got that tack. I looked up the hill. As the Corn Mercantile is set back from the road, I had a clear view of the garbage cans next to the Grand Hotel. And there was Billy beside them with his rifle. My stepfather was standing in front of the hotel. I suppose Billy had missed with his first shot. He was quite drunk. I called to my stepfather, but I was too late. Billy shot a second time and my stepfather went down, as dead as that clout tack you're holding in your hand.'

I studied her.

I saw she believed her story; there wasn't a shred of dissimulation in her manner.

And it seemed a cogent enough synopsis that jibed with at least some of the more established facts surrounding the events of that night. What it didn't take into account was the wound angle. She saw her stepfather standing there. He wasn't on his knees. He wasn't crawling at some preposterous angle toward Billy. Billy had fired at Purcell straight on from the alley, according to Marigold's story, and as such, her story contradicted the scientific evidence.

Yet she knew what she saw.

The question now arose, how was she misinterpreting what she saw to contradict the scientific evidence?

THIRTY-FOUR

I pondered the matter as I went out to the Swinford farm the next day. Given the wound angle, I was now convinced that though Billy had been there, he hadn't fired the fatal round. I was now beginning to wonder if he had fired any round at all. I tied Pythagoras to the hitching post next to the farmhouse, went to the kitchen door, and knocked. Seeing Billy from the front of Flannigan's after falling off her bike, Marigold, in her discombobulated condition, may have misconstrued him as the shooter. But had the shot really come from the hotel roof? From the drugstore window? And Billy just there with an unfired rifle looking like the shooter? I put these questions from my mind as I prepared for what I hoped would be my final interview with the Swinfords.

A few moments later, Clarence answered. 'Dr Deacon,' he said, with some misgiving. 'What are you doing here?'

'Clarence, are your parents home?'

'They're sittin' by the fire, sir.'

'Would you mind if I came in?'

'Course, doctor. You're more than welcome.'

Considering his father had threatened to set his dogs on me last time, I wasn't sure if I was indeed more than welcome, but entered the farmhouse just the same.

In the parlor, Mrs Swinford stared at the flames in the grate. Her arm was in a sling. She didn't turn when I entered, nor did she say hello, but remained oblivious. Albert Swinford, on the other hand, got up – the way a soldier gets up at the sound of distant gunfire.

We stared at each other.

'You look a mite frozen, doc,' he said, but didn't offer a place by the fire or anything hot to drink.

I pulled out the glassine envelope containing the lace curtain with the gunshot hole through it. Having been exposed to the iodide of potassium solution, it was as yellow as ever, revealing the presence of lead.

With no pleasantries or hospitality offered, I got right to my point.

I tapped the envelope. 'This piece of curtain was snipped from the window in Mr and Mrs Wileys' bedroom. You can see a hole through it. The hole is roughly the diameter of a bullet. And – Clarence, you might be interested in this – you see the way it's yellow like that?'

Carefully, and as if suspecting a trap, he said, 'Yes?'

'I wanted to confirm that the hole was indeed a bullet hole so I had to prove the presence of lead. To do this, I caused a chemical reaction using an iodide of potassium solution. When it comes into contact with lead, it turns yellow. So this is indeed a bullet hole. The brighter the yellow the more recent the lead adhesion. I've pretty well timed the hole to the night of Mr Purcell's murder. And Clarence, I know you and your ma were in that bedroom on the night of his murder. Which begs the question, did either of you kill Mr Purcell?'

This got the expected reaction, especially from Mr Swinford. His tone became belligerent. 'What gives you the right to barge in here and accuse my wife and son of murdering that old villain?'

I lifted the yellowed fabric higher. 'This does, Mr Swinford. I've learned the way Mr Purcell compromised your wife. I've heard that he threatened to take away Clarence's college trust fund. Mr Purcell approached Mrs Swinford at the Corn Mercantile Building on the night of his murder and made inappropriate overtures toward her. Melissa, you hurried over to the Wileys' afterward, didn't you? Clarence, you followed fifteen minutes later. Shots were heard. And Mr Purcell was found dead in the street. Now I have a bullet hole through this lace sheer.'

Clarence turned to his father, a questioning look in his eyes. Albert was staring at me. I thought he would continue to be the family voice in this matter, but it was Mrs Swinford who spoke next.

'Much as that monster deserves to be shot dead in the street,' she said, in a fragile haunted tone, 'I'm afraid I can't claim credit. But whoever did shoot him should be honoured as a hero. He or she has done Fairfield a great service. Perhaps because he is now gone, I won't try to kill myself a third time.'

'Melissa, hold your tongue.'

'Albert, it's all right. Dr Deacon's a good man.'

I leaned forward. 'A third time? You mean you've already made two attempts? I know about the one on the night you came to my surgery. When was the other?'

She turned to me and an awful grin came to her face, as if death's handmaiden had taken corporeal substance in the person of Melissa Swinford. 'My other attempt was on the night that wretched beast met his end, almost to the second, as if fate had ordained it.' She turned to her son. 'Isn't that right, Clarence? You were rushing up the stairs when you heard me shoot.'

Clarence's lips tightened. He looked distressed beyond all measure. 'Ma, please.'

Mrs Swinford nodded. 'Tell the doctor what you know, Clarence. He's twisted the truth right around in his head, and he's going to arrest us for that beast's murder if we don't straighten him out.'

Clarence turned to his father.

Mr Swinford hesitated. He stared at his hands. At last he spoke. 'It's something you don't want folks to know about.'

'I can assure you, Mr Swinford, everything I hear today will be held in strictest confidence.'

'Didn't I tell you he was a good man?' said Melissa.

After thinking it through, Swinford's shoulders eased. 'If it'll convince you we're innocent of the man's murder.' He turned to Clarence and gave him a nod. 'Go ahead, son, tell him what you saw.'

Clarence turned to his mother, who had gone back to gazing at the fire. Then, with new earnestness, he addressed me. 'I took it upon myself to protect my ma from Mr Purcell, doc. Whenever she was in town, I always came with her. If he tried anything, I got right up in between them, and put a stop to it, just like that, even though he's my actual pa.'

I nodded. 'Most commendable.'

He took a few seconds. 'On the night he was killed, we were over at the Saturday evenin' auction. Mr Purcell comes stumbling in at quarter to nine, drunk as can be, and starts harassing ma. She's looking at pies, and pa's bidding on a hog, so I go down from the bleachers and walk up to him, and say to him, 'Mr Purcell, I'd like you to leave my ma alone.''

'You're a good son,' I said.

'But he starts talking about my college fund.'

Clarence began to explain about the college fund and I cut him short. 'I'm already aware of the provision that's been made for you.'

Clarence nodded. 'He says he's going to cancel it if my ma don't start playin' ball. I tell my ma to go to the Wileys', so this is what she does. She has this sad look on her face, like she's blaming herself for the cancellation of my college fund. I didn't like that look at all.'

'No.'

'So after fifteen minutes I tell pa I'm going over to check on her. I get there and my ma's upstairs alone in the Wileys' bedroom, and she's managed to find Mr Wiley's Winchester. She's got her shoe off so she can operate the trigger with her toe.' He motioned at her shoulder. 'Just like the time we brought her to you. I go rushing up and she's just about to pull the trigger. She's so startled to see me, her hand gets jerky, and she just plain misses. I guess the bullet went through that lace sheer, and at the time we didn't notice. She'd opened the window so she wouldn't break the glass. A bullet that calibre would have gone right out the back of her head. Ma knows her firearms.'

The only sounds for some time were the crackling of the fire, the wind outside, and the log construction house settling. I turned to Mr Swinford. 'Is this why you were so insistent in telling me there was only one shot, and that it came from the back alley? You figured if you stuck to the one-shot story I wouldn't investigate the second and find out your wife was trying to kill herself?'

He looked away. 'Your wife attempting suicide isn't something you want folks to know about. You know how this town is. No one would buy our produce anymore.'

'And Clarence, you got there and saw the whole thing?'

He nodded. 'I'm only glad I stopped her in time.'

This, then, seemed much likelier: not two attempts on Mr Purcell's life at the same time, but two separate if tangentially linked dramas playing themselves out in different, yet nearby, arenas.

'And so Mr Swinford, did you in fact hear only one shot? Or are you going to change your story now and tell me you heard two shots?'

'I heard two shots, doc. One from out in the alley, like I said, and the other from the Wileys' bedroom window.'

Out in the alley – that would mean Billy was my prime suspect after all. But with the echoes in that alley, the sound could have been hard to pinpoint, even for a Cuban Scout.

'And the Wileys can confirm your wife's suicide attempt?'

He nodded. 'Like good friends, they kept it secret, but I can write a note telling them it's okay now. They can talk to you, and the whole matter can be cleared up. As long as it don't get spread around town and ruin things for us at the Farmer's Market. We count on that money.'

Later in town, Cora Wiley said, 'We were ever so thankful for Clarence's arrival. If it hadn't been for him, Melissa surely would have been dead by now. I've been after Gordon to get rid of that old rifle for years. This whole incident finally made him listen to reason.'

THIRTY-FIVE

Having eliminated Jensen as well as the Swinfords, I was now down to Marigold, Daisy, and Billy. Again, the most direct approach would have been to confront Billy with Marigold's eyewitness account, but I wasn't entirely convinced that her account or other evidence could successfully indict Billy when the wound angle so obviously pointed to a rooftop origin for the firearms discharge. Also, I had Daisy's various omissions, misdirections, and dissimulations to think about.

Upon my return to town, I swung round to her Finch Street home to talk to her again.

We again sat in her parlor. I was in the house alone with her. Her father was down at the cement works and her mother was at the Thanatopsis Club attending a lecture on prehistoric fossils recently discovered in South Dakota.

She gazed at me apprehensively with her unusual blue eyes – eyes the color of Lake Ontario in its darker moods.

I began by telling her that she had been remiss in leading me astray. 'Might I remind you, Miss Pond, that the last time we spoke, you told me you were in your house all evening on the night of Mr Purcell's murder. Now I learn you were in fact visiting Miss Reynolds and that you took a call of a most disturbing nature from Billy Fray around eight forty-five. He told you that he was down at the Grand Hotel and preparing to kill Mr Purcell. I'm afraid this omission is something I can't easily overlook. I'm going to give you one more chance, Miss Pond. I know you're terribly frightened of Miss Reynolds, but you must, absolutely must, cooperate with the authorities in this matter, or you'll find yourself facing dire consequences.'

She wrung her hands, her long blonde hair falling past her face. 'I'm sorry, sir. But you're right. I'm frightened of her. She said I was to tell no one. Can we not just arrest her? She's the one behind it all.'

I was surprised that she would so quickly turn on her friend.

'We're getting close to taking it to Judge Norris, Daisy, but we need further evidence or witness testimony. That's why I'm asking you again for your cooperation. Tell me, why did you lead me to believe Marigold was the one who was responsible for employing Mr Talbert Two-Arrows? She insists it was, and always has been, her father.'

Some bitterness came to her eyes. 'She's trying to save herself any way she can.'

'And she says she never burned you with the cigar. Maybe you burned yourself with a cigar to make your story more convincing?'

Her face reddened. 'That's a lie, too.' But with her cheeks red like that I wasn't so sure.

'So you're telling me you think Marigold is the murderer?'

I could see she was fighting with herself, and that she was torn between being a good friend and a good citizen. 'I'm afraid I must amend my story, Dr Deacon. It's essentially as I told you before, but with some critical differences.'

I could see she was reluctant. 'Go ahead, Daisy.'

She looked away. 'One thing I wasn't lying about was Billy, and how Marigold ensnared him.' She turned back to me. 'Marigold tricked Billy into being her beau, but not because she loved or admired him. She wanted someone to protect her from her stepfather, that's all. She told me this numerous times.'

I nodded. 'She's admitted that Billy's protected her on occasion. But I'm not convinced she doesn't love him.'

Her eyes grew solemn and she stared at me for several moments, using the pause to underline her next words. 'She would joke about killing her stepfather when the three of us were together. She would say, "Wouldn't it be lovely if Ephraim were dead? Billy, why don't you be a good sport and kill him for us?" On another occasion, she said, "He would be very easy prey, Billy. He doesn't deviate from his schedule, not a smidge, and I can give you all the particulars. Be a dear and get rid of him for us, will you?" She would say things like this, and then afterwards she would tell us that she was joking.' Daisy shook her head. 'This went on for some time. I kept telling Billy that no matter what he did, and no matter how deeply in love he was with Marigold, he should never entertain the idea of killing her stepfather for her.'

'A wise counsel, Miss Pond.'

'She would say to him, again as a lark, "When you kill my stepfather, Billy, make sure you're sober. Your aim tends to wander when you drink." I can attest to that. I've seen him at the Shooters Club when he's drunk and he can't hit a thing. That's why I think that even though Alvin Jensen might have seen him down at the hotel with a rifle at the time of the murder, it's unlikely he could have killed Mr Purcell, not only because he was drunk at the time, but also because I know he's not capable of murder. There were two shots, I understand. Maybe there was someone else.' Her voice grew fraught with emotion. 'Maybe someone like Marigold.'

I gave this veiled accusation the time it deserved, then played devil's advocate. 'You understand that much of the evidence points toward Billy as my perpetrator.'

Her face reddened even more, her shoulders straightened, and she became braver. 'Then I will have to change that, won't I, doctor? I will not let my Billy hang for a murder he did not commit. I told him again and again that Marigold was only using him to get rid of her stepfather. Well, sir. The truth shall be known. I'm tired of being frightened of Marigold.'

'If you have information that exonerates Billy, Miss Pond, now's the time to come forth with it. We're very close to drawing up murder charges against him, and I would hate to see him electrocuted for a crime he didn't commit.'

She took a few moments to gather her thoughts, then began with an altered version of events. 'I was over at Marigold's house on the night of the murder. I'll admit to that now. And I did take that call from Billy. And, as you say, he was down at the Grand Hotel. He told me to tell Marigold that he was in position, as he called it, and getting ready to kill her stepfather. He was slurring his words – quite drunk, you see. I became frantic. I ran upstairs to the bathroom. Marigold ordered Flora to leave. I then told Marigold about the call. "And he's drunk?" she asks me. I told her, yes, he was. She grew angry after that. She told me to go home. So that's what I did. I was on my bicycle. I rode up the hill to Erie Boulevard and was just reaching Poplar Avenue when I decided I better go back and see if I could do something to help. So I turned around and I rode back to Marigold's house.'

'You went back?'

'Yes. When I got there, I saw Marigold riding down her drive on her bicycle. She had her Henry rifle in her carrier. I could tell by the brass trim on the butt. And so I really think it was her, because Billy can't hit anything when he's drunk.'

I paused to reflect on this newest information. 'When you saw Marigold with the rifle, did you not try to stop her?'

'I did, sir. I rode after her. But she has longer legs than I do and is able to ride faster. She reached the Cherry Hill Road drawbridge just as Mr Barner was lowering the barrier and flashing the lights. A late barge was coming through. But still Marigold kept on. She went around the barrier and crossed the bridge. By the time I reached the bridge, it was already going up. I had to go around, by the Tonawanda Road bridge. And by that time I was too late. Mr Purcell was already dead. I was so frightened, I just rode away and pretended to everybody, including you, that I had been home all evening.'

I reached the Purcell mansion twenty minutes later.

Mr Leach admitted me into the salon, where I found Marigold reading *Sister Carrie* by Theodore Dreiser.

'I'm going to have to take your Henry rifle into custody, Miss Reynolds.' I told her of Miss Pond's accusations. 'We'll have to test-fire it to see if it was the murder weapon.'

She was livid. She gave me some argument and ended with a question any betrayed person might ask. 'Why would she do that to me?'

'Come, now. I'll need the rifle.'

She ruminated petulantly. 'How convenient for her. Getting me to take the blame so she and Billy can be together at last.'

'An interesting theory, one I'll keep in mind. Could I have the rifle, please?'

'Do I have to give it to you? It actually belonged to my mother.'

'Refusing only makes it look worse for you. I'll take good care of it and return it promptly.'

She stared, her green eyes like pieces of polished beryl. 'Fine. Do what you want with it. The rifle wasn't used. I haven't taken it down to the range since Billy was forced to hide in the Pleasant Hotel. If you need to rule me out, by all means, have Leach put it in its bag and give you a box of ammunition. He knows where everything is. In fact, I absolutely insist you take it now.'

When I finally turned up my drive a half hour later, I was confronted with a lone horseman mounted beside the surgery's side door, an Oneida tribesman in misty silhouette against the wintry dusk. He was cloaked in a native blanket, and wore a derby with a white feather sticking up the back – a vision that reminded me so much of Cross Plains that for several seconds I felt transported eighteen-hundred miles to the southwest and fifteen years into the past. He had a rifle resting across his saddle horn. The butt was distinctive, a Henry, with the brass trim on the back. Snow fell past him, every flake seeming to miss him. He held up his hand serenely, and I knew that this was Jerome Highcloud, at last returned from his Adirondacks hunting expedition.

'Mr Highcloud,' I called. 'So good of you to come.' I nodded toward the rifle. 'Is that the Henry?'

'It is, doctor.'

I now had two weapons to test, Mr Highcloud's, and the one I had just confiscated from Marigold, which presently rested in my saddle holster.

I had Munroe build up the parlor fire for Mr Highcloud. My man then brought him coffee and Christmas cake, and let me know that Henny and my son were over at the church enjoying a Christmas carol sing-along.

I left Highcloud in my parlor and went to my stable to test-fire both weapons. The stable was warm – it had its own pot-belly stove to keep my animals comfortable. It also had a water pump.

I found water a useful ballistics tool. Its density was such that it had extremely good stopping power but also the advantage of keeping slugs relatively intact after impact. I leaned both weapons against the wall, startling a mouse, which darted under some hay. I dragged a water barrel to the pump, and over the next five minutes filled it to the brim.

When I was done, I got my sixteen-foot stepladder, set it up next to the water, and climbed to the top with the weapon Mr Highcloud had brought, Billy Fray's old Henry. I loaded a round into the chamber and fired. My animals jerked, spooked by the discharge, but quickly settled. I got off the ladder, rolled up my sleeve, and fished around the bottom of the barrel until my fingers closed around the slug. I pulled it out and had a look.

The impact had only minimally distorted its shape. It had distinct lands and grooves on its lead body.

I repeated the process with Marigold's weapon and got the same result, a nicely preserved slug with sharp lands and grooves that would be useful in a comparison against the bullet recovered from my victim's body.

Back in the house, I bade Mr Highcloud a hearty Merry Christmas and a Happy New Year and sent him on his way with enough patient-baked Christmas cake to feed the entire reserve at Silver Lake.

I then went to my lab.

Using first my magnifying glass and finally my microscope, I determined, after fifteen minutes, that the lands and grooves from the murder bullet matched not the bullet from Billy's rifle, but that from Marigold's weapon.

I looked up, stunned.

Marigold was the guilty party after all?

I couldn't figure it out. If she was guilty, and she knew she was guilty, why would she so freely surrender the murder weapon and in fact insist that I take it, knowing that it would only serve to incriminate her, and even indict her formally?

THIRTY-SIX

I went into Billy's cell and sat on the bench opposite him. I didn't consider him a suspect anymore. I never really had, not with the wound angle the way it was. And the fact his weapon hadn't been used just confirmed this conviction. No, I didn't think of him as a suspect anymore. On the contrary, I thought he might be my best witness.

At first I just stared at him. His face, with its pleasant mouth, square chin, and handsome forehead was set in its usual expression of intransigence.

'Billy, your court date for assaulting the sheriff is coming up on January second. A new year. A chance to make a fresh start. And you'll be happy to know you're going to make that fresh start. We won't be charging you with Mr Purcell's murder. The sheriff and I apologize for putting you through all this worry. Isn't that right, sheriff?' I called to Stanley, who was sitting at the basswood table doing paperwork.

'That's right,' called the sheriff.

I said to Billy, 'As compensation, we'll be dropping the assault matter against you. New evidence has come to light. We know who our killer is. We'll be arresting Marigold Reynolds later this evening for the murder of her stepfather.'

His eyes went wide, the intransigence left his face like a frightened bird, and he leaned forward on his bench with a lurch, his dark eyes filled with panic. 'You're arresting Marigold?'

'We got her on the evidence. We'll be asking Judge Norris for the death penalty.'

Billy looked like a fish trying to swim its way out of an ice cube. 'But I know for a fact she didn't kill her stepfather.'

'And how do you know that? You've consistently told us that you were nowhere near the Grand Hotel on the night of the murder. You're not a witness.'

He glanced away, desperate now. 'Darn it, doc, maybe I was there after all. Maybe I was the one who killed Purcell. If you want to 'lectrocute someone, 'lectrocute me, but leave Marigold alone.'

I was impressed. He would sacrifice himself for love. I used love like a grape-press – to squeeze as much information out of him as I could.

'You might have been there, Billy – and in fact we've been told about the telephone call you made to Marigold from the Grand Hotel – but we know you didn't kill Purcell. You can't hit the dirt on the ground when you're drunk, and Robert McGlen says you were stuporous with drink. His exact words. Plus the wound angle is all wrong.'

Indignation flashed across his eyes. 'I can hit anything in any condition at any time, and I don't know who told you otherwise. I was there, and I was by myself, and dang it all, doc, I shot him! I shot him with my own rifle!'

'Your Henry rifle?'

'Yes.'

'And in order to get rid of the weapon afterward, you sold it at King's Emporium?'

He now seemed to see salvation in his bid to save Marigold. 'You can ask Mr King himself!'

'And that was the same rifle you shot and killed Mr Purcell with?'

'The exact same one. So you might as well save my spot in the 'lectric chair and tell Marigold she can go free. Marigold ain't had nothing to do with this.'

I studied him some more, curious now for personal reasons. 'You really love her, don't you?'

He was adamant. 'I love her more than anything. She's my girl.'

'You love her so much that you'd go to the electric chair for her?'

'All I know is I shot and killed her stepfather with my own Henry rifle.'

I paused. 'Funny, Billy. Because we found your rifle. Mr King sold it to Jerome Highcloud.'

He paused, now wary. 'He one of them Indian fellers on the reserve?'

'He is.'

'He got a dang fine rifle, then.'

'We tested that rifle.' I briefly went into the science of ballistics for him, how I could compare bullets. 'It's a relatively new field, Billy, but it's doing wonders for the science of criminology. The lands and grooves on the bullet fired into the victim didn't compare to the test round fired from your own rifle. Therefore, we know you didn't kill him. Unless you used a different rifle, and you just told me you didn't. I also compared a test-fired round from Marigold's rifle. It matched. So we know her rifle was used. Other evidence puts her in the area on the night of the murder. There was a tack in her boot from the scene. We know she did it.'

Billy was breathing in a fragmented and agitated way now. His eyes were wide, panicked. He glanced around the jail as if he wanted to escape as quickly as possible, perhaps to rescue Marigold physically. At last his shoulders sank and he scrutinized me. I could tell he was thinking hard. He then heaved a great sigh. I felt I had broken a big intemperate horse.

'She wasn't there. I would have seen her if she was.'

'Why don't you tell me what really happened, Billy? It's the only way we might save Marigold's life.'

He stared at me, leaning forward, his back straight, his spine like a girder, his eyes wide, bulging as his brow grew shiny with moisture. 'She didn't do it!'

'Just start from the beginning, Billy.'

For several seconds he seemed at a loss. More weakly he said, 'She didn't do it.'

'Come, Billy, how did it start? What set the whole chain of events off? If we can untangle that, Marigold might stand a chance.'

He didn't speak for several seconds. Then his whole body sagged and tears came to his eyes.

'It all started because of that dang promissory note.'

I stared, considered this, and admitted to myself that I might have been wrong about the promissory note. I wasn't infallible, after all; something Stanley loved to point out on occasion.

'So you did forge the promissory note?'

He looked at me sheepishly. 'I reckon I lied to you about that. I admit, I tried some stupid things to save the smithy.' His brow stiffened and he sucked at his lower lip. 'The night of the promissory note, I went up to the mansion to forge the dang thing, and the old man caught me red-handed and took it from me at gunpoint. Then he fired a few rounds at me as I lit out the back. He yells out them French doors that the next time he sees me he's going to shoot me down like a dog. Way I reckoned, we was coming to a showdown, and it was going to be either me or him. I figured it was better him than me, so I made my plan. I waited for him at the Grand Hotel by those garbage cans two nights later. I was going to ambush him. He comes out, and I call to him and he turns around, and I don't know how he did it, but he shoots first, and I don't even see him pull his revolver, that's how fast he is, the sly old geezer.'

This revelation left me mystified for a moment. 'He shot at you first?'

'Dang right, he did. The man's a quick draw, I'll give him that. But his aim warn't that great because his shot went way high.' As examination of Mr Purcell's hammerless revolver had revealed no discharged rounds, I quickly understood and could only conclude that the shot Billy had heard had been Mrs Swinford's from the Wileys' bedroom window, and that he had mistaken it for the old man firing. 'Then, before I could figure out what was what, I heard another shot from the hotel roof, and I reckon he had one of his cronies up there from the Welland Street Club spotting for him, come down to the hotel to guard him because of all the ruckus I'd made at the club earlier. It sure warn't no Marigold.'

Of course it was perfectly apparent to any reasonable man that it very well could have been Marigold, but Billy wasn't a reasonable man at the present moment, and it appeared as if he couldn't admit to that possibility.

I glanced at Stanley. He was staring at me. I turned back to Billy. 'And when you heard the second shot, what did you do?'

Billy shrugged dismally. 'I figured I was outgunned so I got plum out of there. Bullet fell out of my pocket but I couldn't go back for it.'

Here, then, was the source of my live Henry round. 'And what did Mr Purcell do once he had fired the first round?'

'Took cover on the ground. He was in the Civil War, so knows his soldierin'.'

A man taking cover on the ground to Billy, at least that's what he thought at the time.

'Then you found out he was dead.'

'I know, I know. But I didn't kill him.'

'So even though you thought it was one of his cronies up on the roof, it could have been Marigold?'

'It warn't no Marigold. She ain't no killer.' Yes, love was making this particular scenario impossible for him, even though I had told him it was Marigold's rifle that had been used.

I left it for the time being.

'What happened next?'

'I ran. I spent the night out at the Allegheny caves, and let me tell you, it was a cold night because I didn't want to light no fire in case somebody saw it. Then in the morning I came back to town and read about the whole thing in the *Newspacket*. I figured I was in trouble, even though I wasn't the one who shot him. So I did what I could to protect myself. I sold my rifle to raise some money and holed up in the Pleasant Hotel.'

THIRTY-SEVEN

After I finished with Billy, the sheriff and I went for an evening stroll along Court Street toward the railroad tracks to talk things through. It was now dark, and there were hardly any buggies or carriages about, and only a few pedestrians.

'So it's Marigold after all,' said Stanley. 'Who'd have thunk?'

He took out his case of cheroots, gave me one, took one for himself, and we lit up. We turned east along North Railway Street, where the buildings on the south side couldn't decide whether they wanted to be shabby or well-to-do, situated, as they were, on the border of Hoopertown. We passed the closed-down Fray smithy. Such a sad place now.

Stanley continued. 'Here's a girl who's told both her best friend and her beau that she wants to kill her stepfather. We know her stepfather has pilfered her trust account. Now we hear he was putting his paws all over her. We have Flora Winters telling us she left the house. We have the tack. Daisy Pond saw her leave with the rifle. Then the test-fired bullet from her Henry matches the bullet that killed our victim.' He shook his head. 'I think we ought to make an arrest, Clyde.'

I took a meditative draw on my cheroot. 'I'm not so sure, Stanley.'

Stanley kicked an ice chunk out of the way with mild irritation. 'That second shot didn't come from no club crony Mr Purcell put up on the hotel roof. That was Marigold up there. She could have easily gotten a key to that back door. She didn't want a drunk Billy to make a mess of things so got on her bicycle to make sure he got the job done right. Then she turned around and blamed him for the whole thing.' Stanley sighed and stopped. 'Clyde, it's nearly Christmas. I've finished my case in West Shelby and nearly done the one in Burkville, too. The town's clamouring for a conviction. The mayor himself called me today about it. It would be mighty nice to get this one out of the way before December twenty-fifth. Why don't you go over to Ray's house, get him into his deputy's gear, and the two of you ride up and arrest her? We'll put her in the cell right next to Billy. That would be fit justice, wouldn't it?'

'I think it would be premature, Stanley.'

'Premature?' He puffed on his cheroot. 'You've ruled out Isaac Jensen. You've ruled out the Swinfords. The bullet came from her rifle and she was seen riding down to the hotel at the time of the murder. She's even admitted to riding down that way. She's got that tack in her boot. What else could be holding us up?'

I took a pull on my cheroot and let the smoke out slowly. 'The bridge, Stanley. The bridge.'

'The bridge?' He stopped. 'What bridge?'

'The Cherry Hill Road drawbridge.'

'What's the Cherry Hill Road drawbridge got to do with any of it?'

'Daisy said Marigold crossed it.'

'So?'

'There weren't any tacks down that way. The tacks were in front of Flannigan's.'

Stanley paused. 'What are you getting at, Clyde?'

'Daisy said she saw Marigold cross the drawbridge. But Marigold says she crossed the span bridge at Tonawanda. And she's got the tack to prove it. If Daisy's innocent in all this, why would she lie about that, or at least be wrong about it? Plus Flora says Daisy was rummaging about the house after the phone call, just before she left. Was she getting the rifle? Was she getting the hotel key?'

It took Stanley a few moments to figure out what I was suggesting, but he soon caught on and he didn't sound too pleased. 'Yes, but, Clyde, what would Daisy stand to gain from shooting the old man?'

'I don't know.'

'You're not thinking because of the assault thing back in October, are you? Seems like an awful slim reason to kill a man.'

'There could be any number of reasons. Then you have Marigold giving up her rifle just like that. Why would she so easily surrender her Henry if she knew I was going to test it? A guilty person wouldn't do that. Why would she even keep it? Any murderer with any sense would have gotten rid of it a long time ago.'

Wilmer Barner, the evening bridge-keeper, lived on my street, Culver, only further west, at the corner of Onondaga, a block away from the Cherry Hill Road drawbridge. As the bridge was now closed for the season, with both day and evening shifts suspended because of ice, I found the septuagenarian ensconced in front of his fire in his small but scrupulously tidy wood-frame bungalow. At one time an ensign in the Union Navy, he was spry, alert, with a bald head and a captain's beard. His beard was white, bushy, like the froth of wind-whipped waves. The bungalow's primary décor was ships in bottles.

When his wife led me into the parlor I saw him studiously working on another.

He looked up from his work, a slight frown on his face. 'Dr Deacon, to what do I owe this unrequested pleasure?' His frown deepening, he asked, 'Am I sick?'

'On the contrary, Mr Barner, I seem to find you in perfect health.'

With some exasperation, he said, 'Then I can't understand why you should come to this end of Culver Street when your end seems just as hospitable.'

'Mr Barner, I come on a matter of bridge business.'

He grew abruptly worried. 'Bridge business? Is there something wrong with it? Are the Cruishank brothers climbing the girders again?'

'No, the Cruishank brothers aren't climbing the girders again, Mr Barner. The matter I'm concerned with would be one of observation and record-keeping.'

He seemed immensely relieved that the young mischief-makers weren't up to their simian antics again. 'Ah. Well! Have a seat, doctor. Audrey, get the man some coffee. He's come on a matter of bridge records.'

Mrs Barner soon had me settled with my hot beverage.

By this time, the old man had taken down his logbook, a narrow leather-bound volume, and made room for it on the table. 'Every freighter, barge, or boat that goes under that bridge you'll find in here, doctor. In this column, the name of the ship, in this one the captain, in this one the time and date, and this last one, the toll charge. Of course, if it's a day-time passage, you would have to check with the day-time fellows, and I'm sorry to report that I can't vouch for the record-keeping of those young hooligans.'

'No, it's an evening record, Mr Barner. The evening of Saturday, November twenty-second. It would have been somewhere between eight thirty and nine.'

He flipped pages. 'Let's see, let's see, a late one trying to get by before close. Ah, yes, here we are. A coal freighter, the *Orland*. What a night that was, I can assure you!'

My curiosity piqued, I asked, 'In what way?'

He sat back, now comfortable with the unrequested pleasure of my company. 'I heard the *Orland* blowing her horn from the Fifth Country Road just as she was entering the town. She was late because there was a problem down at the locks, and I'm thinking to myself, here she is at last. So I'm about to lower the barriers and raise the bridge when this girl comes along, riding her bicycle down Cherry Hill Road like fury. She doesn't stop at Cattaraugus Avenue, but keeps coming right along, dodging around the barrier just as it's going down, riding on to the bridge even though I've got the bells ringing and the lights flashing. I leave the tower-house and go out to the railing. I call to her to go back because I must start lifting the bridge immediately or the *Orland* will surely crash into it. But she keeps coming, right across the bridge, pedalling like mad, as if she were on her way to a fire. It was the most extraordinary thing I'd ever seen. I barely got the bridge up in time.'

I leaned forward. 'And do you know who this girl was, Mr Barner?'

'Know her? My wife, Audrey, used to babysit her when she was no more than a wee one. It was Miss Daisy Pond, of Finch Street, riding like she might take flight. And a rifle in her carrier to boot! I don't know what's happened to young people these days, doctor. They've become reckless, the lot of them. And in my opinion it's because the schools don't cane them soundly anymore.'

THIRTY-EIGHT

From Mr Barner's bungalow, I rode Pythagoras across the exact same bridge after I had finished my interview with the old man and climbed the steep slope up Cherry Hill.

I soon reached the Purcell mansion.

By this time it was close to eight o'clock, and only a few lights burned in the house. I rapped on the door. Leach answered a minute later.

'Can I help you, doctor?'

'I must speak to Miss Reynolds at once. It's urgent.'

Professor Herschel Purcell now came from the back. 'Leach, who's there? I'm expecting parcels from New York, but the devil take it if Hepiner delivers them this late.'

Leach backed away. 'It's Dr Deacon, sir. He says he has urgent business with your step-niece.'

The professor peered at me from above the brass rims of his pince-nez. He hesitated, then nodded. He looked worn out by the ordeal of his brother's passing. 'Yes, doctor, of course. I'll fetch her directly.' His brow rose wearily. 'Is it in regard to Ephraim? I should so like to give him some peace before Christmas.'

'All I can tell you, professor, is that I think I'm close to concluding my investigation.'

He stared at me, then nodded. He motioned at the bench under the full-length portrait of Mrs Purcell. 'Please, sit, doctor. I'll find her.'

Five minutes later, Marigold and her step-uncle descended the stairs.

Marigold's red hair was down, and without its usual sophisticated Gibson-Girl style, she looked young, far too young to be pawed by her stepfather. Her eyes were cautious, and she came down the steps in a halting manner, staring at me all the while like I was a wild animal who might at any moment pounce.

'Doctor, my Uncle Herschel says you're close to concluding your investigation. I thought we had already established that Billy was my stepfather's killer.'

'You'll be relieved to hear that Billy is innocent, Marigold. Of this we are now certain.'

Tears of relief glimmered in her eyes, and for a few seconds she couldn't catch her breath. 'That's wonderful news, doctor! Absolutely splendid!' But then her joy faded. Her face reddened, then blanched, and in a tentative tone, she said, 'You don't think it was me, do you?'

'At this point, Miss Reynolds, I think you'll serve better as a witness. In that capacity, I'm hoping you might help me with two outstanding items in my investigation.'

From tentative she became curious, then earnest. 'I'll do whatever I can to help, doctor.'

'Good. Could you show me where you keep the key to the back door of the Grand Hotel?'

A knit came to her brow. Her step-uncle looked perplexed as well.

She said, 'All the keys are in a special cabinet in my stepfather's study.'

'Could you show me?'

After a moment's hesitation, she shrugged. 'Right this way.'

Professor Purcell and I followed her along the corridor, and we soon entered her stepfather's study.

The room was dominated by two large combination steel safes on either side of an expansive mahogany desk, each safe bolted to the floor. The walls consisted of trays and slots, with all manner of business papers, invoices, and receipts. It was singularly bereft of personal ornamentation – no photographs of any family members, no artwork, and certainly no parlor organ, such as the old man had in his office at the New York Emporium. To wit, the room was one big brain, a sad and lonely counting house for Ephraim Purcell's many holdings and assets.

Marigold walked to a cabinet to the right and opened it. Within, I saw an array of keys hanging on hooks. The young woman inspected the keys, then grew still.

She turned to her uncle. 'Did you take the hotel keys, uncle?'

The professor's brow rose. 'No, my dear. The hotel's always open. Why would I need keys?'

Marigold glanced at the key rack again. 'Strange. Very strange.' She turned to me. 'I'm sorry, doctor, but the hotel keys aren't here.'

I had been merely trying to confirm that the keys were available for possible access. That they weren't here raised the suspiciousness of the matter to a whole new level. 'Would your stepfather put them anywhere else?'

Marigold shook her head. 'No. He always said that as long as a man knows where his keys and pocketbook are, he'll be as sound as a house. All keys were kept in this cabinet. He never varied in this matter.'

I now viewed the missing keys as a stroke of luck. The only puzzle was why they hadn't been put back after the crime.

'Very well, Miss Reynolds. If we could proceed to your studio.'

'My studio?'

'Yes.'

She scrutinized me, shrugged again, then led the way.

We exited her father's study and soon came to her studio.

I walked over to the three French doors looking out on to the extensive snow-covered grounds. 'Do you ever use these doors in winter, Miss Reynolds?'

'No. And only the closest is used in summer. Those others with the curtains in front of them remain locked year round.'

I walked past the first two French doors to the last one and pulled the heavy damask curtain aside. I looked at the bolt-locks top and bottom. I observed that they had been slid into the unlocked position. I again remembered Miss Winters's statement, how, after trying to ring the police, Miss Pond had mysteriously gone from room to room, looking for something. Turning the latch, I gently pulled the door open so that the cold night air crept into the studio. I turned back to Marigold and Professor Purcell, who were staring at me, stunned.

'This door appears to have been unbolted by someone,' I said.

THIRTY NINE

Early next morning, I visited the offices of the *Fairfield Newspacket*. In Fairfield, the news rarely got bigger than who was marrying whom, who was burying whom, and where the fish were biting at Silver Lake. So Ira Connelly, his recent editorially contrary opinions about me notwithstanding, greeted me like a dignitary of the highest order. Being a former presidential physician, I was news all on my own.

'Mr Connelly, I wish to announce that we've made an arrest in the Ephraim Purcell murder case.'

'You have?' He pulled his pencil from his ear and jotted down some preliminary notes. At the end of this first feverish spate of scribesmanship, he looked up, and in his characteristic sibilant delivery, a verbal style much moulded by two front teeth that were as prominent as the White Cliffs of Dover, he said, 'I thought you'd already made an arrest in the case, doctor. Isn't Mr William Fray in custody?'

'Mr Fray has been cleared of all charges. We have now arrested Miss Marigold Reynolds, the victim's stepdaughter.'

Mr Connelly stared at me in astonishment, excitement, and perhaps unhealthy editorial ambition.

He then walked to his office door with a curious lurch, as if in his enthusiasm his blood pressure had begun playing tricks with his balance, and called out to the bull pen. 'Felix, have Mr Cragg pull the front page. We've got bigger news than the Christmas bazaar.'

Daisy Pond, with a lover's giddy smile, had her hand ensconced in the crook of Billy Fray's elbow. They were about to enter Jensen's Hat Shop. Daisy had no doubt read Ira Connelly's lurid copy describing how the *Newspacket* had learned that 'a most dastardly daughter had killed in cold blood her own innocent and noble stepfather.' Stanley and I were in a room on the second floor of the Grand Hotel observing Daisy and Billy. The cement factory heiress had most obviously learned that the 'gallant and assiduous Dr Deacon had untangled a most fiendish plot, and had put together a case against Marigold Reynolds the likes of which is unparalleled in the annals of criminal justice.' Lastly, she must have read how 'Mr William Fray, our esteemed and trusted smithy, has been released and absolved of all charges.' Oh, yes, the poor dear was in heaven, and had no idea how I had laid this trap for her.

Billy was going to buy her a hat at Jensen's Hat Shop, probably one of the last the shop would ever sell. He was pretending, now that Marigold had apparently been arrested, that he had suddenly and miraculously fallen in love with Daisy. Intelligent though she was, I could see that she wanted Billy so much she was easily allowing herself to be fooled by the ruse. Billy played the role well, shoulders up and proud, a young man in love.

Stanley said, 'He knows how to make a deal, the rotter. We let him off for my shiner, and he gets a pretty woman on his arm.'

They went into the hat shop. Stanley and I waited. It was the twenty-fourth of December, and I was eager to deliver, in person, my pearl necklace and my Jensen Hat Shop hat to Miss Olive Wade. I prayed for a Christmas truce with the estranged object of my affection, perhaps even an amicable renaissance in 1903, but needed to get this murder case out of the way first. Once the necklace, hat, and truce were accomplished, I would get down on bended knee with my engagement ring.

We waited fifteen minutes. The pair at last came out.

Daisy still had her lover's giddy smile, even more so now that she carried a tinsel-spangled hatbox. What startled me was the way Billy had a lover's smile as well. Much to my consternation, I realized he was not acting.

Stanley came to the same conclusion. 'He's actually falling for her,' said the sheriff.

As we were both afraid Billy might now tell Daisy to run off, we left the room quickly and started down to the street, double-timing it.

In Tonawanda Road, Stanley kept his eye on the pair, following them toward the river.

I, on the other hand, entered the hat shop.

Tilda Jensen was there with her son, Alvin. There was no sign of Isaac, still in Milwaukee, as far as Tilda was concerned, but so tragically in Manhattan with Hattie Whitmore.

I gave the mother a grin. 'So, then. Did young Alvin get a good look at Miss Pond?'

'He did, doctor.'

I knelt next to the boy. 'Do you remember seeing the lady on the night Mr Fray shot Mr Purcell?'

He nodded.

'And where do you remember seeing her?'

'Up on the hotel roof.'

'And you saw her from that distance when it was so dark out?'

He nodded. 'The light from the sign lit her up.'

I was puzzled. 'Why didn't you mention the lady when you first told me about the man behind the garbage cans?'

The boy looked nervously toward his mother.

Tilda rushed to explain. 'He was told by his father not to say anything about the lady. Isaac thought it might damage the credibility of Alvie's story.' She shrugged. 'A lady on the roof too? Isaac thought he was making the whole thing up. Alvie does tend to tell stories sometimes. You can ask Miss Wharry, the schoolteacher, about that.'

So. There had been a little coaching after all, not just about Miss Pond's involvement on the scene but also about the flask robbery.

I turned to Alvin. 'And who was this lady?'

'Her pa owns the cement factory.'

'And what did she do up on the roof?'

Alvin thought. 'She was looking down at everything.'

'And did you see her rifle?'

'Yes.'

'And did you see her fire the rifle?'

'After the man by the garbage cans fired his.'

Here was another witness fooled by the discharge next door. Mrs Swinford trying to kill herself was mistaken for Billy firing his own rifle. I could discount it because of the ballistics evidence. Added to Mr Barner's witness account, I had what I hoped I needed, enough to convince Judge Norris to give me a warrant for Daisy's arrest.

'Thank you, Alvin.' I pulled out a stick of candy and gave it to the boy. 'Merry Christmas. May your new future in Elmira be a bright one.'

His eyes shone as he spied the candy and a big smile came to his face. 'Merry Christmas, sir!'

*   *   *

As Miss Reynolds had said, Miss Pond was prone to fainting.

When the sheriff and I went to arrest her, armed with a warrant Judge Norris, considering town pressure, was only all too eager to grant, I found I had to immediately suspend my duties as deputy and commence my ones as doctor.

The shock of her arrest made her face turn red, then white, then gray. Her eyes twitched upward toward her blonde brow, her neck grew as limp as boiled pasta, and her head lolled toward her left shoulder. Her legs gave out by increments and she went down like the *Thomas Wilson* in Duluth Harbor.

Her parents hurried to help, but they weren't in much better shape. Mr Pond looked as ashen as the cement he sold, and Mrs Pond, a stout matron of forty-five, had to sit quickly on the damask-upholstered chair.

I stepped forward to catch Daisy. I carried her to the sofa. I opened the window and had a servant bring smelling salts.

Miss Pond revived before the smelling salts arrived, but remained pale. She couldn't sit up for the next several minutes. When she did, she was unsteady and sobbed in a most horrible way. 'I only ever wanted to save Billy.'

She kept saying these words – or variations of the same – as we brought her to the Sheriff's Office in the police wagon, her parents following in their motorcar, Mr Pond at the tiller, Mrs Pond, in goggles, fretful beside him.

At the Sheriff's Office, we had her sit at the basswood table. Billy was now released, and the only one in jail was Rupert Scales, the town drunk, who watched the proceedings with great, if bleary-eyed, interest. Mr and Mrs Pond took the bench off to the side. They were inconsolable, holding each other, fearful for their only daughter – shocked, doting parents.

Daisy wept in a breathless, clutching way.

'Daisy, dear, you admit to the crime?' I asked. 'Confession is your first step to the judge's lenience.'

She struggled to regain herself, but was having a difficult time. 'I had no choice. I had to protect him.'

'And you used Marigold's rifle?'

She nodded woefully. 'I did.'

'And you got the hotel's back door key from Mr Purcell's key cabinet in his study?'

'I did.'

'And then you made sure one of the French doors in Marigold's studio was open so afterward you could return the rifle?'

She nodded pitifully. 'I waited a long time out in the cold. I wanted to make sure everyone was in bed. And I couldn't leave by the front, so I couldn't lock the French door behind me after I left. I've been frightened ever since.'

'And you've had no opportunity to lock the French door since?'

'No. There's always been a servant down the hall, or Marigold in her studio, or the professor in Mr Purcell's study.' She cried a bit more. 'And I was afraid you would find the key missing.'

'We did.' I was curious. 'Why didn't you put the key back when you returned the rifle?'

'I got back and couldn't find it. It must have fallen out of my pocket during my bicycle ride. I was riding so fast.'

Stanley said, 'The thing I don't understand is why you killed Mr Purcell in the first place. You weren't sore at him for hitting you back in October, were you?'

'No. At least, yes, I was. But that's not the reason. I had to save Billy.'

'You keep saying that.'

In a tiny voice, she said, 'Mr Purcell has threatened Billy again and again. He's fired upon him with his revolver on three different occasions.' Stanley and I glanced at each other; this was news to both of us. 'The promissory note incident was the most recent. On that particular occasion, he threatened to kill Billy the next time he met him in the street. When Billy telephoned Marigold from the hotel, I went up and told Marigold about it but she just frowned and said that she would go downtown and put a stop to it, and that I was to go home. She didn't seem to understand the urgency of the situation the way I did. So I went back downstairs and tried to phone you at the Sheriff's Office to let you know what was going on so you could go over and put a stop to it, but the line was in use. So I did the only thing I could think of to save his life. I took Marigold's rifle and Mr Purcell's key and went to watch over him on the roof of the Grand Hotel like a guardian angel.'

I thought of Ernie Mulroy talking to his sweetheart in the Sheriff's Office; maybe all this could have been avoided.

'And so you rode your bicycle down Cherry Hill Road and crossed the drawbridge just as Mr Barner was getting ready to lift it.'

She looked surprised. 'How do you know about that?'

'Because I've spoken to Mr Barner. He saw you.'

She nodded fretfully. 'I'm sure he'll never forgive me. He's so particular about his bridge.' She seemed lost in thought for a moment. 'Once I crossed the bridge and reached the hotel, I went round to the back and climbed to the roof. I saw Billy kneeling behind the garbage cans. Mr Purcell was out on the street. I was going to try and stop the whole thing by calling to them. But then Mr Purcell fired at Billy, and I knew I had to take action.'

At this point, all talk came to a stop. Stanley and I stared at the girl, then turned to each other.

I leaned forward. 'You actually saw Mr Purcell take out his revolver and shoot Billy?'

'Didn't see him, because I was focusing on Billy at that precise moment, but I heard him, and knew Mr Purcell was going to keep his word and kill Billy if I didn't do something to stop him. I had no choice. The man I loved was in mortal danger.'

The poor girl of course didn't realize the shot had come from the Wileys' bedroom window: Mrs Swinford trying to kill herself.

'And then you tried to blame Marigold for the whole thing,' said Stanley, in a flat and unforgiving tone of voice.

She looked away. 'It was a horrible thing to do. I'm so sorry. I just couldn't stand the thought of going away to jail and not being able to see Billy anymore.'

FORTY

I got home from the Sheriff's Office late.

As it was now the afternoon of Christmas Eve day, I saw only a few more patients, then closed the surgery early for the holiday.

I was just putting my DOCTOR IS OUT sign in the window when I noticed a hired cab come up the drive. The coachman reined in his horses. Looking more closely, I saw – curiously – that no fare rode inside the covered conveyance. The coachman wasn't in dropping-off mode; he was in picking-up mode.

Thinking he may have made a mistake, and that perhaps it was my neighbours, the Caines, who needed a cab, I made for the front door, only to find Henny waiting in the vestibule in her traveling cloak with all her luggage packed.

Her face reddened. 'Oh! Doctor. I left a note. I was trying to slip out unnoticed. I do so hate goodbyes.'

'Henny, where are you going?'

For several seconds she couldn't speak. Her face was suffused with conflicting emotions. 'I've made such a fool of myself, falling in love with you like a schoolgirl.'

I regarded her kindly. 'There's a cab waiting for someone in the drive. You've no doubt made alternate Christmas arrangements?'

A broad grin came to her face and her eyes moistened. 'How can I ever thank you?'

'For what?'

'For writing that letter to Mr and Mrs Booth. I don't know what you said, or how you framed your appeal, but they've forgiven me, and want me to spend the holiday with them. I daresay I won't be there in time for Christmas, as my train doesn't arrive until the morning of the twenty-seventh. But then I shall be in Wisconsin for the rest of the holiday, perhaps even longer. They say they have a town doctor who's looking for a nurse. They've put in a good word for me. Oh, Clyde, I'm ever so happy. All of Martin's sisters and brothers, and even some of his cousins, aunts, and uncles are there, and they're welcoming me as part of the family. So you see, I really don't think I'll be coming back. I'm sorry. You must think it entirely unprofessional of me.'

'Nonsense, my dear girl. Everything's worked out for the best. You have a home to go to for Christmas. I'm most cheered to hear it.'

In a surfeit of feeling she flung her arms around me and kissed me full on the lips, a big romantic goodbye kiss. My arms went rigid at my sides, my fingers splayed, and my eyes sprang wide as if I had just been latched on to by a diamondback rattler. She kissed me that way for several seconds. I at last clasped her shoulder and, with some gentle pressure, bade her desist.

She pulled away and looked at me with half-hooded ecstatic eyes. 'Don't think I'll ever forget you, Clyde Deacon. As a man – and a mentor – I've never met anyone like you. And please tell me that you'll allow me to write to you.'

'Of course, Miss Gregsby. I should be delighted.'

'And always think of me as Henny. Not as Miss Gregsby.'

'As you wish, Henny.'

'And should you finally marry Miss Wade, I would be ever so honoured if you would invite me to your wedding.'

I looked away. Great sadness stole over me. 'Of course.' Shaking away my sudden emotion, I said, 'Come, now. I'll have Munroe help you with your bags.'

Fifteen minutes later, Munroe had her luggage loaded into the cab. The driver turned around and headed out to Culver Street. Henny gave me one last wave from under the canopy, blew a kiss, then disappeared into the dusky light of the wintry evening.

I was going to miss her.

Not only as a nurse, but as a woman.

On Christmas morning, Munroe and my son and I spent a happy time by the tree opening presents. Jeremiah unwrapped a B-flat cornet. I opened a hand-crafted rosewood pipe with accompanying tobacco pouch. And Munroe received a complete set of J. Fenimore Cooper's novels – I'd learned the young man was an avid reader of adventure stories.

Two gifts remained conspicuously unopened: the pearl necklace I had bought for Miss Wade, and the hat I had purchased for her at Jensen's Hat Shop. As for the engagement ring, it was snug in my pocket.

After our Christmas celebration in the parlor, we got dressed for the holiday service at Fairfield Congregationalist Church. Munroe stayed home and prepared the turkey.

My son and I arrived in the church a short while later.

We immediately looked for Miss Wade – Jeremiah knew my plans.

I glanced up and down the pews, into the transepts, as well as the choir – she was sometimes an occasional substitute soprano when one of the regular ladies was sick. Jeremiah glanced everywhere as well. I could see that he was as anxious as I was; I would gain a wife, but he would gain a mother.

With a tone I could only call plaintive, he said, 'I don't see her.'

I continued to look, but after another minute, gave up. 'She's not here.' I was beginning to feel dejected but maintained a façade of hope. 'Never mind. I'll ride up to her house afterward.'

Reverend Eric Porteous, always generous when it came to his sermons, didn't finish his particularly lavish and extensive ode to

the coming of the Messiah until nearly noon. Much as I gloried
in the Christ-child's birth, I was nevertheless the first one out of
my pew when the aging minister concluded with a solemn 'Amen.'
No Christmas fellowship for me in the church basement. I was off
like a spooked buck in hunting season, out the front doors, turning
right across the Court Street bridge, left on Cattaraugus Avenue,
then up Cherry Hill along Poplar Avenue until I reached its summit,
where the wind coming down from Lake Ontario hit me like a herd
of incensed mastodons.

Miss Wade's house, a three-story wood-frame Victorian model
with white clapboard and blue trim, stylish mansard roofs, and many
dormers, looked bereft and deserted. All its shutters were closed
and the front steps had been left uncleared of snow. The bare poplar
trees around her house swayed violently in the wind. The sky was
clear, cold, but laced with windblown ice crystals.

I rode up her drive to the old-style portico and tied Pythagoras
to the hitching post. I made sure the engagement ring and the
necklace were in suitably accessible pockets, and the hatbox
securely under my arm. I then climbed the stairs and knocked on
the door.

I felt nervous. As I waited for Miss Wade's servant, Freda, to
answer, I realized I stood at a crossroads in my life, that I had finally
put Emily to rest, Henny to Wisconsin, and was now ready to take
someone else's hand.

But when Freda answered, I knew immediately that something
was wrong. For one thing, she wasn't in her servant's uniform but
just in ordinary street clothes. For another, she regarded me as if I
were Mephistopheles himself, risen from the underworld to collect
her soul.

'Doctor! Merry Christmas!' Her tone was forced, nervous.

'Merry Christmas, Freda. I've come to pay my respects to your
mistress. Is she at home?'

Even more flustered, she said, 'Why, no, doctor. Her train left
three days ago. I'm afraid she's gone to Boston.' More fretfully,
she added, 'Her stay there will be indefinite.'

My disappointment was acute. I of course understood that there
had been this risk, but had believed, perhaps foolishly, that the force
and passion of our kiss in front of Dr Thorensen's house would
secure for me a permanent place in her heart.

Struggling to maintain my composure, I said in a quavering voice,

'Perhaps you can give me her address, then. I have a small Christmas package I'd like to send to her.'

'Oh, dear. She's sworn me not to give you her address.'

I stared at the maid. 'Why ever not?'

'She was quite emphatic, sir. I'm not to reveal her address to you.' Seeing that I was dashed, Freda added, 'If it's any consolation, doctor, I told her you were ten times the man Edgar Keenan is.'

I looked up with a jerk. 'She's gone to Keenan?'

'I'm afraid she has.'

I stood there for a few more seconds, my emotions at war, then came up with a plan. 'On my behalf, could you send the parcel? That way, you won't have to divulge her address.'

She thought this through and after she was done with some momentary reluctance, gave me a timid nod. 'I suppose that would be all right.'

'I would like to write a letter to her as well. Could I impose upon you for writing materials?'

Freda now entered more heartily into my amorous plot. 'Of course, doctor. If you would kindly follow me. We'll put you at my secretary.'

She showed me to her bird's-eye maple secretary in a back room – her own office.

'My nieces and nephews, doctor,' she said, when she saw me looking at the photographs on the wall. 'I'll be taking the three-o'clock train to Albany to see them. You caught me just in time.'

She left me to my letter.

I tried to explain to Miss Wade how, though I felt a brother's tenderness toward Miss Gregsby, my connection to my nurse had never been anything more than one of collegial regard. I admitted that Miss Gregsby had suffered a small – or perhaps not-so-small – infatuation for me while employed at the surgery, but that I had rectified matters with a letter to the Booths, and had subsequently packed her off to Wisconsin permanently. I finished by telling her that I wanted to marry her, that I was in fact offering a proposal of marriage, and that I hoped she would take my apology and proposal in good faith and return to me at once before Edgar Keenan made her life miserable again. I then put the letter in an envelope, packed the engagement ring and the pearl necklace in the hat box, and presented the whole to the housemaid for mailing.

FORTY-ONE

On December twenty-seventh, Stanley and I discussed the Daisy Pond arrest with Judge Norris.

At this time of the season, his honour was out of his robes. A man of sixty, he was considerably shorter than me or Stanley, his bodily design taking as its inspiration a cannonball; he was exceedingly round, so much so his arms and legs were like afterthoughts to his general rotundity.

Perhaps I was biased. Perhaps my own recent misfortunes with love were making me take a more compassionate view toward Daisy than I should have. Having given the judge an overview of events on the night of the murder, particularly stressing how Mrs Swinford's misguided attempt to take her own life had coincided with Daisy's altruistic efforts to protect the life of the man she loved, I now did my best for the unlucky young maiden.

'The facts of the case are unique, Judge Norris. We have Ephraim Purcell making several threats against Billy Fray's life prior to the murder. We have him actually shooting at Billy on three different occasions, the promissory note episode being the most recent. Miss Pond knew Mr Purcell wanted to kill Mr Fray. She couldn't let that happen because she's desperately in love with Billy. When Billy called her from the hotel, Daisy feared for his life. She tried to telephone the Sheriff but the town operator has confirmed the line was engaged. Rest assured, we've spoken to Deputy Mulroy about that. Daisy felt she had to take matters into her own hands. I've given you the circumstances of how she obtained the Henry rifle and gained access to the hotel roof. I've explained to you how things happened so fast once she got there. I've outlined for you how there came a shot out of the Wileys' bedroom window – Mrs Swinford's attempted suicide – and how Daisy misconstrued this as a shot fired from Mr Purcell's revolver at Billy. She was under the dire misapprehension that Billy's life was in danger. She did what any good citizen would do – she tried to protect him. Since such is the case, I believe that what we have here is a justifiable homicide.'

The line on the judge's brow deepened. 'I don't doubt for a minute that Miss Pond was prompted to shoot Ephraim Purcell in defense of Billy Fray, Clyde.' He now lifted himself from the edge of his desk and looked out the window where he got a good view of the church grounds. 'What I don't like about the whole thing is how she attempted to blame Marigold afterward. Yes, I realize she was scared, and that she didn't want to go to jail for fear that she would never see Billy again. But she told you Marigold rode across the drawbridge with her rifle to deliberately kill her stepfather when it's abundantly clear by the evidence that she didn't, and it's put rather a stain on the whole thing, hasn't it? She saved Billy's life only to forfeit Marigold's. Her love, as you call it, went a little too far.'

'Desperation often nurtures contradictory impulses, judge.'

'I know it does, Clyde. But it often nurtures criminality as well.'

'It was plain bad luck, Mrs Swinford trying to kill herself at that exact moment. Without the suicide attempt, it's unlikely Daisy would have fired.'

'Yes, but we have to view the case within the defined framework of the criminal justice system. The shot wasn't fired in defense of another. We know this because Ephraim's revolver was still fully loaded when you found it on his person. And so, disregarding Mrs Swinford's sad attempt on her life, we have to decide who's criminally responsible for Mr Purcell's death. I would have to think that Billy Fray is.' Judge Norris let Stanley and I mull on this for a few seconds, then continued. 'He was the one who conspired to lay in wait for Mr Purcell. He was the one who telephoned Miss Pond, prompting her to her rash actions.' He tapped his chin a few times with his fingers. 'Tell me, has he shown any remorse at all for his part in this?'

'Yes, judge, he has,' I said. 'He's been down at the jailhouse every day since Daisy's arrest, visiting her. He's apologized to her in a most profound way. As much as he might have originally been in love with Marigold, it appears he's now transferred his affections to Miss Pond.'

The judge nodded. 'I guess he thinks she saved his life.'

'He's been disabused of that notion, and so has she, but the affection persists.'

'Well, well, well. Love conquers all.'

Stanley broke in. 'Judge, you're not thinking of letting Daisy go, are you? The town won't stand for it. Ephraim Purcell was an important man in Fairfield.'

Norris stared out the window some more. He finally scratched his right temple and turned to us. 'I know she did it for love, Clyde. But she also betrayed Miss Reynolds. And I can't easily overlook that. In my opinion, I don't think it was a justifiable homicide.' He lifted his index finger. 'But neither do I think it was capital murder. I believe it was a crime of passion. And so I think the best we can do for the poor girl is a lesser charge. The same goes for Billy. If they love each other, they can wait for each other.'

On New Year's Eve I went to the Welland Street Club for supper at six. I tried to be as convivial with other club members as I could, but as I hadn't yet received a response from Miss Wade, my spirits were struggling as 1902 counted down its final hours.

Present among the company was Professor Herschel Purcell. He spotted me and Stanley. He came over, a tired smile on his face.

'Happy New Year.' He motioned at an extra chair. 'Do you mind?'

Stanley said, 'Be our guest.'

He sat. I poured whisky for him. He accepted gratefully.

The professor said, 'I thought I'd let you know that we had a big meeting with the lawyers today. It looks like we've come up with an arrangement to avoid a trial. Judge Norris has decided that no one is entirely blameless in the matter. Daisy, after all, pulled the trigger and conspired to get my step-niece to take the blame. Billy was there behind the garbage cans, the powder-keg who set the whole thing off. After having a good long discussion about it, Daisy has agreed to do the sensible thing and serve ten years. With good behaviour, she might be out before she's thirty. I'm afraid Billy must also serve ten years, for conspiracy to commit murder. The pair of them have grown desperately in love, and have vowed to wait for each other. Considering he'll be surrounded by men and she'll be surrounded by women, true love should prevail.'

I wasn't happy with these sentences, susceptible as I currently was to the idea of love, but they did instil in me the notion that I might have to wait for Olive Wade. Surely if Billy and Daisy could wait ten years, I could endure whatever indefinite period I faced while Olive came to her senses and realized I was the man she should marry.

*   *   *

I didn't feel like celebrating the New Year much, so left the Welland well before midnight.

At home, I found a note from Munroe and Jeremiah – they had taken their skates to the Green and were going to stay at the rink for the fireworks at midnight.

I also found a package addressed to me, a late delivery, waiting in my study. My heart sank. It was the hatbox. On the label, I recognized Olive's fair hand, just my own address, with no return address. My hands began to shake. Love. It was like a strong medicine. It could induce in the patient adverse physiological effects, and even worse psychological ones.

I tore the package open and found first the hat, then my pearl necklace, and finally the engagement ring.

Fishing further, I pulled out a letter.

Trying to quell the trembling in my hands, I read.

Dearest Clyde:

It is with great regret and sadness that I must decline your proposal of marriage. My father, before he passed away last year, used to say that timing was everything, and it's tragic that the timing wasn't right for us. He would also say, 'Olive, keep a level head.' I must confess, I've found this advice hard to follow, particularly in the last few years, when I've had to contend with not only the passing in quick succession of my dear parents but also the unfortunate demise of my beloved Aunt Tabitha in Fairfield. Add to this my emotional entanglement with first Edgar Keenan, then Everett Howse, then you, and you might understand why I've found it difficult to keep a level head.

Clyde, I have never felt for a man what I feel toward you. To put it succinctly, I love you, and love you still. If it hadn't been for my own erroneous misconceptions – and lack of level-headedness – in regard to Miss Gregsby, maybe the timing would have been right for us. But because I so obstinately misconstrued circumstances, I'm afraid I've gone ahead and done a rather rash thing.

As you know, Mr Keenan's cousin arrived in Fairfield shortly before Christmas. He came to tell me Edgar had recently undertaken divorce proceedings against his wife. Edgar has begged me for his hand in marriage and because I believed I was losing you, I accepted. I now find myself engaged to Mr Keenan, even though the current divorce proceedings haven't yet been finalized. Consequently, I'm not in a position to accept your own proposal. To that end, I return the ring, the pearl necklace, and the hat.

Please forgive me, Clyde. We are so often the inventors of our own misfortune.

In a more practical vein, I should tell you that I will be returning to Fairfield on January fifteenth. It is my sincere desire that you will continue to count me as one of your friends. Edgar will be coming with me and taking rooms at the Grand Hotel. He feels he cannot stay in Boston at present, as the scrutiny and censure he now endures for launching these proceedings against his wife have become intolerable. I beg you treat him kindly, with compassion, and a selfless heart. It is my hope that with time, you and Edgar might become amicable.

I wish you and Jeremiah the best for a happy 1903.

Sincerely, Olive.

My hands stopped shaking.

I repeated her words in the stillness of my study. 'I love you, and love you still.'

Yes, I understood she was engaged to Edgar Keenan, and that the man would be taking rooms at the Grand Hotel, but that didn't matter.

It didn't matter because I was passionately convinced there remained a chance.

She loved me still!

I poured myself a large bourbon and drank it in one go. I walked to the window and looked outside. The clock in the parlor chimed the hour of midnight: 1902 ended and 1903 began. Through the window I heard the band in the park strike up 'Auld Lang Syne' just as the church bells started peeling. I heard people cheering. And then fireworks lifted into the sky. A moment later, several booms shook the house, and the sky brightened in a myriad of colours.

As far as I was concerned, the time was right.

She was coming home.

As far as I was concerned, I had a level head.

She would be here on the fifteenth.

As far as I was concerned, she would be mine, come what may – even with Mr Keenan staying at the Grand Hotel!